THE EXILED IMMORTALS

BREAKING ROGUE

BY

CAMILIA JOHN

This book is a work of fiction. The names, characters, places and incidents are products of the writer's imagination or have been used fictitiously and are not to be construed as real. Any resemblance to persons living or dead, actual events, locale or organizations is entirely coincidental.

InTown Books

245 North Highland Avenue
Atlanta, Georgia 30307
http://www.intownbooks.net

The Exiled Immortals:
BREAKING ROGUE

ISBN-13: 978-0692538069

E-book ISBN-10: 0692538067

Editor: William Dyson

Cover Art: Michael Dyson
www.coroflot.com/guerrilla808

DEDICATION

To my husband, Greg, who kept alive my passion for
writing, with all my love.

ACKNOWLEDGMENTS

To Mr. William Dyson, my friend and my mentor
who always believed in me.

Book 2

The Legend of the Silver Sword

PROLOGUE

FIVE THOUSAND YEARS AGO, to keep the peace and avoid an uprising, our King exiled three Orders of Immortals: the Warriors, the Defenders and the Enforcers to the mortal realm.

We came from the future and into your past.

Today, we are still here, among you.

These are our stories.

We are the Warriors.

1

THE WAR HAD STARTED.

My war. Our war.

My first battle was against a renegade Amestec prince and his immortal mother, who raised an army of semi-immortal hybrid soldiers and hunted me. He also intended to invade Liechtenstein, the Secret Mountain and the sanctuary for the old Order of Immortals. I stopped him.

One of the precious relics I was sent to find, the Fire Sword, was back in our possession.

But the victory came with a price. Julian Grant, the mortal man I fell in love with, was injured and died as he joined my fight. I brought him back to life and made him immortal. This had never done before, and my disobedience almost cost me my own life.

Gallbor allowed me to stay alive, but I am not certain what I have become.

So, my haven was only temporary. Keeping Julian Grant safe meant to let go of him–this time forever. The mortal man I loved, now an immortal, had no claim to my heart as he did before.

Rules had changed and I was certain that he was aware of them. A Healer is second only to Gallbor, our Spirit Master.

I was destined to be the almighty creature that cannot be defeated. But instead, an uneasy feeling of predestination grew strongly in my spirit. To assure the survival and stability of what was left of my kind and to rule an order, I had to accept the domination of a Master. Somewhere out there, an Immortal male was chosen by Gallbor to be my king and I was to be his queen. I felt his presence like a shadow, stronger every day—he was closer than ever.

It was time for my destiny to be fulfilled and without a doubt, my master was coming.

Does he even exist? I was a singular being, one of a kind, and except for my own brother, Octavian, who could be the immortal man stronger than me?

A year had passed after the battle with Prince Albert and his hybrids, and I was still waiting. Waiting for another war? Or just simply waiting for something…anything…

*   *   *

"Safira, I need your help," I heard my brother's anxious and loud voice in my ear piece. I dropped the TV remote, startled.

"What's going on?" I asked, almost with a shameless hope. My home was also my prison for the past year. Octavian knew that was just a matter of time before I would be found again. But my spirit needed action.

"Nelda was abducted about ten minutes ago," came his answer. "She managed to text me. They just turned onto Hwy 74, most likely heading to the interstate. She's in a black Tahoe, tied up in the back seat. I'm on my way, but I'm more than five miles behind. I'm returning from Newnan and I don't know what to do!"

"I'm going after her," I answered firmly. I felt the same rush of adrenaline like I used to, and that made me feel good against the gravity of the situation. "I'll take the motorcycle."

I opened the third garage door and I put on my helmet, merely to disguise my identity. I strapped two guns onto my waist belt and mounted my Ninja ZX motorcycle. The Kawasaki would be a faster ride for me. I planned to catch up with the car and take it down, preferably before it reached the interstate.

But, four minutes later, once I reached the highway, the Peachtree City traffic was not in my favor.

"Octavian, how far behind are you?" I asked my brother, swinging hard to the right and passing an eighteen wheeler, and he wasn't that far behind me.

"I'm driving the truck," he said, and his voice sounded a bit frustrated. "This isn't a sports car."

He feared for his mortal girlfriend's life. This was the second attempt against this girl's life in a short amount of time. At that moment I had no clue about the identity of her kidnappers.

But if I eliminated a hybrid from this equation, the only other possibility, although very improbable, was an Amestec.

"I'm riding fast," I assured him, "she's, maybe, five minutes ahead."

As always, some slow drivers got comfortable in the fast lane, holding back traffic. I had to make an unwise decision and drive between the cars. Some of the people honked at me in rage because of my daring act.

"Octavian, get on the shoulder and try to keep up with me," I instructed him. "I think it's going to decongest in about half a mile."

"There's a red light up on the hill! What should I do?" he asked, alarmed.

"Run it," I answered, "but try not to kill anybody."

Luckily the red light wasn't on too long and we could continue our pursuit. Also, it seemed that we could drive a bit faster now, as many cars turned onto that last exit.

"I've got eyes on her," he said. "You're only four cars behind her in the left lane. Hurry, it's only one mile left before they reach the interstate to Atlanta."

"I see them," I said, raising my head. "I'll pass them and go for a forced stop. I still need you to drive on the shoulder so you'll be ready to take us in when the car stops. But make sure you slow down the vehicles behind them."

"Understood," responded Octavian.

Looking in my rear view mirror I saw the traffic in the left lane growing distant. Some unhappy drivers moved into the right lane, honking at my brother. I passed ahead between the black Tahoe and another car, and I slowed down until the SUV almost bumped into me. But the vehicle attempted to move to the right and I couldn't allow that.

I increased my speed, catching up with the car in front of me. I slammed on my brakes and turned the motorcycle facing oncoming traffic, bracing myself for the impact.

As the driver saw the unexpected obstacle, he hesitated for a second, but he didn't slow down. The large SUV wouldn't be an easy target to disable.

I laid my motorcycle flat on the ground, knowing that it would be completely smashed, and I stood up on top. The noise of the collision produced a bit of commotion with the vehicles on my right side and many motorists attempted to stop their cars. Octavian was rear ended by the car behind him and moved to the shoulder.

As the SUV tried to drive over me and my motorcycle, I jumped on its hood and started to shoot the driver with both guns. In any other circumstances, the Amestec would die. This time the bullets wouldn't kill him because of the healing energy he was exposed to that was coming from me. But the wounds would incapacitate him for a while.

I smashed the windshield with my gun and jumped on the driver. Indeed, judging from his look—the long hair and brown eyes—he was an Amestec. He had four bullets in his forehead and two in his chest. The front bumper of the SUV was smashed into the radiator and the car was barely moving.

I threw him out of the SUV into the grassy median, and I hit the brakes.

By this time, Octavian had arrived. He picked up the Amestec and dropped him into the back bed of his truck. I opened the back door of the SUV. Nelda was on the floorboard with her hands and feet bound with rope and her mouth closed tightly with duct tape. I freed her of her restraints, but she didn't move from her fetal position.

The girl looked at me with terrified eyes, unable to speak, and shaking from the horrifying experience of her abduction. She was still holding her cell phone tight with both hands. I helped her into the truck and I motioned for Octavian to make a U turn through the median between the double lane highway.

Nelda's rescue had taken less than two minutes. We plunged onto the opposite side of the road and headed rapidly back to Peachtree City, leaving the witnesses to our accident screaming in disbelief. Four miles later, we saw three police cars traveling in the opposite direction, zooming to the scene of the accident.

* * *

At home, the gate was already open. We rushed into the garage and shut the door. Octavian hurried to check on Nelda and the girl started to cry nervously in his arms. He tried to calm her down, but

13

she was still trembling. I could read so much anger and outrage on his pale face.

After he took her inside and laid her on the couch, he came looking for me. I was in the process of the Amestec to the basement.

"It's solely my fault," he answered, agitated, holding the kitchen island tight with both hands. Rivulets of sweat were dripping from his forehead and down his shirt. I stepped towards him but he backed away.

"Octavian, I am afraid that I'm guilty of the greater fault here."

"Safira, it doesn't matter. This has to come to an end. My life with Nelda must come to an end as yours and Grant did, or I need to leave Georgia."

"Octavian, I'm sorry," I whispered with remorse.

"She isn't safe with me; somehow she carries my scent and she looks like one of *us*. She should have started college last year and pursued her dream like any other mortal does, but she chose to stay home to be with me. If I love her—and I do—I must let her go. I must break her heart—and break mine too, but it's for her own good. Next time, I may not find her alive."

"Octavian, be gentle with Nelda; she's just been through a horrifying experience. I think you should wait a little, give her more time."

"And give her more chances to die? No! I hope for her sake that our separation will happen soon."

Octavian passed by me on the way to the garage with Nelda hanging onto his arm. I could tell that he was extremely upset, but he was determined to finish the task at hand.

I couldn't deny that I didn't felt guilty for his grief. But we both had disobeyed our orders by falling in love with mortals, and we took the risk of endangering the ones we loved.

* * *

A strong knock at the door interrupted my anguished inner debate. Lord Arthur, my German shepherd, barked loudly and scratched the door. I checked the security monitor and I immediately recognized the man with short ash blonde hair and dark blue eyes—Detective John Morris, my neighbor.

After a moment of regulating my breathing and forcing Lord Arthur to sit still, I went to answer the door.

"Good evening, Safira," he said in a very serious tone of voice. His demeanor raised a red flag in my mind.

"Detective John, what a surprise!" I said, standing in the door.

"May I come in?" he asked, and then he signaled to the police officer behind him. The man turned around and took his post at the front door. I moved away from the door and Detective John Morris stepped into the hallway. My German shepherd immediately jumped on him, licking his hands and face, and he first had to take a few moments to calm the happy dog.

"What can I do for you, sir?" I asked politely, putting on a large smile without having any intention of inviting him further into the house. It wasn't the right time to have an uninvited guest, especially one who carried a badge.

"I believe one of the vehicles registered to you was involved in a hit and run accident, about twenty minutes ago on Highway 74," he said with an austere face, somehow unimpressed by my attitude.

"Did you find my motorcycle?" I asked, pretending to be surprised.

Morris hesitated for a moment, staring at me. Perhaps he

was trying to analyze my reaction and to read beneath my cool composure, of which I knew he was aware. He appeared to look so much older than when I saw him last. It seemed to me that he had lost his perpetual smile, and he was a bit tired and worried. That made me feel so guilty about my deceit.

"The accident is under investigation since both participants inexplicably fled the scene after they fired their guns. Do you have any idea who might be behind all of this?"

I shook my head, continuing to look down to my feet. I couldn't look at the detective anymore and play this stupid game with him; it was beneath us both. I wished he could understand my thoughts. That would be less aggravating, rather than to admit to him that I had nothing to say that would be realistic and credible.

"Be very careful, Safira."

He turned his back on me to leave, but I still remained silent, standing by the wall with my arms folded on my chest.

"By the way," he said, returning to me and lifting my chin to look straight and deep into my eyes, "if you ever need someone to help you, please, come to *me*."

He stretched out his hand and touched my forehead with his fingers. I held my breath, astonished. But I knew that it was impossible for him, a mortal, to have known the real significance of his gesture, although his touch made me a bit dizzy.

"You had a piece of glass on your forehead," he explained, smiling. "And if I were you, I would ditch the truck, too. I'll keep in touch."

* * *

After Detective John and the patrolman had driven away, an inexplicable exhaustion came over me. I thought that it was one of my old episodes of weakness, so I went to rest.

As I lay on the bed, I felt for a moment that I had lost connection with time and reality. When I became aware again—I wasn't sure if I fell asleep (but how could I?)—I was conscious of a warm muscular form lying against my body, and it felt so good.

I lifted my head to look around the room, but a hand reached over from beside me and pulled me back to the bed. I rolled over into his strong embrace. It wasn't a dream—it was real. Julian Grant was back.

The warm body beside me rose and walked away, so I turned on my right side, closed my eyes, and waited patiently for him. When he returned, he started to caress me once more, gently brushing his fingers down my back and my hips.

I really wanted him to continue that, but his attention shifted from my body to my face. His soft little fairy kisses on my eyes, my nose, and my lips, tickled me.

"Julian, what are you doing?" I giggled, but the man didn't have any intention of stopping. At that moment I opened my eyes.

It wasn't Julian Grant! But it was someone who mirrored him almost exactly.

2

"ANDREAS!"

Was this a dream? Was it reality? How could be this real?

I feared that this illusion was a just a side effect of other things that I had started to experience during and after coming back from Greece. I had the time to analyze them and they didn't make sense afterwards to me or Octavian. The fact that my spirit transferred from me to my brother was beyond my comprehension. It was not an ordinary power that was within our reach, not even to us, the most powerful immortals.

But the young man standing in front of me was not a ghost or an apparition. It was indeed Andreas, still looking the way I remembered him–tall, long dark hair, gorgeous blue eyes and quite well-built—just dressed differently, more modern and not like I had seen him last in 1885.

Actually he was only half dressed, wearing just a pair of dark jeans.

I realized that I was naked, and the thought of being seen like this, even by the man I once loved, made me blush. My eyes searched the room for my clothes but they weren't there. As I pulled the sheet around my body and got out of bed, he smiled and bowed to me.

"Welcome back to us, Lady Safira," he said to me in English, and I ran to touch his face and body.

"Andreas! It's really you!"

He grabbed me and hugged me tight and I felt myself melting under his embrace. This was the man who I had waited for a century to return to me, the man that I thought had forsaken me, and the man I could not forget.

"I missed you so much," he whispered. "I never stopped thinking about you, never."

"Andreas, this is impossible," I said, still refusing to believe that he was real. But as I looked around the room, I didn't recognize it. It wasn't my bedroom and we weren't in my home. "How did I get here? Where am I?"

"Wellington," he answered as he caressed my face.

"Wellington! Which one?"

"Florida."

At that moment I heard the noise of a dog and I recognized Lord Arthur's bark. How could it be possible that my dog was here, too? Still suspicious, I stepped towards the window and looked outside. The sight of two tall palm trees covering the entire view from the second floor convinced me quickly that I was indeed in Florida. There were no palm trees in Peachtree City!

"So I'm in Florida, but how did I get here, and why is my dog here too," I continued to interrogate Andreas, who put on a shirt in the meantime. "No one has these kind of powers, certainly not you!"

"You're right," he agreed with me. "It was Gallbor who made you unconscious for the past two days; I was just the transporter, as I was before."

"Do you mean to tell me that it's been two days since you took me away from my own bed? Andreas, why am I naked? Where's my purse?"

He didn't answer me but pointed to the dresser.

Since I had been missing for two days, I was sure Octavian had already caught my signal by now and he was heading for my location. But the very next second I realized that I did not have my ear piece in place, and after a frantic search I couldn't find my cell phone in the purse. Someone wanted to be sure that my brother wouldn't find me too soon.

"Andreas, where's my cell phone?"

"Who would you like to call?" he asked, with a guilty look. "I'm sorry, perhaps it's lost."

I wanted so ardently to call Octavian and tell him where I was, but obviously that choice was taken from me.

Why would Gallbor, our Spirit Master do this to me? Why now? After more than a century of expecting an answer and a sign from him, he had ignored me completely.

Obviously, he didn't care about me until I disobeyed. So perhaps that's why I was here. I had gotten his attention now, and he chose to embarrass me by bringing me here to Florida naked, in a nineteenth century style abduction, to a man to whom I no longer belonged.

"You were very hard to find," said Andreas, coming closer to me. "I looked for you everywhere, but many times I was too late because you had moved. But I did what I promised."

"I had to move for my own sake. Andreas, you look the same as you always have," I said to him, and I touched his beautiful lips. In the past, those lips were the object of my lust and affection. He kissed my fingers and moved to kiss me too, but I turned my head slightly. My reaction seemed to anger him even more.

"I told you to wait for me because I was going to find you again," he said harshly. "But you didn't. Instead, you gave yourself to a mortal man, broke a sacred rule, and made him immortal."

"He was a mortal man who looked like you, Andreas," I answered calmly. "He fought by my side and sacrificed his life for me."

This time Andreas turned his face away. I could only imagine how painful my betrayal was to him, but I was disappointed too. This was definitely not the way I had always wished for our reunion to take place.

Looking back at our time together, I realized that there was a very thin line between love and lust, and I was not at all sure of my feelings for him. Maybe, because of Grant, I couldn't return to my old feelings again. Still, our moments together after I awakened this morning bothered me a bit.

"Why were you with me in bed," I asked him straightforwardly and a bit too petulantly.

Andreas closed his eyes. "We didn't make love, if this is what you want to know—you were asleep. True, I was very tempted and you are so beautiful, but my only wish is that you will love me and choose to be with me, like before. I thought you were destined to be my wife."

"My destiny is uncertain. I don't know who is going to be my master."

"Now that we're together again, you don't ever have to leave me," he insisted, with a pleading voice. "You still have the right to choose your lover."

"Well, other than that, I am sure there must be another motive behind my presence here, isn't there?" I asked, hoping to move on from this tense and awkward moment between two former lovers. "It looks like I've been relocated. I really could use some clothes."

"There are some in the closet," he responded coldly, walking to the door. "Dress and come down. Your brother, Serban, is here. He'll be the one to tell you everything you need to know. By the way, coffee is ready for you."

The room I was in was modern, painted in a chic style, but after taking a peek in the closet, I realized that the wardrobe must have belonged to a teenager before I arrived. None of the clothes that were left behind were to my taste, and they were a bit too small for me. I managed to find a pair of navy shorts, and a white blouse that almost fit me.

I couldn't think straight. I should have been happy, but I had to admit that after more than a century of waiting for Andreas, I had discovered a part of me that discriminated against him and against our past together.

* * *

I was born in 1865 in Transylvania. When I was a child, my mother was forced to leave me behind, with Lord Fers Martuzon, the Prince and Governor of Transylvania. He kept me in his palace and raised me. When he died, his son, Milos Martuzon, became the Governor. He took me away to his castle in Oradea, a city in the western part of Transylvania. I didn't know who I was or why I was there. I never knew my father.

I was led to believe that I had been abandoned by my family, so I was willing to beg for affection from the one who pretended to be my protector, but who was actually my jailer.

One night I was able to sneak out of the palace alone, and a man with eyes that glowed in the dark saved me from being killed by

Gypsies. At that time I was sure he was part of a dream I had while I was sleepwalking. But I couldn't free my mind of his presence.

Lord Martuzon was visited by an old friend of his, the Archduke Rudolph. Not long after the Archduke's arrival, a gala ball was held in the palace. The Archduke had seen me in the palace courtyard and he was smitten with me, so he took me with him to the ball as his guest. He wanted to take me away with him as his wife's companion when he returned to his homeland, or so he said. I know now that he really wanted to make me his mistress. I wanted to go with him to escape my captivity, but Milos told me on the night of the ball that he knew my mother. She had been his father's mistress, so in a way, he was my only family.

Later that night, someone kidnapped me and took me to an old castle outside the city. It was the same man who saved me from the Gypsies. His name was Andreas, and I felt in love with him.

Soon, the other residents of the castle arrived. All six men looked alike—they had dark hair and blue eyes, like me.

Two of them, Serban and Rares, were my older brothers. They told me that I belong to an Order of Immortals from another world and we had the same father, a Warrior Prince named Gavril.

But Lord Martuzon's army caught up with us and I stayed behind with him to save my brothers and the rest of the warriors. I was captured and imprisoned in the dark cellar of the Black Eagle Castle.

Milos Martuzon beheaded me and inherited everlasting life. But only part of my spirit went into my killer. The other part went into the shadows.

It was my mother, Lady Amara, the former Healer of the Order, who found me before I was to be buried. When she gave birth to me, all of her powers transferred to me. She united me with my younger brother, Octavian, her son, who brought me back to life.

I was to keep Octavian's identity a secret–no other Immortal Warrior knew about his existence, not even my older brothers. My mother never disclosed the identity of Octavian's father to me.

My family history was complicated, but nothing could change the fact that I was born a Healer and a Warrior. I had Prince Gavril as a father and Lady Amara as mother, two older brothers after my father and a younger brother from my mother.

*   *   *

I stepped to the window again and looking outside, to my amazement, I saw a cemetery not far from the house. What a strange choice for a place to build a house, but I knew by now my older brother's taste for unusual dwelling places. The thought of reuniting with Serban added even more excitement in my heart.

Serban waited for me in the hallway at the bottom of the stairs. My older brother—I haven't seen since 1885—hadn't changed, either. I shouldn't have had an expectation of that sort—we don't get old. Only his clothes were different, so different from those in the nineteenth century. Now he was wearing blue chinos and a white golf shirt.

I ran and jumped into his arms, and my emotional gesture took my brother by surprise. He hugged me closely but then he immediately stepped back and bowed deeply to me.

"Lady Safira," he said with his beautiful deep voice I remembered so well. "It's so wonderful to be in your presence again. I'm so happy to see you alive. "

"Oh, Serban," I said, holding his strong arm, "I missed you, my brother. I suppose that Gallbor didn't allow me to remain dead. But why I have been sleeping for two days? Where are the others? How is my mother? Please, tell me everything."

In the meantime, Lord Arthur came straight to me. He jumped on my chest, forcing me to lie on the floor and give him a more deserving hug, along with a belly rub. I didn't understand why my dog was here, but his presence had a calming effect on my spirit.

"Patience, my Lady, all in good time," added Serban, helping me to get up from the floor. Lord Arthur left us in a hurry, most likely heading to a couch somewhere, his favorite place.

"Serban, for you I am just Safira; please, we're in 21st century."

"You are still my Queen," he responded, smiling gently. "Come, first I want you to meet the rest of us."

I followed him into the family room, expecting to find the ones I had known before, but three young men and a female I had never seen stood up, apparently waiting for me. My eyes grew bigger at the sight of those creatures—I knew what they were—they were Immortals.

"Lady Safira, I would like to introduce you to Ditmar, Lars, Codrin and Raluca."

Two were Germans and two were Transylvanians. Each of them raised their right hands and touched their foreheads with the tip of their fingers before bowing and lowering their hands with their palms open towards me. Their salute was unmistakably for me—it was the way that the Immortal Warriors had used to honor me long ago.

But despite their respectful salute for me, I immediately felt in my spirit that these Immortals didn't truly believe in anything they had been told about me. It only took me a minute to read them all. This was not a craft that I had possessed with accuracy before, but lately it had become very easy for me.

Ditmar was handsome and arrogant, a bit phlegmatic too. His eyes tried to look through me and he stood indifferently, tolerating my quick attempt to search into his soul.

Lars, who had no intention to be dominated by anyone, had a well-hidden instinct of superiority. I assumed his made him less popular in the group.

Codrin was charming; he smiled courteously and politely, but his thoughts were not on impressing me. His concern was but how to con me with his seemingly harmless demeanor.

They all looked to be in their twenties. Fashion was a strong element in their life—they were not wearing jeans, but dress pants and expensive designer shirts. The men had their hair pulled back into ponytails, and each had a Ruger P345 attached to their belts. Their choice of weapons may have changed, but we still die in the same way.

Raluca was stunning in her short green dress, tall and slim, with a very attractive body. The girl colored her waist long curly hair in a light blonde shade. It flowed around her perfectly oval face, pink chin, heart shaped lips, and sparkling blue eyes. I sensed a strong will and stubbornness behind her sweetness, but I liked her.

"Nice choice of hair color," I said to her, and Raluca smiled at me with sincerity as she handed me a large cup of coffee with a lot of cream and sugar in it.

"So, you are Lady Safira," said Ditmar, openly examining my body. "I thought you were older."

"Well, I am," I answered, sipping the delicious coffee, and everyone started to laugh. "But I detect that something else is bothering you, isn't that right?"

Serban nodded towards them in a way of saying *I told you so*, but he rushed to explain: "Lady Safira, these are the young ones, all born after you, the new rise of the Warriors."

"The *new* rise—that's a very accurate statement." Lars intervened, crossing his hands over his chest. "Most of the *old* remaining Immortals, those who fought for so called humanity, are wounded— not only physically, but mentally, too. Now, they are all holed up in an old castle doing nothing but proclaiming the glorious past. And all of that for what reason? To be deprived of a great everlasting life because of the absence of a Healer?"

"It wasn't my choice to be far from you," I responded before Serban had the chance to rebuke Lars. I set my cup on the dresser, convinced that something was about to happen. "This is what you want to know, right? Whether or not I'm the real Healer?"

"I can explain everything," said Serban. "I apologize for their behavior."

But before my brother finished his words, Lars pulled out his gun and started to shoot in my direction.

I saw the bullets coming towards me, appearing to be in slow motion.

I stopped to think for a fraction of a second—should I allow myself to be wounded and prove who I was by healing myself, or do what I do best. I liked the second option, and my body gained elevation and floated high above their heads, rotating in the air to avoid the shots. By the time my feet landed back on the floor, I wasn't hit but I caught the last bullet in my palm.

It was the right choice. These were Warriors and nothing else would impress them. Lars shook his head when I handed him his bullet. But his whole attitude reflected that he wasn't done with me.

"I don't like to be interrupted," I said, returning to finish my coffee, but my cup wasn't where I had left it and it wasn't anywhere in my sight.

"Perhaps our information was a bit inaccurate" he said unapologetically. "So you have some skills—you are a Warrior. But are you the Healer? You haven't proven that to us."

"Why would I have to prove that to *you*?" I asked him with irritation, but his inquiry found an ally in the others. "It's very important to us," added Ditmar. "We want to believe that you exist, but so many of our kind have lost hope."

"It's not that we don't believe Serban," said Raluca, pushing Lars out of her way, "but it's been so long since you two parted ways, and the legend said that you've been murdered. You were brought back to life by Lady Amara, your Mother. You could have lost those powers as she did. We just don't know anymore."

I opened my mouth to correct her by admitting that Octavian brought me to life, but at that very moment I realized that Octavian, my younger brother, was unknown to them. After all, he was to remain anonymous.

"Fair enough," I agreed. "I will prove to you who I am, but first, who are you? Are you what you declared yourselves to be or was that just an empty suggestion? So far, all I can see are some contestants in a fashion show, and one of you tried to shoot me with a gun. Indeed, a gun can wound us, but doesn't remove our immortality. Are you up to the challenge, or are you young ones just a cheap imitation of James Bond?"

My little speech wasn't all that serious to me, but struck a sensible chord with them. My little game of words, as I planned, sent the right signal to their minds—Octavian would have been proud of me.

Serban opened the cabinet behind him and pulled out a few swords.

"You got to be kidding!" protested Lars. "Are you going to challenge us with swords?"

"Everybody outside," Serban ordered, and one by one we went to the back yard. This brought some memories back to me, as I remembered a similar circumstance when Serban wanted to prove to me who I really was.

The sun was up; the thermometer read 75 degrees, at ten in the morning, in June, in South Florida. This back yard was perfect—there were no back yard neighbors. All that could be seen was a large field of head stones in the cemetery.

Serban kept a sword for himself and handed one each to Lars and Ditmar. Ditmar flashed a calm and reassuring smile and took the sword, but Lars was still hostile. Their swords were different from mine, a bit shorter and not as wide, but every bit as sharp. As I expected, Lars was the attacker but Ditmar was good at defense.

I liked their style. They were aggressive but more skilled than I expected. It seemed to me that they had practiced their fighting skills. They had improved themselves by stretching their movements diagonally and going for a faster thrust. Ditmar responded to Lars' aggressiveness with a fast swing to the right, blocking his sword with a downward motion and punching him with his left fist.

Lars used his foot to kick Ditmar in the stomach, forcing him to back away so he could keep his balance. Then, pretending to raise his sword and stab towards Ditmar, he turned his back to him, thrusting at me.

I bent down on one knee and grabbed Serban's sword and I swung it upwards, cutting Lars' hand above the wrist. His sword and hand fell to the ground. The blood coagulated fast—we, the Immortals, do not bleed like the ones we were sent to protect.

Lars gazed at me with unbelief, and then his eyes froze on his missing limb. The others remained unmoved, as if the whole world stood still. Only Serban crossed his arms over his chest in a posture of assured expectation. I dropped my sword and stood up, picking up Lars' hand as I rose.

As I got close to Lars, the others gathered around to witness my failure or my redemption. I asked him to relax and I slowly attached his limb to his arm, perfectly matching the place where it was cut.

Suddenly, I felt a little tingling in my fingers, and light gray ashes appeared throughout my skin and pores, as my palm rested on his wound. The bones, arteries, and blood vessels reattached and rebuilt. When I removed my hand, he was completely healed; there was not even the evidence of a scar that remained.

Lars stood intimidated for a moment, but then I forced him to move his wrist.

"Next time I'll aim for your head!"

3

BESIDES SERBAN, NO ONE dared to smile at my threat.

"I need a word with my sister," he said to the others and they all made their way quietly into the house.

"You have quite an unusual place to live," I started the conversation, surprised that my brother had kept quiet for a few moments.

"It suits us perfectly," he said without rushing to answer me, pointing to the cemetery. "There weren't too many takers for this property and we've got the place all to ourselves. Except for St. John's Church down in the cemetery, we only have a few neighbors. Aside from that, we're only a hundred feet from our work place."

"You work at the funeral parlor?"

"Yes, we all do, and may I add that this is the perfect place to bury someone you've killed by decapitation. Mortals aren't ready to deal with the consequences of our war. Besides, we know this job well and we are very much appreciated by our employer."

This thought painted a vivid picture in my mind. I could only imagine the effect on the mourners of this parade of handsome young men and a woman serving as the undertakers.

"How long have you been here?"

"About five years. We've been all over the south looking for you. Lady Safira, please accept my apologies for the kids' behavior. I've been telling them about you for so long, now; they thought you were just a legend, as our true origins are to them, and not real."

"You needed to know, too," I said to him as I bent to smell a bush of pink oleanders.

"I didn't doubt you," responded my brother as he was collecting the swords.

"I doubted myself many times, lately."

"All right," he admitted, "it's so good to know that you're still my dear sister, the Healer."

"I sense that you, my dear brother, are still the storyteller I love to listen to. You always have a great story for me," I provoked him, but I knew he was ready to talk.

"I'm also the one brother that could never forgive himself for leaving you behind."

"It was my own choice and it was meant to happen that way. That past is all gone from our lives and it can't be changed. Only the future matters."

"You're right; it's time for you to know all about us.

"After we left you behind, we were ordered by Gallbor to find and kill all the Impostor Immortals. We suffered so much as the news of your death reached us. Andreas suffered the most. He wanted to leave and find you, but I had to detain him. It was the darkest moment in our lives. Before she was forced to return to the Secret Mountain, Lady Amara informed us that she brought you back to life. I can't tell you how much we rejoiced.

"There was nothing for the other Warriors to do anymore—just stay and wait. We found shelter for everyone in an abandoned castle in a Transylvanian village. We were secluded and safe since Liechtenstein was no longer accessible to us.

"For so long in the past we didn't procreate because all male and female warriors were fighting in wars along with the mortals. Times had changed—we no longer blended with the modern army. Those who were masters of a female Immortal had nothing better to do but mate, creating a brand new generation. That was when the first of the young ones were born—nine boys and seven girls.

"As soon as the youngsters were grown and ready for action, I asked Gallbor's permission to take them out on a new mission, clearing the path for your return. He agreed.

"We left Europe twenty-four years ago and came to America. At first there were twelve of us. We set out to kill the troublesome Amestec. Our logic was that the fewer there are, the better—there wouldn't be as many of them hunting you. Our intelligence was that all the remaining Immortals from Europe had crossed the Atlantic, looking for you here in your new country. So now we have a whole new generation of enemy here, too."

"Well, unfortunately, not all the Immortals followed the instruction manual," I said, and this was sad a reality. "Loneliness is a hard pill to swallow."

"Indeed. But an Amestec is an Amestec and we didn't spare them. Some were killed by their offspring, and we also killed those who killed them. We used Raluca as bait—she would set the trap. It worked for the first ten years, but then, the rumor spread among them about us and they figured out our strategy. But at that time we had killed about two hundred Amestec and Impostor Immortals.

"Raluca didn't give up—she colored her hair blonde and for the next ten years we continued to do our best to eliminate the Amestec. But everything changed when we encountered a new breed of Amestec, a bit strange and more powerful. They stayed together in their enclave and they are seeking us. This new rise of

Amestec is powerful and they have their own army, too—as you are already aware. Some of these powerful Amestec killed six of us and we need to take them out. They are all here, in south Florida."

"I know who they are. Their mother was Anda Kovack, my foe, and the wife of Milos Martuzon. He married her after he killed me. She decapitated him and became immortal, too. Then she used the powers she inherited from Lord Martuzon. She killed former soldiers from Transylvania and made an army of hybrids for her son, a renegade Liechtenstein prince. He was in the possession of the Fire Sword, too. I stopped them in time, before they could complete their mischief and retrieved the sword. But her children and the hybrids she made are still at large with the rest of her offspring. That's why they're so strong—they're a part of me."

"Lady Safira, we're building a new army and now we have the second new generation: ten boys and sixteen girls. But America is now the battleground. Before we can be united and fulfill our purpose among the mortals, this is where we need to make our last stand."

"You know a lot about me, but I had no knowledge about your presence here. How is that possible?"

"Don't be angry," murmured Serban peacefully. "It was only Gallbor. He was always around you, even if you didn't know it."

"I didn't know it, indeed," I said, upset, "I never even felt that he existed. I'm not sure that I have any faith in him—not because he is who he is, but because he abandoned me."

"I assure you that he didn't abandon you."

"Did you ever see him in real life?" For so long I had been dying to ask someone this particular question about an unknown Spirit Master, one who I had never seen but one who demanded blind obedience from me. "How often did you see him? How do you communicate? Where is he right now?"

"Gallbor was an omnipresent powerful Warrior," responded Serban, perhaps not too amused by my questions. "I have seen him many times and I fought by his side many times. Your fighting reminds me of him. I haven't seen anyone capable of doing things like that, except for him."

Saying this, Serban bowed his head in a respectful attitude and his features profiled an inexplicable sadness. His narrative suddenly faded in power and substance and he became quiet. His spirit wasn't approving what his mind believed to be true. I refused to comprehend what I was sensing from him.

"We need you Safira," he said a moment later, and I felt compelled not to interrupt his quietness. "We need you more than ever. We need you desperately. We need a new Master. All Immortals will follow your lead."

"Gallbor is our Master, Serban. I sense that you are about to tell me something dreadful and I need to know the truth."

Serban nodded. "Your coming here was Gallbor's last act as our Spirit Master. It all came to an end for him. He can't stay among us in human form for more than seven days' time. After that, he needs to change into spirit form and return to the Secret Mountain. One hundred and fifty years ago, he disobeyed. For the love of a woman, he refused to return on the seventh day, so he remained among us. But he slowly began to lose his powers, becoming like one of us. With the last of his strength, he helped us to find you and bring you to us."

"Where is he now?" I asked, feeling a cold rush in my soul. I felt betrayed, thrown to the lions, and worse—left to die.

"His reign is over, Safira. I haven't seen him physically in fifteen years. We are crossing the valley of the shadows and we are alone. Please don't have evil feelings about him, as you said before— perhaps it was meant to happen. This is not for you to judge—you are now our Queen."

It was me who was looking away, now. The prospect of the absence of a Master at this crucial point in our history, when we seemed to have no more glory and future, was impossible to absorb. And Serban's request for me to take Gallbor's place was no less controversial. I was not born for this.

"There must be someone else who has the right to reign over us."

"Gallbor said that our spirit and souls will recognize the new Master. You are the Healer, the most powerful Immortal we have. You are the only one who can save us."

My lips moved to say something, but no words came out— my mind stopped them in time. The realization that my younger brother Octavian, the anonymous powerful Immortal Warrior, could and would be the chosen one to reign in Gallbor's place, changed my disposition right away.

Yes, perhaps some things were meant to happen. Mother warned me that one day Octavian's time would come and he would rise for a purpose. And Gallbor knew it all along.

I never doubted that Lady Amara was our mother, but we never brought out into the open the subject of the identity of Octavian's father—it was suggested that it might be Prince Gavril but this wasn't confirmed. Sometimes I wondered about it, but I had no one to ask.

Yes, it was Octavian who was born for this purpose, not me. But how could I tell the others the truth about him?

I didn't want to ponder this situation anymore. Everything would be revealed and set in place at the right time, and not a moment sooner. Now was the time to concentrate on my mission here, in Florida. I was sent to fight the Amestec, find one more lost magical sword, and I was supposed to be conquered by my own Master—not to become one.

"Serban, I need a cell phone. Mine was purposely lost and I need to call my neighbor and check on my place in Atlanta. My house is loaded with state of the art technology and the Fire Sword is there."

"You don't have a home in Atlanta, Safira. I am sorry to tell you this, but two days ago, someone set your house on fire and it burned to the ground—there's nothing left of it."

"That's impossible," I said in disbelief. "Who could do something like that? What happened with…?"

I took a deep breath because I was going to ask about Octavian, but I stopped. The thought that he could have been in harm's way sent a cold rush of blood through my veins. One thing I was sure of—it would take more than fire to destroy Octavian, and I prayed that he had been gone long before the devastation.

"Andreas saved you and your dog in time," Serban answered delicately. "But there's no need to worry, there was no one else in your house at the time of the fire. Your neighbor from the house for sale across the street confirmed it to the firefighters who first responded."

A small stroke of light came out from my eyes. Octavian was safe and he took shelter in the Samson's empty house. Very smart. I hoped he still had the Fire Sword with him, an object that we had fought fiercely to regain. I could only assume that everything that happened with my house had something to do with that magic relic. Still, I had no way of knowing and that was frustrating to me.

"The Amestec are after you," concluded Serban, "and they will destroy everything in their path. And one among them wants to reign over our race."

"One among them? Who?" I held my breath for a second.

"He's just an impostor. We don't fear him, although he's very smart and he's been eluding us for many years. He's responsible for having killed many of us."

"What about Rares?" Suddenly, my heart started to race against my will and I felt my own breath burning. "Serban, where is our brother, Rares?"

His answer came slowly as his deep voice shook: "He is no more."

"No more? Serban, what happened to him?"

But my brother was not willing to talk to me anymore. He bowed, turned his back to me and went inside.

* * *

"Rares' spirit was stolen a year ago, in Orlando," I heard Andreas speaking behind me. One of this Immortal's particular gifts was that he could move around you, unseen and unheard.

"A year ago?"

I had lost people I loved before, many mortals who I have been so attached to, and I almost lost Grant, the man with whom I fell in love. But what I feared the most was the loss of my own brother and my own blood in the war with the Amestec.

And it had happened. It was Rares. My emotions betrayed me and I closed my eyes in agony. I couldn't keep them still too long; they lightened up into a blue striking thunder. The burst freed my anger, but the urgent need for revenge remained strong.

But why hadn't I felt his passing at all? I should have felt that his spirit was gone into the shadows or into a different body.

"I would advise you to never to ask Serban about it. He blames himself for Rares' loss. When he left Rares behind to guard our safe house there, Rares was captured by an Amestec named Valli. We haven't been able to find him to kill him because he has a large number of guardians and several brothers."

Andreas gently touched my shoulder while his eyes were watching me curiously but affectionately at the same time. "I'm so sorry," he said, and his voice warmed my heart.

"Valli will be punished," I said, and my voice came out rough and unpleasant, like a bark.

"I have no doubt," Andreas replied, and taking advantage of my vulnerability he pulled me into his arms. I didn't resist nor did I wish it to be any other way. His chest was robust and he still smelled so delightful, like fresh lilac flowers.

But I did have a volcanic heart and his presence around me increased my struggle to keep a grip on my feelings. I must admit that I was weak and confused. I had loved Andreas' memory for so long. Now that he was back, I loved the memory of the man I fell in love with to replace him.

Indeed, I missed Grant, and the fact that I was far from him. I struggled to stay indifferent to my past. And he, Andreas, had saved my life for a second time.

"We've got to go." Raluca interrupted our moment as her blond head appeared behind the patio glass door. "It's time to meet the others."

"Where?" asked Andreas, still holding me.

"They called for us," she answered smiling. "Let's get ready, Lady Safira."

"Ready for what?"

"Tonight we meet the Americans."

4

"I THINK RED'S A good color for you," said Raluca as she slipped some latex gloves over her hands. "Will you dare to try it? What about bands? And don't worry—I'm actually a licensed beautician. It a good craft, especially in a funeral parlor."

* * *

My hair didn't come out as red as I had dreaded. It was now a beautiful dark burgundy that made the color of my eyes even more vivid. "Oh! Well, why not," I answered courageously, giving her permission to color my hair.

Truth be said, I had had the hidden desire to try this before but I cowardly continued to postpone the event, fearing that the change would create such a big trauma in my mind, regardless of the fact that I had imposed it on Octavian.

"So, what kind of meeting do we have tonight? Who are the Americans?"

"Our local Immortals. I am thinking that they may have found some evidence of the Amestec. They have their spies in the night clubs."

"Raluca, why are you chasing the Amestec in night clubs?" The notion was so ridiculous and annoying to me, but I had to admit that I had been sheltering myself for so long, I had lost connection with the outside world.

"Because, that's where most of them like to spend their time—drinking, chasing girls, having the time of their lives."

Raluca's hands were moving fast, brushing the cream over my hair. She was talkative at the same time, behaving like a true hair dresser, determined to impress me with her skills. But I sensed that there was more to our time alone together than just changing my appearance. There was something that she needed to ask me, so I let her to do all the talking.

"At first they didn't want me, they only wanted my brother, Codrin," she said. "There were seven of us, girls who wanted to join, but they had stubborn minds. Their goal was to keep all the Warriors in the group male. I challenged them to fight me. Needless to say that I stood up to Serban and Rares. Rares was a great friend, also like a brother to me; I mourned his death deeply and I still do."

"His death will be avenged," I assured her with confidence.

"I know the Amestec who killed him," declared the young girl, gathering my hair on the top of my head. "Lady Safira, I think Rares' death was my fault."

Raluca's disposition became increasingly lethargic and she stopped rubbing my hair. Her eyes were large, but they darkened while she forcefully fought back tears.

"I made a mistake with Valli," she said, sitting on the edge of the tub. "He was one handsome half-immortal. I thought he might be different, so I didn't have him killed right away. As time passed, I was naïve enough to hope he wouldn't turn out to be our enemy. But ultimately he wanted the same thing, as all Amestec do— immortality. And that forced me to leave him."

"I told him to stay away from me but he refused. He came looking for me and found one of our safe houses. Unfortunately, we had already left, all except Rares. Valli took him down with hired guns. They were some strange soldiers who were made by a rogue Immortal woman that was his mother. He told me the story about his brothers and himself. Believe it or not, they all know about your existence and they are constantly looking for you."

"Surely they're not looking for me in a night club," I said, laughing at the whole idea of being expected to frequent such a place. "Such habits are strange to me. It may come as a surprise to you, but my life is quite simple."

"And your love life is lonely?" she asked without hesitation, and I felt this particular subject was quite troubling to her.

"Indeed, my life has been quite lonesome at times. Did you hope that Valli would truly love you?"

"Perhaps I did. I was tired of everything and everybody. Every Immortal male was too ancient for me. I grew up with the younger ones, but I couldn't entertain any feelings of affection for them. Many tried to be my master, but they couldn't measure up— they failed to win the fight. But one in particular caught my eye and I would have accepted him freely, but he never asked. Now I know why."

I was certain that she was speaking of Andreas. To hear that he was desired by her weakened even more my aversion towards him.

"It's him," she admitted, smiling with guilt. "Andreas was one Immortal I could care for, but the rumor was that he was your man."

"He was at one time," I answered, not fearing that my confession to her would hurt me in any way. This girl to girl conversation in this old bathroom in a house by a cemetery was surprisingly comforting to me. "But that was a very long time ago; I have no claim over him any longer. I was sent to live among the mortals and sometimes the love for them found its way into my heart. Many times we all turned to the mortals for love – they were sincere and passionate, but too fragile. They wanted to keep us but we couldn't keep them."

Raluca's features remained cold and her eyebrows rose in an angle on her forehead like they were attempting to unite.

"I thought Valli's love for me was real, but I wanted the impossible. I crossed the line and someone died. Serban doesn't know that I had feelings for Valli. I don't deserve to be your warrior Lady Safira, and I wanted you to know my horrible shortcomings. If you wished to send me away, I would understand."

"Raluca, do not call me Lady, please."

"But you are our Queen, now. Nothing can change that. You are who you are and you have proven to us that you deserve the title."

"But do you wish to remain a Warrior?" I asked her firmly.

"Absolutely." She again raised her eyebrows, but this time a sincere smile lightened her beautiful face. But what I was about to ask of her would be something so hard that it would grieve her spirit and trouble her judgment.

"Then, you will have to help me to catch Valli," I said to her, and I expected nothing less. "Would you be willing to do that?"

The girl looked straight at me and her eyes lightened with a fast stroke of blue thunder. They were filled with pain and surprise and I felt the emotions in my own spirit, too. How many times had I told myself that if I hadn't healed Grant, it would be like I had killed him myself? I gave Grant immortality because I loved him and then I sent him away to protect him from the Amestec.

Love had blinded me in many ways and I couldn't cast judgment on anyone else. But our enemies had corrupted our hearts and minds and we now have no other choice but to eliminate their existence, or they will replace us. What I was asking of her I hadn't embraced myself yet, not at that level.

"I won't demand that you to do it. It must be of your own will."

"Yes, I'll do it" she barely whispered, and her vague murmur pretended to sound heartless. "But at this moment, I am sure he's already forgotten about me."

I had expected this reaction from her, but I knew better. Valli hadn't forgotten her and most likely, now that he was an immortal, he would come looking for her as he did when he killed Rares. I was counting on Valli being here soon to take her.

"I think I'm done," I said to Raluca, heading for the shower. "Thank you! I will see you later."

Raluca bowed and left me, but not before her eyes involuntarily tried to search for approval from my attitude. But her peace of mind was radically compromised. What I demanded of her to do instantly changed her affection for her lover into a mercenary ground for a new battle. But my brother's killer must be punished at all costs.

* * *

"Pretty color."

Serban stood in the bathroom door, collected and confident as always. It seemed that he had intentionally passed on to Andreas the burden of telling me about Rares. Now that the awful news been brought out into the open, he was ready for action.

"I'm so sad to hear about Rares," I said, trying to sound rather more dignified than anguished. "I don't understand why I hadn't felt his passing. I feel like I let all of you down by not coming out into the open. I am so sorry."

Serban looked like he was thinking of something beyond what I was saying, and his face involuntarily turned from grave to warmth.

"I know. Follow me, Lady Safira." I proceeded to walk behind him, convinced that against my wishes and demands, none of them were going to stop calling me Lady.

We passed the staircase on the first floor of the house and stepped inside a small room painted plainly in white, in the back of the kitchen. This room had served as a large pantry to the former owners, but it was now filled with containers. Serban pulled one closer and opened it for me. I looked inside, but instead of guns or swords, or the regular ammunition I would have stored in there, I saw some unusual steel objects. They were some sort of weapons, but these were things I wasn't familiar with.

"These things are odd. Are this Shurikens?" I asked, surprised by their massive bulk.

"Bigger and better than any I've ever seen. They were hand made specifically to kill us."

The basic idea behind their design was stolen from the weapons of the Shurikens, but these were bigger and more dangerous. There were made to be thrown in the air, take out a limb, and kill fast. My brother took them out one by one and they all had different forms and sizes.

"We've got the famous Tri Blade, very sharp and efficient, the Cyclone disk, the Silver Spin, the Dragon and the Saw Cutter. They average from eight to twelve inches—double the normal size."

The container was empty, now, with the exception of one.

"You see all these weapons? We confiscated them from the Amestec we killed. I don't know who made them, but they're everywhere."

"I don't understand—why would the Amestec possess these obsolete Japanese weapons? These are too big and too hard to fight with, and from the twentieth century. Isn't it easier to just use guns on us?"

"Two words—fast and quiet," responded Serban calmly, amused by my indignation. "Guns are loud and we shoot back at them. They got smarter, hoping to have our heads chopped off with these weapons rather than fight us with a sword.

"They can't win over us! They aren't warriors, but they could be trained to use the Shurikens. The secret behind the technique is that before you throw, you turn them with your fingers in a circular rotation and make them spin in your hand so they have more power to cut into your enemy's flesh."

"Spin them with your fingers—that's pretty hard because they're so heavy," I said, checking the Tri Blade. "Especially one like this. It has to be something more like the Dragon or Cyclone, but with an even surface. You use less grip and it's sharp enough to go through skin and bones."

"Indeed, the weapons are far from being able to decapitate us—but we *can* get hurt and lose a limb. However, this one in the container is the most dangerous, like you mentioned—it cuts straight through flesh and bone. It's called the Vortex of Death. None of us can touch it or fight with it."

He pointed to the weapon. It was round, about twelve inches in diameter, with a four inch wide blade. Both surfaces, inside and out, were very sharp. It was highly polished and it glistened, but it had no connecting grip at the interior, leaving its user no other choice but to hold the blade. I bent down to pick it up, but Serban stopped me when my hand was half way inside the container.

"I have seen it cutting off a head. It's the perfect weapon—you don't have to shoot a gun or fight with a sword. The surface has sharpened ridges, and you can't hold it in your hand. No one can! Don't touch it—it could cut off your hand!"

I turned to my brother, surprised by his reaction, but then I remembered that he doesn't know all the things I can do.

"How did it get into your possession?"

"Six months ago we chased an Amestec behind a hotel in Miami. Raluca brought him into our sight and it was Lars' turn to fight him. Suddenly, out of nowhere, a man threw something at us from behind an SUV. It was the Vortex. It decapitated the Amestec, like his neck was hot rubber. Then it continued to fly until got stuck in a massive tree trunk. The man attempted to recover it, shooting at us, but we fired back. He escaped on a motorcycle before we could follow him. None of us could touch it, we all got cuts on our hands and arms. We used metal cable to take it down and bring it here."

"Strange indeed," I said intrigued, considering that besides me, only Octavian could have been capable of throwing such a thing. But I was certain it wasn't him. But then, who else had similar powers? Could it have been another Immortal of whom we weren't aware, one who was on the same mission to kill our enemy?

Intrigued, I bent again to lift the weapon and see it for myself, against Serban's vehement warning and disapproval.

It was very sharp. I felt the cold metal running through my fingers as I attempted to hold it in my hand. The edges cut straight through my bones and cartilages until it almost took my fingers off. I didn't felt any pain, but I knew I was about to lose my fingers. I could use my other hand to pull the metal out of my flesh, but instead, I let my mind do it.

Slowly, the flesh and the cartilages grew back around the blade of the weapon and propelled the metal away. The next moment I held it in my hand like any other weapon.

"How is that possible?" Serban looked at me in admiration and surprise, with an unsatisfied hunger for more demonstration.

I knew then that this was to be my weapon from now on. I would be its new master. I must find its old master—if he is out there fighting for our cause.

What was his story, anyway?

5

SOME MAY SAY THAT people can change. If something dramatic happens in their life, then they change the path they are on and revise their thinking for a new course.

That may be true in some instances but the reality is that nobody changes. You may do things differently for a while, but in essence, everyone remains the same, hiding who they are and covering their malice. And that is because most people know who they truly are and what their purpose in life is.

Except for me. My name is Artamian.

In my world, not being who you are was a condition of surviving.

All I could remember from the time I was a small boy was the continuous traveling. My mother and I did not have much materially, but she took care of me as best she could. It never occurred to me to ask my mother about the circumstances that provoked this drastic situation for us. I just accepted them as a fact. Many times it felt like we were hiding, or running away from someone or something.

I never asked about my father, either—not even about his name. It seemed to me that the subject saddened my mother too deeply and I just assumed that he was dead. My beginnings were a life of misery—not having anything at all, not knowing my father, and not having any protection from anyone. From Vienna to Madrid and on to Paris, our home was the night sky or a rundown castle—until one day when a man offered my mother a shelter in his home.

I was only nine at the time. We had moved into1220 Rochelle Avenue, a splendid home with magnificent large rooms, a great kitchen, and quite a few servants. At first I thought that mother would be a servant as well, but it turned out that she married the owner of that mansion. Our gypsy life was over.

* * *

Mother was young and beautiful. Her blonde hair flowed down her back in shiny curls, and her silhouette was very attractive. She loved to laugh, and these good things and our new situation made her laugh a lot. I was happy for her. I was given good food and I was starting to receive some education.

But the man of the house did not like to have another candidate for my mother's heart, and soon I saw my mother only on special occasions. At his first opportunity, the owner made arrangements to send me away to school and had me moved out of the house.

That infuriated me a bit. I felt like something was stolen from me, the only thing I had truly possessed for the past ten years, and the one anchor I had in my life—my mother. I was terribly disappointed that she did not object to my being sent away but I remained calm, hoping that it would be just temporary. It should have been—I couldn't foresee a reason for mother to want me away from her for too long.

But the day I said goodbye to her I understood—she was carrying the child of the owner. I swallowed my anger and I left for Berlin to start what I felt to be an unjust punishment.

* * *

It was the fall of 1900, the turn of the century.

The name under whom I was registered at school was Artamian Gutierre. The rich Frenchman my mother had married gave me his last name so I would have a good reputation and prestige at the school. These qualities immediately started to diminish upon my arrival.

First, for such a young boy, I had unusually dark long hair that fell to my shoulders. An attempt to cut it short in order to follow the established rules

*was not an easy task—it grew back in the next few days, to everyone's amaze-
ment. I was indifferent to the school and much of the time I was angry to be
surrounded by so many other strange males.*

*But my schooling was paid in full for the next ten years (a fact I didn't
know it at the time), so the school's director made strenuous efforts to handle me.
Apparently, I could not be disciplined and I was constantly accused of bad behavior and starting fights. Was it just a deliberate act of rebellion to attempt to
establish communication with my mother?*

*But after more than two years of not receiving any sign of interest from
her, I realized that I was on my own. Of course, I had an excuse for my mother
- she might be so busy now, raising the siblings I never met.*

*Sadness and anger were my companions for a long while. I realized
that in spite of the fact that I was totally exiled from my family, I had a place to
stay, nice clothes and food to eat—more than I ever had before when I was a
small child. And if other parents kept a strong grip on their sons, I had the
liberty to do whatever I wanted. So, the bad behavior suited me well, especially in
a place full of spoiled, obnoxious sons of nobles.*

I had no friends.

*I was taller and smarter for my age, at least according to the school
standards. The professors didn't know what to make of me at first. Learning
was an easy task, but this created another problem—I was not accustomed to an
indolent life in the same place. I wanted to get out and explore the city and its
surroundings, but that was impossible. Our only time for such fun excursions
was on Sundays, to church services. Life on the street was tempting, but I had no
strength and courage for it, at least not yet—I was only twelve.*

*I cannot remember much that happened to me for the next five years. I
was bored but I studied more, toning down my rebellious attitude a little. Regardless of my anonymous past, I realized that I could accomplish much more by
applying myself to my studies and trying to improve my social life. Mother's
marriage with Mr. Gutierre was not bad for us after all. I started to see things
through the eyes of a more mature person and not an angry, abandoned boy.*

*Being older now, we were allowed longer trips into the town and I de-
lighted in the beautiful streets, houses and gardens. I, too, wanted to become rich*

and have a comfortable situation as I imagined the inhabitants of the beautiful houses enjoyed.

It was clear to me that Mr. Gutierre would not have had my beautiful mother in any other circumstances except for his wealth. And I absolutely wanted a beautiful girl with whom to share my wealth.

This was a great plan and I was determined to accomplish it. Some people were just lucky, and I was one of them. Or so I thought.

*   *   *

It all started one afternoon of a warm day in July, 1907—I had just turned eighteen. Herbert Walden, one of the few classmates that I tolerated at a certain distance, had invited me for the hundredth time to have dinner with his family. I never understood the arrangement for Herbert to live at school when his family's estate was just an hour away. But like always, if such information was not freely offered to me, I never had the curiosity to ask. Herbert was a large young man, quiet and a bit slow in his movements, but he suited me well at the time.

So, finally I agreed to the dinner invitation, just because I felt the need to see a normal family.

Mr. Walden sent the carriage out for us and that made a distinct and positive impression on me. They lived out in the country, in an old home that I immediately liked. I was welcomed and introduced to everyone: mother, father, and younger sister, Renate, a girl of fifteen, with long blond hair and sparkling green eyes.

She was my focus the whole time I spent there.

The dinner was set out like a feast to me, with a lot of meat—a luxury not given to us in abundance at the school. I was trying so hard to eat properly and to focus on my host's avalanche of questions.

"Mr. Gutierre, my son tells me that your family lives in Paris," said Herbert's courteous father, motioning for a servant to put more meat in my plate.

"Indeed," I agreed, "but is has been quite some time since I had the opportunity to go home."

"And why is that?" asked the sweet and enchanting voice of Renate.

"I am focusing on my studies, so I can ensure a better future for myself," I answered proudly. "I cannot merely rely on my family; I must accomplish certain goals for myself."

"That is very commendable," said the mother. "I am sure your mother is very proud of you."

"I would think so," I responded, trying to keep a steady tone of voice. There was absolutely no need for this stranger to be aware of my nonexistent family situation. To me, the word 'family' was not a part of my vocabulary.

"Herbert admires you a lot," continued the father. "Your friendship means the world to him and I thank you for that."

Involuntarily I turned my head to Herbert, surprised by these flattering words coming from his father. But the truth was that Herbert and I were not friends. I merely left him alone and didn't rebuke him when we were in the school surroundings. He was only a little less noisy and obnoxious than the rest of the students.

I never paid attention to anything happening around me as long I was not involved in any way. Perhaps, behind my back, they were talking about me, too, but in whisper so I wouldn't be provoked to an angry altercation. Herbert bowed his head, closing his eyes.

"I am not sure I understand," I said. "Isn't what…"

"Mr. Gutierre," his father interrupted me, "our son is constantly the subject of ridicule from other young gentlemen and you are the only one who has showed kindness to him."

"You are so sweet and gentle," I heard Renate say, and her voice sounded like birds chirping in my soul. No one since my mother had such wonderful words for me. I was eighteen and felt a wind of passion sweeping through my body.

The rest of the afternoon was pleasant and they treated me like a king. I accepted everything without restraint and wished only to be adored by Renate.

* * *

For her sake and because of all the complements she had in store for me, I started to pay more attention at school to her brother. It was not long until the same group I had despised and ignored for so long poured out their disgusting remarks on Herbert.

They had cornered him by the library door. I was some distance from them but this time I paid attention and I heard them clearly.

"Herb, the blob," started Johan, "I see you have a new shirt. Did you lose the buttons from your old one?"

"I saw him in his old shirt yesterday," mocked Sebastian. "It was so tight on him! His blubber made all the buttons pop right off!"

The other two started to laugh while Edward attempted to unbutton Herbert's shirt. The first two buttons unfastened. The shirt opened widely, uncovering part of Herbert's chest.

"Oh, look, hair on his chest," Sebastian pointed out loudly, "we have ourselves a little man here. Where else do you have hair, Herb?"

The boys were still laughing while Herbert tried to move away and leave, but they blocked the corridor. In the meantime more were gathering to join the fun.

"That would not be any of your concern," I answered in Herbert's behalf, who had turned red and started to sweat.

"I apologize," started Edward, with a smirk on his face, "but I do not recall including you in our discussion."

The crowd suddenly became quiet in expectation. I acted like I always had since I arrived at the school. I still held a very well established reputation among them, not to mention that I was the tallest there and I was allowed to have long hair.

"Not that I wish to have a discussion with you. I don't associate myself with such a poor mind as yours," I answered boldly.

Sebastian closed his fists and came closer to me. "What are you implying? That we are all stupid except for you?"

"You said it for me."

"If you think you are funny," Johan retorted, "then think twice, you bastard. Yes, that is true—your own family abandoned you because you are a bastard." A long, surprising murmur flowed over my head from the crowd.

His terrible words cut deeply into my heart and made my blood boil. If I had ever asked myself the same question, it was unimportant at that moment. It was being said in front of everyone and that raised my anger again. So, this was what they were whispering behind my back.

I stepped into their circle, agitated but still in control.

"Such frail and inferior creatures you are," I responded, raising my voice, "that believe themselves above others just because you cannot see beyond your impotency and mental deficit. You laugh at others in the hope that no one will look closely at you and discover your true sick minds. I am not a bastard. And if I am, it would not be your concern, as Herbert's chest hair is also not your concern. Perhaps you are jealous of him, Sebastian, because hair is absent everywhere else on your body."

There could have been a hundred ways to finish this discourse peacefully, but that was not my intention. I could not forget or forgive that I was insulted and I wanted them to know their limitations. I had not fought in a while, but I felt such a strong need to do so.

It wasn't long before the first punch came from Sebastian, as I had planned. I blocked it so easily and punched him back on his face. I didn't know how much force I had used, but he fell immediately to the ground. Edward was next, trying to push me into the crowd while Johan attempted to jump on my back.

I hit Edward hard in his stomach and I stretched my right leg high, hitting Johan behind his neck. It happened so rapidly as I put them both on the ground. I was the only one left standing. My anger and adrenaline was not consumed yet, but the boys would not get up.

Someone called for the director.

* * *

I was sent back home—to Paris, along with a letter of apology for Mr. Gutierre, my benefactor. Apparently Sebastian, suffered a concussion and lost some teeth, and Johan had some trouble hearing. It was all too drastic for their injuries to be just the result of my punches, but once again my reputation of being the bad boy climbed to the highest level.

Unfortunately, it was necessary to be sent away from school, perhaps indefinitely. I was to wait at home for the school's decision on my behalf. And that was my reward for standing up to protect Herbert.

All the way to Paris I rejoiced over my incredible powers, and I hoped that an opportunity to put them to the test would occur quite soon. I barely contained myself to not provoke anyone else into a fist fight.

But sadness emerged into my soul again. I was to leave Berlin and Renate behind, perhaps forever, and I was emotionally conflicted to go home to my mother after so many years of being absent. And two days later, here I was again at 1220 Rochelle Avenue, holding a small bag and waiting in the hallway to be announced.

The first person to welcome me was not my own mother but a boy approximately seven years old, blond with reddish hair. He looked at me with large dark eyes and asked me my name. I answered and I could easily guess that he was my half-brother.

His name was Pierre. Then, my mother came. I was astonished. Eight years had passed since I saw her last but she hadn't seemed to age a day. She was still so beautiful and young looking, even though she might be in her late thirties. She was wearing a dress the color of cornflowers, and she was apparently pregnant again.

Smiling and happy, I took a step forward to embrace her. But when she looked at me, she screamed for her husband. It was indescribable panic that I could see on her face when our eyes met.

She stepped back, her hands pressing tightly on her chest. I was totally surprised and confused by her disturbing reaction. Could she not recognize her own son anymore?

"I want him out of my house," she begged her husband.

"Mother it's me, Artamian!" I said in a desperate voice.

"Oh my Lord!" she yelled. "Go away. You are Milos Martuzon."

"Who is Milos Martuzon?"

6

"THIS IS MY CAR!" I exclaimed, as I watched Andreas driving my old Land Rover out of the garage.

"Yes it is," he admitted ironically. "Sorry, but I don't have a horse anymore. I had to use your car to bring you and your dog here. Your guns are still in it, and I just put in some more."

"Thank you," I said, as I opened the trunk and laid the Vortex over the guns and rifles. I also loaded up some other weapons, including a few Dragons and Tri Blades.

I chose to take a seat in the back as Andreas got behind the wheel. Raluca got in beside me and Serban sat in the passenger seat. The rest of our young men were traveling in a black Escalade. It looked as if the funeral business was doing well.

The road was heavily congested and I thought that was uncommon for a Thursday night. I didn't have a good feeling about meeting with people who were strangers to me, and I wasn't thrilled, either, about the idea of chasing Amestec in a place where a fight could be dangerous for any mortals who might be present.

"Where are we going?" I asked my brother, and I tried to hide how irritated I was by the fact that I had been in control of everything for so long. But I trusted Serban. He had been doing this for so long. But so had I.

"It's pretty far to Deerfield Beach, but we'll get there soon. It'll be dark when we get there, so no one should light up—we don't want trouble."

The air conditioning was blasting cold air on the boys in the front, so I opened the window a bit. I don't like feeling cold at all. Raluca had let me borrow her blue dress, and I disliked the fact that I wasn't even in control of my own wardrobe—specifically, my own undergarments. What irritated me most was that I *could* buy my own stuff—I was rich, after all. Andreas stared at me in the rear view mirror all the way to our destination, and he didn't lose that expression of confusion that came over him after he saw me handling the Vortex.

I hadn't made up my mind about him yet, but I couldn't justify—not even to myself—what the reasoning would be to accept him back into my life, when the future wasn't in his favor.

Truthfully, this reunion with my past was not the way I had always imagined it, and it had started to become a little uncomfortable, at least on my part. There were five men too many, for starters.

My comfort zone for the past century had been composed of just Octavian and me. For now, only Raluca was an acceptable addition to this zone, merely because I could feel her emotions and they weren't a threat to me.

* * *

After we exited the interstate, we didn't turn towards the beach as I would have liked, but we turned onto a side road and drove into a rundown area that I didn't think could exist in South Florida. Some of the buildings appeared to be abandoned, and some were just severely damaged by the weather or vandals.

We stopped at a place that seemed to be a restaurant at one time, and I could barely read its name on a faded sign that was hanging out over the sidewalk: *Grecian Steak House*. I hesitated—anything that was connected with Greeks wasn't good news in my mind, since my earlier battle with the Amestec.

"Why're we meeting here," I asked again, somewhat alarmed over the fact that Serban would so be so eager to attend this peculiar summit. I wasn't given a detailed explanation and Serban was already out of the car while I was still waiting for an answer to my question. He walked rapidly to the entrance. Someone inside was apparently waiting for him, and as he approached the door, it opened.

"Hello, Cedric," said my brother, saluting the man who had opened the door for him.

Everyone exited from the cars and gathered behind me. To my dismay, they were armed only with their regular guns. Friend or foe—they were still vulnerable to an unexpected Amestec's attack. Because Serban had said earlier that none of us should make our eyes glow, I followed him blindly inside as the door immediately opened for us.

The decrepit outside appearance of the restaurant was only a cover, a deceit. The interior was entirely different. I found myself looking at the most modern restaurant I had seen in many years. Along with seven large flat screen TV's hanging from the bar, directly ahead of us were solid oak tables arranged in four rows, with chairs that had an interesting design carved into the back supports. The entire restaurant had a Grecian style décor, although it was a bit too colorful for my taste.

A massive mural on the right wall represented a white house on the shore, but the other walls were painted in a muted peach color. The water in the mural was a clear blue that truly showed the beauty of Greece. The floor was solid wood, which was quite unusual for Florida. But the minute I walked in the door, I understood why—every step we took caused the wood to make a loud squeak.

If you were concerned about intruders, this was a subtle way of being made aware of them.

My biggest surprise came when I saw the hosts of this place. Sitting on stools, facing us, were five male Immortals. The one that Serban called Cedric was African American, with dark blue eyes and dreadlocks pulled back into a ponytail. The other four had the same signature look as most of us: tall, long dark hair (but kept loose) and sparkling blue eyes. The men had a darker skin tone than mine, proof that they either enjoyed Florida's sun or they spent much time outdoors in other activities. That made their appearance even more fascinating. Unlike the Europeans, they were wearing jeans and black t-shirts.

I had expected something like that, but not that the fourth man among them was Julian Grant. Nothing had prepared me for encountering him, just months after we had parted ways.

I just stood there, motionless, thinking that a disappearing act on my part would be welcomed if I could pull off something like that. But the innocent surprise from Julian's face was a sign that he didn't knew about my coming here.

Although Serban positioned himself between me and the other guys, I could sense now that my brother had accepted this invitation only because he was aware that something unusual was on the agenda.

"Alex, what's this all about?" asked Serban, turning to the male on his right.

The one called Alex, acting like the leader of the group, got up and came straight towards me. He was followed closely by Julian, who appeared to be a bit confused and baffled.

"This is a matter that concerns her," Alex responded, and he saluted me by lifting two fingers to his forehead. "You are quite a surprise, Safira! Dark red hair—I like it."

"Lady Safira, these are the American Immortals. Meet Alex, Kyle, Cedric, Luke and a new one," Serban said, calling me by my formal name and pointing at Julian. As he was introduced, he got so close to me that a jealous Andreas put his gun to Grant's temple.

"Get away from her," Andreas threatened him, with unrequited anger.

Andreas and Julian together, the two men I loved. Strangely enough, I didn't feel their presence in the same way. Seeing them together stirred a feeling of confusion inside me, as I expected, in spite of their close resemblance. At this moment I had to keep calm, and allow myself time to confront my own emotions later.

"He's one of us," said Alex, "I'm not sure your gun will kill him. His name is Julian. He just joined us yesterday. He's American, too."

Julian.

I was accustomed to calling him 'Grant', but Immortals do not carry a last name. We all take a last name eventually, but only for the sake of staying safe among the mortals.

"Yesterday?" mumbled Andreas. "And you've already brought him to our meeting?"

"Yes. Because he knows her."

Everyone turned to look at me. My tongue was still numb, but my demeanor was steady and composed. There was no point in denying knowing Julian, and especially our involvement. But I resented his presence here. The fact that he came to join the other Americans so soon after his conversion was a sign of ingratitude. Ignoring all my precautions in this regard was a blow that gradually began to harden my heart.

Andreas, who at this point realized Julian's true relationship to me, forcefully pushed him back a few more feet. However, the men reacted exactly as I thought they would. Julian didn't dare to look into my eyes anymore; he understood how much trouble he had gotten himself into and that I was so unhappy.

"I must say that I couldn't make myself believe his story at first," continued Alex, addressing Serban, "but that little message you sent this morning made me a halfway believer."

"I don't care how much you believe or not," said Serban a bit irritated, "what was the urgency of our meeting now?"

"This morning I made a certain discovery of such severity that I can only disclose it to Lady Safira."

Saying that, he turned to me, waiting for my reaction. His face opened into a radiant smile. His eyes were close to each other, but intense, as they guarded a narrow straight nose. But Alex's vital interest was not to tell me his finding. The man seemed to wrestle with an instant and vain temptation to test my powers, the same way Lars and Ditmar had done.

I could have diffused the moment, but then, an altercation, as stupid as might have been, was a welcomed distraction from the present situation.

"Why is that only you, the Europeans, could have her," he asked, continuing to walk around me.

"Alex, this is not the right time for this," said Serban and he gave me a worried look. Behind him, Lars, Ditmar and Codrin moved closer towards the Americans.

Kyle was still sitting at the bar with his arms crossed over his chest, while Luke and Cedric jumped over the counter. Luke grabbed a gun from under the counter before he made his leap. Serban turned to me, pressing his lips together like he was uncertain of the severity of Alex's intentions.

"We're great warriors, too," continued Alex, continuing his orbit around me. "We fought for the country's independence; we paid our dues to humanity. Why wouldn't she stay with us instead of with you? I have an equal right to claim her and I am challenging you to a fight. The prize will be her!"

I pressed my hands against my hips, appalled by Alex's insolent request and ready to intervene in this conversation, but it seemed to me that neither of the two men was interested in my consent. Raluca grabbed my hand and pulled me back towards the door.

"You must be crazy," said Serban, and his voice sounded like thunder. I could tell that he was becoming enraged and he regretted coming here. "Are you insane? We are not here to fight for her."

"Oh, that's an understatement; I'm sure you all wanted this—and it's long overdue."

"Your conduct is unacceptable, Alex. Why aren't you saying what you really want? You really want to fight *her*, don't you?"

"Then let him fight her," proposed Ditmar. "Let him embarrass himself."

"Sure," agreed Lars with an ironic smile, "he has a reputation to uphold. Imagine if all the Americans should hear about this."

'Shut up, all of you," commanded Alex, as he rapidly ran over to the bar and grabbed a sword from underneath it.

Suddenly all the men pulled out their guns and started to shout at each other, and the building stated to shake from the ground up. In the moment's panic I saw that Julian had dropped to the floor. He wasn't armed and he tried to stay away from the rain of bullets.

They weren't fighting with each other because of their rivalry but because the need to fight had boiled inside them for so long. It was Serban who started the shooting and I knew why—they had me now, and they weren't afraid to be hurt.

Kyle, Cedric and Luke took cover behind the bar. Only Alex was still out in the open. He used his left hand with the sword to defend against the bullets, and fired his gun with his other hand.

Some of the tables and the chairs were turned on their sides and used as shields. In a matter of minutes, drinking glasses, the mirrors behind the bar, and a couple of TV screens were destroyed. The walls in front of me and behind me were full of holes. It reminded me of a gun fight in a bar in an old western movie, and that was even more annoying. I didn't move because no one aimed their gun at me.

My first impulse was to break up the fight by getting in the way of the bullets as I had done in Greece, but something told me that that would not be enough. In order to stop them, I had to use a weapon and I didn't have one—not a gun or a sword on me.

In my mind I went back at the moment when I laid the Vortex on top of the other weapons. I saw it with my spiritual eyes and I wished for it. The side window of the car was open and I levitated the Vortex out through it.

A moment later, one of the restaurant's windows exploded as something powerful came through and straight to me. I raised my hand and caught it—the Vortex. The weapon was alive and moving in the direction that my mind commanded it.

I stepped up on a chair and then onto a table to gain more height in order to fly over Codrin's head in the middle of the room. I swung the Vortex and it orbited around the combatants at their eye level, and then it returned back to me.

The men stopped shooting. Their faces froze in astonishment. The Americans and the Europeans all dropped their guns and raised their hands at my command.

"I am no one's property," I shouted, and I pointed my weapon at Alex and his men. "You *all* owe me your allegiance."

In the corner of my eye I saw Serban's face grimace with a spasm of aggressiveness. I saw a power problem emerging: two men—always in charge, making decisions and accustomed to being obeyed.

And me.

We couldn't be a trinity.

"You still want to fight me?" I asked Alex, but his eyes moved from me to the floor. Apparently, the sharp object in my hand was all too well known to him. He was conflicted about it, but he chose to be wise.

7

THREE MORE HOUSE SERVANTS *joined Mr. Gutierre to force me to leave their house. I had no intention of staying there against my mother's will. Her reaction to my presence made me understand that now, as a grown young man, I did resemble someone from her past—someone of whom she was terrified.*

Perhaps it was my father, but I had no way of asking her and learning the truth.

Mr. Gutierre handed me some money, a considerable sum, and asked me to leave. I was back on the street and I didn't know if I needed to turn left or right—neither direction would have made a substantial difference in my life at this point.

"What is happening, sir?" I dared to ask Mr. Gutierre. "Why is my mother denying me and who is Milos Martuzon?"

The man looked at me with pity. After taking a moment to analyze my situation he concluded, "You are not welcome in her life anymore. I can only suspect that Milos Martuzon was your father. The money will take you as far as Transylvania."

"Where is Transylvania?" I asked, intrigued. "Why would I go there?"

"You are not a very smart boy," he said, frustrated. "All I can tell you is that Transylvania is a small province in the Austrian Empire and that is where your mother was born. That is all I can do for you. Go now and never come back."

Saying that, he turned his back to me and locked the massive front door. The three story building was closed to me forever.

I was eighteen and now I was suddenly homeless. It was a bit different than before—even if I didn't have much connection with my family, at least I had a good situation because of my step-father.

But Mr. Gutierre was wrong—I was smart and even if my qualifications wouldn't take me very far, I would survive. At that point I had no intention to go to such an insignificant place as Transylvania, to search for my mother's relatives or for my father—who obviously had abandoned me. My sole goal was to find a place to sleep that night.

I rented a comfortable room at the Royal Hotel in downtown Paris and the next morning I was at the train station purchasing a ticket to Berlin. As I prepared to pay, my attention was diverted by an old man at the next window who was frantically searching in his wallet for his money. I saw his desperate face and I turned and handed him a few bills without considering that I was barely left with anything for myself.

But wherever this man was going, I was pretty much in his shoes as well. This money in my pocket was not my money and my future was close to nonexistent—so why worry? The old man bowed deeply to me and thanked me, long after I left the ticket window.

*   *   *

I took the train to Berlin. I had a friend there and I was hoping Herbert and his father would still consider me a part of the family, as they had declared before. I was also anxious to see Renate again and pursue her love. Now, of course, without Mr. Gutierre's money, I was not considered a good catch, but I thought that all would change soon.

My planning was interrupted by a young man who made his way up the aisle and deliberately took a seat across from me; then he saluted me as if we were acquaintances. I stared back at him but I was not in the mood to start a conversation.

To my surprise, the stranger had features similar to mine—dark shoulder length long hair, a Roman nose, a wide forehead, and intense blue eyes that looked directly and boldly into mine. He was also taller than average, perhaps in his late twenties.

"I think this is a great day for traveling," he said without a smile or intending to be overly friendly. I nodded, but in reality I didn't care. "What is your destination, sir?"

"Berlin," I answered, looking out through the window. The young man appeared to be very well dressed, like a nobleman, and with good manners. At this point, I could use a friend.

"Berlin's a great city," he continued politely. "I have some family there."

"I'm visiting friends," I answered. "I am sorry to ask, but did we ever meet before? You look somewhat familiar."

"Well, I saw you in the train station giving money to that poor old man—a great philanthropic gesture to help a complete stranger. I very much admire you for it."

"It was nothing," I said with sincere modesty, "He needed it and I happened to have it—perhaps anyone else would have done the same. I wasn't aware that someone was watching."

"My mane is Gallbor, John Gallbor," he introduced himself. "I'm from Liechtenstein."

"Artamian. My last name was Gutierre, but I am unsure of that, now. So just call me Artamian. I'm from Paris."

"It's a pleasure to meet you Artamian. But you are wrong in one matte—many men passed him by without helping."

The young man didn't expect an invitation from me to continue a conversation. He started to talk about his numerous relatives, friends, and places I had never heard of, and it was not too long before I fell asleep. Once in a while I would be awakened for a few moments, but I could still hear him talking.

At one point I could vaguely see him getting up and lightly touching my forehead—but perhaps that was only my imagination. When the conductor woke me up at the Berlin station, John Gallbor was gone.

When I asked the other passengers, no one knew where he went or remembered seeing him.

* * *

Renate stood by the window seat smiling, and I hoped she was happy with my presence. Her father scratched his forehead, at a loss for words and puzzled because I was at their dinner table a week after I had been expelled.

"Mr. Gutierre, I don't know what to say," he said with a puzzled look.

"Indeed, this is so unfortunate," added Mrs. Walden with a sad voice.

"Well, I must accept the reality that my family could not accept my intolerable behavior in protecting Herbert," I said. At that point I was lying about the real reason my family had banned me, saying they were furious because of the whole incident regarding Herbert.

I needed them and this was my primary motive—to gain their appreciation and gratitude in the hope that they would allow me to remain with them for a while. My soul was strongly conflicted by my actions, but nevertheless, I also needed for Renate to admire me and give me affection.

"Well, I do have some good news for you," said Herbert, and his eyes shone with excitement after he had waited patiently for me to pour out my misfortunes. "I think that you still have some family that wants you."

"What are you saying, Herbert?" I asked my so called friend, wondering if I needed to worry or not.

"About two days after you left the school that morning, your grandfather came looking for you."

"My grandfather?"

I was stunned. I had no knowledge of the identity of my father until a day ago, and now an unknown member of my family was suddenly looking for me.

"Three days ago I was in the director's waiting room with the intent to inquire about you and plead for your return, when I saw an old gentleman in the office. He said that his name is Mr. Johan Lutz and he was looking for you regarding a matter of inheritance. Isn't that a great news?"

I got up and turned to Herbert, who was standing beside me, and I involuntarily hugged him strongly. Herbert's large body shook under my pressure. I didn't know who this old man was, but to me he was definitely a godsend.

"Tell me more," I begged. "What was it that he said about me?"

"Well, the director told him that you had returned to Paris. Mr. Lutz said that unfortunately he must return home, that he was in poor health and unable to continue to travel."

"Ohhh," whispered Renate, and that moment all my hopes degenerated and I turned to desperation again.

"Mr. Lutz mentioned that you are the sole owner of a palace in the city of Oradea, wherever that is. Perhaps you know where your grandfather resides," suggested Herbert, and I had to admit that my large friend was wiser than I thought.

"Yes, I do indeed," I said, thinking that Transylvania must be the first place I should start my search. "Unfortunately, my finances are too limited to take on such expensive travels."

"I am more than willing to contribute to such a venture," added Mr. Walden with dignity, but I was sure that the fact that I was to inherit a castle was also a determining factor in his decision. "You are a friend to our son and for now we are your family."

"I accept with gratitude," I said and for the first time in my life, I truly considered myself lucky to a have Herbert as a friend. That boy, who was too slow in his movements and too large for anybody to befriend him, was by all means my savior.

Everything, starting with the day he invited me to dinner and continuing with my return to his home, homeless and helpless—this young man with freckles and pimples, was a crucial intermediary in my destiny.

* * *

That evening we both stood on the veranda drinking refreshments made by Renate and smoking some sort of strange cigars from Mr. Walden's collection.

"Artamian," started Herbert and he was already sweating in his new shirt, even though it wasn't all that hot outside, *"I must say that I have never encountered anyone who knows how to fight like you. Where did you learn that?"*

"It must be just the fact that I am so tall and muscular."

"Not at all," Herbert disagreed. *"I meant that you do have the knowledge, as well as the ability, to fight. You put down three boys in three moves—that isn't normal. Please teach me to fight like you."*

I turned to Herbert, who stood up and removed his vest in the expectation of his first fighting lesson.

"I am tired of being mocked," he said, raising his arms toward me, *"If I can fight them, they will all leave me alone."*

"Herbert, you have no reason to be afraid of them anymore," I said, with no intention of giving in to my friend's ridiculous request. *"It's all over, now."*

"What do you mean?"

"You have less than a year to finish the school and leave that place behind you. None of the troublesome boys are there anymore, and all the others

will remember the incident—you can walk around with your head held up and proud. Besides, you have no idea how hard it is to learn to fight like me."

I kept a serious face while Herbert tried to decide if would worth it for him to learn to fight, or just keep a low profile for another year. The second choice was more appealing to my massive friend. It was settled then, and we were both satisfied, although his compliment about my fighting skills made me think that somehow I must possess some special powers and I was lucky to be born so big and powerful.

*   *   *

They prepared a nice room for me on the third floor of the house and thinking that my coming here was such a lucky turn of events, I considered that I could stay with them a bit longer before I would go to Transylvania and take over my palace.

My Palace.

I repeated this word over and over the whole evening. And even if Mr. Johan Lutz was my grandfather or not, I was sure that he wouldn't take the trouble to find me unless I was truly the rightful owner of that castle. Perhaps that meant that my own father or someone else passed away, but it didn't matter to me.

I heard the faint noise of someone walking on the hallway and my door opened slowly. It was Renate. She was holding a small candle and dressed only in her night gown. Her surprise visit stirred up my instincts. I became overexcited and I had to mask both the awakening in my whole body and my erection that her presence produced.

She came closer and crawled in bed with me with a wild provoking smile.

"I came to kiss you good night," she said, laying her head on my pillow.

I bent over her and kissed her dimples. I felt a frantic need to remove her clothes. If she had come to my room to show me some innocent affection, there was nothing innocent about my intentions for her.

73

Something was igniting inside me like a fire. But she was the one who took my hand and pressed it on her bare chest. Her small breast was resting in my palm, like a bird. Her skin was so white and her lips so fragile, and my whole body started to vibrate with lust.

By this time I was almost delirious as I started to kiss her lips, while my hand searched between her legs for places that had been previously unknown to me.

I was ready. But the moment I closed my eyes, the image of an unknown girl with long dark hair and fiery blue eyes replaced the sweet childlike image of Renate in my mind. I stopped kissing Renate and I opened my eyes quickly.

The girl looked at me puzzled and I tried again—and again it happened.

Surely I was going crazy, or my mind was too fatigued, that I wouldn't enjoy kissing a girl. How could I have this stranger's image in my mind when I was holding another girl in my arms, ready and willing to give herself to me? This time I started to kiss her with my eyes open and soon my hands were caressing her hips.

But before I could continue with my quest, I felt a sudden burden overflowing into my soul.

I got up and left the room, and Renate remained there, lying on the bed alone. It would be so wrong for me to act on my predatory instincts with this young girl, and betray the family who trusted and embraced me.

Early the next morning I left for Transylvania. I couldn't stay there a day longer. I was certain that it wouldn't be the last time that Renate would crawl into my bed, and when it happened again, I wouldn't stop in my quest to conquer her.

8

"I APOLOGIZE TO YOU," started Serban, after a moment of awkward silence. He retrieved his gun from the floor and stuck it behind his back in his belt. "It was a mistake to bring you here, even though I thought that everyone would behave."

"God, this was so foolish," I said, furiously. "Are you all feeling better now?"

Alex nodded, visibly embarrassed, but I pretended not to acknowledge that. I knew immediately what was happening. They all desired to fight—It was in their nature—and they had grown restless in their spirit. Even a fight among themselves was welcomed at times.

This would have to change. Our purpose in this world would have to change very soon.

"This place is a mess," I complained, stepping on a carpet of bullet shells. "Are any of you hurt?" I dropped the Vortex on one of the tables and I motioned for them to check their bodies.

Each of them had been shot, with the exception of Julian and Raluca, and when they took off their shirts, all of them had bullet holes in their chests. One by one they came to me, and I patiently removed the bullets and erased the evidence of the holes. Their eyes watched me with gratitude and submission.

Until that moment, the Americans, had no idea what a Healer was all about.

The last to be checked, and the worst hit, was Alex, with seventeen bullets in his chest, arms, and abdomen. He had been the target of six guns—I remembered that even Raluca shot at him. I touched his skin and he trembled. His body had many more signs of unhealed wounds. I pressed harder on his heart and I felt something in there, too.

This was serious—he needed my help. He covered my palm with his and his eyes were imploring. I understood his feelings; although to me, male pride was usually beyond my understanding.

"Serban, you may return to Wellington. I'm coming later—I need a word with Alex."

"You shouldn't stay behind alone," he said, most likely concerned about leaving me behind and alone with three males—one who was too new for his liking. Too, he didn't trust that Alex's impulsive nature wouldn't show itself again.

"Luke, Cedric and Kyle, you should leave, too," said Alex to the other three Immortals. "We'll clean up this place in the morning before we start our shift on the beach. We're lifeguards, Lady Safira, and we work for the Coast Guard, too. It's a good job and we're in place to spot enemies. Only Julian can stay, I need him."

The men hesitated a moment, perhaps out of prudent curiosity. Then they took their guns and left.

"Raluca can stay with me," I said to my own crew, who until that moment didn't listen to me telling them to leave. "The rest of you are five too many."

"When should we expect you back?" asked Andreas, very displeased by my request.

His body turned involuntarily to Julian, who stood silent, leaning against the wall, and he became tense. In the future, this would be a matter for me to resolve. These confrontations would become too frequent and unbearable. For now, I thought that Julian had accepted defeat.

"You stay away from her," said Andreas and threatened Julian with his gun again.

"Come on, Andreas," demanded Serban and he bowed to me and turned, walking towards the door. "All of you, let's go. Alex, don't do anything stupid."

Saying this Serban slammed the door behind him. A few seconds later I heard the engine of the Escalade rev up and the crunch of the tires as they left the parking lot. Raluca took a seat on a bar stool, keeping a cautious eyes on Julian and Alex. I knew that she was anxious to find out the reason I stayed behind, but my first priority was to take care of Alex.

I saw hope in his eyes, a new connection with his true identity, a notion that was lost to him for the last century. He longed for a spiritual renewal and he was tired of his condition, absent of all glory.

"I need to operate on you," I said to him as I handed back his tattered T- shirt. He didn't put it back on, but he disposed of it in the trash, quite confident in showing me his perfectly fit and tanned upper body. "I can extract that bullet. Right now it's acting like its alive and it's moving. I've located it one inch away from your heart."

"It's not going to kill me," he said, walking away and stopping by one of the tables where I had laid the Vortex. His fingers moved closer to the blade like he wanted to touch it.

"Are you familiar with this weapon?" I asked him, intrigued.

"I saw it in action on one of our 'hunting' trips, I think. It's a pretty powerful thing, like nothing I've ever seen before. I know that no one else can handle it. It was quite amazing how you were able to maneuver it with your mind."

"Who's its owner?" I asked, and I couldn't mask the excitement in my voice. "Is he an American?"

"I don't know his name. He appears to be a loner, and he's quite comfortable with that. I tried recruiting him for our team, but he refused. Regardless, he seemed to be there for us a few times when we needed help. The only detail we know about him is his place of origin. We simply call him *the Transylvanian*. He may be one of yours."

"Describe him to me," I continued to ask, annoying the man; no one else from my land could possibly be unknown to me— I had already met all the known Transylvanians, old and new.

"Describe him? We all look alike, except that he's taller, not at all talkative, and muscular, like one of those pumped up wrestlers on TV."

Alex smiled at his own comment, satisfied that he was keeping me interested. But to me, every detail about his identity was all too serious and I even was more determined to find him. Somehow, it was impossible to acknowledge the possibility of the existence of another Transylvanians as powerful as he was described. Unless he was the one…but I pushed that thought out of my mind.

"I'm glad you're here," Alex continued. "Julian's told us some amazing things about you."

Julian.

My soul melted, but I didn't let it show.

"I'm sure he did," I said sadly, suspicious that Julian had most likely bragged about me and our relationship. My conduct was icy towards him. I had to remain passive.

"I'm sorry, Lady Safira, I didn't mean to upset you," Julian said with a despairing voice. "After returning to my unit I was so unhappy. It was a long, unhappy year. I thought hard about joining this group, and it's the one place where I thought I could really help. And, it'll help me with the pain of losing you. I *am* a soldier, after all."

"You're too new to this kind of life to be involved in any of this," I said harshly, refusing to look at him.

Raluca placed her hand over Julian's mouth so he would keep silent. She quickly understood that Julian was, at one time, the mortal man had I loved. I could tell that she was puzzled by the close resemblance between Julian and Andreas and the fact that he was one of us now.

This wasn't the right time to analyze my situation, but I couldn't wrap my mind around this situation any more. Julian Grant must stay away from me. There was no doubt in my mind that learning to let go of Julian would not be as easy as I thought, now that he was here. With Andreas, it had only been a matter of time, but now that he was here too, I had to admit that I never actually got over losing him, either.

The answer was simple: I had lived a life that was vulnerable, hovering over a lost love.

"Well, I explained to Julian a lot of things last night," Alex broke into my thoughts. "When he called me, I had to see him for myself. These days, every one of us who is alive needs to stay that way—we need to stick together. I've lost over a hundred men, Immortals whose spirits were savagely ripped from their bodies by the Amestec."

"I gave him a new life," I said, but only addressing Alex.

"And now, let him choose how to live it."

"I need to cut you open and take that bullet out," I said, changing the subject and annoyed to conclude that Alex was right.

"I'm sure you're not going to die, but that bullet could stop your heart at any time. When it does, the timing will be bad for you."

"Oh, so here ends my reign as a tough warrior. I've survived every battle I have ever been in."

"Including a stupid one just this night. Look at all this destruction!"

"Well, that was just a brotherly squabble. I had to see for myself what you can do. The restaurant is bullet and sound proof—we shoot a lot in here. When I got a message from Serban telling me that you were here, I humbly admit that nothing else mattered but you."

"You said that you made a discovery that concerns only me."

"Yes, I did. Follow me."

* * *

The back room didn't look at all like a kitchen. It was obvious that there was no cooking being done in there, but the room had a close resemblance to my old basement. To the right were computer screens with hundreds of images from satellites, with the capability to monitor every street camera in the country, x-ray machines, and an array of weapons—including swords. To the left was something similar to a laboratory.

"We've been working from this place for the last twelve years" said Alex, proudly. "It was getting harder to distinguish the real Immortals from the impostor Amestec because many of us had changed our appearance to blend in. We are obviously hunted because of our appearance. So, we have a DNA lab. It wasn't always necessary to use it—chasing them for saliva or a blood sample wasn't fun—but there's a more powerful breed out there that's harder to detect after it's been transformed.

"Somewhere down the line they all acquired a root of your DNA. At first I didn't understand all of this and I blamed Gallbor for it, until last night when Julian told me an amazing story about your being killed with a sword. He said you were brought back to life by your brother, Octavian. I have never heard about Octavian, an Immortal with such incredible powers. Why is that?"

"Alex, did you tell Serban about Octavian?" I asked him in a whisper, moving closer to his face until I could feel his breath. The young man deeply inhaled my scent for a second before to answer.

"Jesus, you smell so wonderful. No, I haven't told him anything, yet. I was about to when you sent him away."

I turned again towards Julian who gazed at me with a sorrowful look. He wasn't at fault here—it was just a matter of time before Octavian would be known to everyone—if he could just find me.

"Octavian is my younger brother," I whispered to Alex, hoping that Raluca didn't hear him the first time. "He was born after me and he's unknown to rest of the Order. He was sent to protect me and fight for me, and I was entrusted to keep his existence a secret."

"Safira, your secret will be safe with me. Anyway, this morning, Serban, sent me this."

"My coffee cup," I exclaimed unpleasantly, surprised at recognizing the object in Alex's hand. My pupils changed in size and my eyes wanted to glow thunder.

"Don't be mad," Alex remarked peacefully. "He just wanted to be sure. These are dangerous times; nothing or no one is to be trusted anymore. Look at Raluca. She could pass for the hot trophy wife of a movie star—no one could guess who or what she is. Or you, for that matter, with your red hair."

Raluca looked at me, bothered by his comment about her looks. I sensed that she was not proud of it, but it suited her mission in the best way. They didn't become cowards by doing that, perhaps just a bit more wise. I had used the same trick on Octavian to mask his appearance, so I didn't feel any differently about myself, and the change in my appearance was welcome.

"Shut up, Alex," Raluca said, still protecting Julian.

"I'm just telling the truth," he replied. "Lady Safira has to know what's out there! The Amestec have a leader now, and they've started to gather—and they outnumber us. I'm trying to learn where they have their camp so we can hit them all at once."

"How many of us are left?"

"Perhaps fifty. I summoned everyone to gather here in Florida after I realized that they were hunted down in their own homes. Someone knew their precise locations. The ones still capable of fighting are here with me. The rest are in the safe place I built for them. It's a great place to hide and raise the young ones. Like the Europeans, we too, have offspring. It's about time for a new generation. You are a young Queen and we need young Warriors."

"Alex, are there more than two hundred Amestec?

"Yes and some are old and impatient."

"Well, than, this it's a matter of math," I theorized. "There are not enough of us to kill all of them. So, we'll have to put some of them on the back burner unless they start killing each other."

"I hadn't thought about that, but I am afraid that they have another alternative."

"Me."

Alex touched his forehead with his right hand fingers, and bowed to me, a sign of devotion and commitment. I read him: he was smart, motivated, disciplined, but afraid to commit errors. A true warrior, but a proud man at heart. And right now his heart had a bullet in it, and I must convince him to allow me to take it out.

"Alex, you are a fearless warrior, but if you don't let me do surgery on you, you're going to become a heartless one."

He turned and looked quickly at Julian, who nodded in agreement. Then he smiled at me and removed a small knife from one of the drawers, handing it to me.

"I need for you to lie down on something—a desk would do it."

"I prefer to stand."

"I'm telling you, you can't stand up for this. I hope you won't provoke me to force you to lie down." And with a serious face I laid my hands on his shoulder and pushed him down on the desk.

Alex smiled again. My so called forceful intervention was pleasing to him. I circled his chest with my fingers in clockwise motion until I could feel the metal. He took my hand and rested it over his heart for a moment longer. It wasn't meant to seek pleasure, but a reflection of his sensible hidden nature.

"I once abandoned hope of winning this battle," he said, closing his eyes. "But now I desire victory above all, and here you are with me."

"You know that I'm a Warrior and a Healer, Alex. I'll do my part and fight alongside you."

"No. You must be protected so you can take care of us. You can't be in danger of becoming their prisoner."

"Stay still," I ordered him, "we'll talk about this later. This isn't going to hurt."

I cut deep and just a drop of blood erupted from his chest before it started to coagulate. The sharp narrow knife was bulky, but it did the job. I could feel when the blade hit the bullet. By now, Alex's eyes were open very wide and they were hanging on my every movement. He wasn't afraid or concerned. It was more like he wanted this moment to last longer. I cut one more inch to the right until my fingers were able to get into the wound, and pulled it out.

Not long ago I had done the same thing for Julian. Now, Julian watched me as if he were in a trance, and those memories became painful for both of us.

I released my grayish healing dust and reconnected all the veins and arteries. I put some pressure on the incision and I removed my hand. It was done. Alex stood upright and immediately checked his chest.

"Incredible," he said. "It's like I've never been hurt."

9

MR. LUTZ BROUGHT DINNER *to my room that evening. I was given my father's old apartment while some other rooms were still occupied by people who had been renting the castle for the past hundred years. Some were the governor's aides, and some were noblemen.*

So, I learned that my father was Milos Martuzon, once the imperial governor of the province of Transylvania, and my mother's real name was Anda Kovack. I wanted to find out everything about him upon my arrival and I wanted the knowledge immediately, but Mr. Lutz promised he would talk about my father later. He was an older gentleman in his late sixties, a bit short and very slim, with white hair, a white curly mustache, hard of hearing, and slow in his movements. He presented himself to me as my father's personal servant, aiding him for almost fifty years.

The money I had received from Mr. Walden took me all the way to Budapest. There I inquired about a city called Oradea and soon I was able to find out more details about my family from a very informed librarian. He told me to look for the Black Eagle Palace or the governor's palace.

When I arrived, it was late in the evening, and before I could introduce myself, the man who answered the door quickly pulled me inside.

"Welcome home, Lord Martuzon," he said to me, and I was certain that I had found the right place.

"Thank you," I responded to his greetings. *"This is my home, now."*

After a restful night, I started to learn about the Black Eagle Palace. The part of the palace I was living in seemed to be abandoned. I toured it with Mr. Lutz, who proudly showed me all the palace's grand rooms. We continued into the private apartments and we finished with the servants' rooms. But on the last floor, he carefully avoided showing me a certain room and he didn't attempt to open the door. I didn't ask much about the room at the time, but I was curious if something was being hidden from me.

In the next few days I was taken for a detailed tour of the city—the palaces, the theatre, The Church with the Moon, the multitude of stores, and not the least of the attractions, the peaceful Crisu River.

I was presented to all the inhabitants one by one. I was received politely, but at the same time, with some uncertainties. I could understand why—I was the new master and they were not sure of my intentions.

Finally, I was told that my father had been attacked in his own room and was killed by some renegade soldiers. That forced my mother to run away to save my life. Mr. Lutz had spent the last twenty years looking for me.

As he told me these things, not once did he look me in my eyes. It must have been a dreadful situation for him to be forced to tell me this sad story about my family, but all in all I was happy to be wrong about my being a bastard or abandoned. I felt proud and not sad at all—I never knew my father, so his passing didn't affect me at all.

I started to enjoy a life of free living, having money, and good situation. Perhaps Mr. Lutz expected me to ask more details about my father's killers. After all the time that had passed, however, I was certain there was no chance that I could revenge his death—not that it was imperative for me to do so. Staying in his room was not uncomfortable to me because I didn't feel any connection to the things he had left behind.

There was only one thing I did not have an answer for—my own mother's behavior and the secret she kept for so long about our identity. We were *royals, and this was nothing of which we should be ashamed. If maintaining secrecy was only to protect me from unknown enemies, why would she disregard me when I seemed to grow into a resemblance of my father? There was something in Mr. Lutz's story and my mother's past that didn't seem to connect, but I was too young to care.*

Soon I gained new friends in town—at least those few who could speak German or French. I became a regular at the Theatre and I began to accumulate a rich wardrobe. I didn't consider myself to be a handsome young man, but the girls started to notice me.

One in particular, Francesca, was young, pretty, and blonde. I was very attracted to her, even though we couldn't communicate much because I didn't speak Romanian or Hungarian at that time.

One evening, after a ball held by me for those who resided in the palace, she followed me into my living quarters and she openly gave herself to me. I was so eager to make love with her that I forgot what had happened when I was with Renate. The moment I closed my eyes to kiss her, a beautiful brunette's image appeared in my mind. Her presence was so strong that I had to stand up and gasp for air.

Francesca rushed to bring me some wine. She had an attractive body with long, soft legs, large breasts and a tiny waist. I didn't give up! She wouldn't escape me like Renate did—but I couldn't close my eyes as we became more intimate.

After Francesca left, I felt dissatisfied, empty of feelings, and disturbed as I drank more wine. I grabbed the entire bottle and started to walk the palace corridors without a certain destination in mind. But there was one door in the palace that still intrigued me, and after a month of residence, no one had opened it for me—the last apartment on the third floor beside the service stairs.

I thought I would have to force myself into the apartment, but the door was actually unlocked. When I stepped across the threshold I walked around the room. As I judged the furniture and the color of curtains, I could guess that long ago it had belonged to a female. Could it have been my mother's? Somehow, I doubted it.

I could feel sadness and loneliness here, feelings I couldn't shake, even after I consumed the entire bottle. It was certainly a mistake for me to want to come here. My curiosity was fulfilled—it was just an empty room, and it didn't merit my attention.

But I was wrong! As I was leaving the room, I saw a young girl with brown hair and big blue eyes looking at me from one of the pictures hanging on the wall. I dropped my empty bottle and it shattered on the floor.

It was the girl I had seen every time had I closed my eyes, when I wanted to make love with other girls.

I screamed for Mr. Lutz. It was quite late, after midnight, but I continued to scream his name until after a few minutes he managed to discover my location. The old man was quite winded from running up the steps, and he was a bit frightened as well.

"What has happened my Lord?" he asked, but instantly his eyes turned to the portrait.

"Who is she? Who does this room belong to? Where is she?"

"She died before you were born," whispered Mr. Lutz, answering my avalanche of questions. "Her name was Lady Safira. She was your father's goddaughter and he loved her very much. She was only nineteen when she died."

I was nineteen, too. Why would she be on my mind when I had never met her? But the fact that my own father had loved her swirled in my soul, and I wrestled with the sickening feeling that something wasn't right.

"How did she die?"

"I believe that she fell down the stairs to the cellars and broke her neck."

I turned to Mr. Lutz in dismay. "Please show me," I said, and his intention to decline my request was met with my insistent, almost forceful push of him towards the steps.

"My Lord," he implored, "it is such a late hour to venture into that dark place."

The steps were narrow and unlighted, made from massive blocks of uneven rocks. But it wasn't too dark for me—it seemed that I could see my way down there. Mr. Lutz guided me half way down, and after I turned him around to return to the light, I continued to go further down. I could only imagine how easy it would be for a young girl to lose her balance and fall down.

But what business would she have to come here in the first place?

The room was immense, cold, and smelled bad with the aroma of the deaths of rodents and other creatures throughout the centuries. The air was thick, difficult to breathe, and permeated with the smell of vinegar. Indeed, what a dreadful place to die—the poor girl. Even without any lamp light, I could swear that there was something emerging from my own body that was illuminating the place.

As I passed by on old door with dirty glass, I suddenly stopped walking—the reflection in the glass was mine. My own eyes were shining like two bright blue flames on a clear night. I turned and ran up the steps, terrified of my discovery.

* * *

That was the night I had the first of my nightmares, the beginning of the knowledge that the spirit of the dead girl would be with me for a long time.

In my dream I was in the cellar again. This time I could see as if I were outside in the daylight. A young girl was standing in the middle of the room with her back towards me. I called her name—I knew who she was. It was her—with dark hair and mesmerizing blue eyes. She was so beautiful, I felt my heart stirring and coming alive. I had never experienced this sensation before now.

"Safira," I said, so happy to see her alive.

The girl tuned to me and smiled. But the next moment, out of nowhere, a stranger came into the room, armed with a sword. Safira looked at me, calm and unafraid, but her smile died. She closed her eyes as if she were saying goodbye.

The man lifted his sword over his head and with a wide swing, he decapitated her. I was horrified, but I ran toward the man to kill him myself.

When he turned to me, my spirit froze—that man was me.

10

"I'M QUITE IMPRESSED WITH what you've got here," I said to Alex. Everything about his back room reminded me of my basement back in Peachtree City, where Octavian kept a vigilant eye on things in order to protect me. I could use this place to find Rares' killer and the Silver Sword.

"Luke is excellent at running this place," said Alex proudly. "This is how we were able to discover the identity of the Amestec' new leader."

I turned to him with an admiring look and Alex felt encouraged to continue.

"His name is Nagoshi, a former Amestec himself. He migrated here from the north ten years ago. He's a bit loony. He wants to reign over us, be our Master, and he's declared war against all Immortals. Since he's just an impostor, we aren't afraid of him, but we need to find him first."

"Nagoshi!" I held my breath.

He was the same man Octavian and I were hunting because he was in the possession of the Silver Sword. And of course, he had to be an Immortal. We had advanced in the power potential of our enemies. Prince Albert was an Amestec, with an army of hybrids and a crazy mother, and now Nagoshi, an impostor Immortal, commanded an army of Amestec and had a dangerous weapon at his disposal.

"Alex, you're wonderful," I said to him, and I softly touched his forehead. "I've been looking for Nagoshi because he has the Silver Sword, one of the last relics I need to bring back to the Order."

"You can count on me for this," said Alex with confidence. "He keeps sending out his soldiers to fight us, but he doesn't come out himself. It's only a matter of time before we'll find Nagoshi's hiding place. The coast isn't that large, and he can't hide forever. Just keep your cell phone on and I'll keep you informed."

"I *am* counting on you. Alex, I don't have too much time to linger here with you; it's past midnight. What else have you discovered that concerns me?"

"It can wait, perhaps until we meet the next time."

Alex lowered his head and unhurriedly shut down all the computers, with the exception of the satellites and monitors. I could see that his display of indifference was a facade. His concerns, whatever they were, plagued him on the inside.

"Raluca and Julian, please step outside for a second. I need a private word with Alex."

Julian stood in the door for a moment, but then he looked at me. Now his smile was unselfish. He had surprised me again.

"Come, Julian," Raluca said, and gently took his hand. I liked my sweet but tough Warrior girl—she was taking her role as my guardian so seriously.

"I think you two should talk," suggested Alex, walking over to the door and pointing to Julian. Raluca shook her head, perhaps in disagreement.

"We've talked enough already," I said to Alex. "Nothing else remains to be discussed. Julian is well aware his the new circumstances."

"He needs healing, too," insisted Alex. "Those kinds of wounds don't heal easily. Listen to him."

"I'm not *that kind* of Healer. I don't have another option to offer."

One condition for my demands was that I had to be followed blindly, turning me into a despot. I didn't know when I became that way—I had no right to act in such manner. For so long, Octavian and I always fought and thought in harmony. That was because he left me be in absolute control.

"I couldn't function any longer as a commander in the Navy," said Julian as he became more daring. "I'm sorry to break my promise to you, but I had to find my place, and my place is no longer with mortals."

"I sent you away because…"

"Safira!" Julian interrupted me, but with a soft voice, coming closer to me. "I don't regret what happened to me and I wouldn't change what I am right now for anything in the world. I am the luckiest man who was ever born, a mortal who fought with you and was loved by you, even for the short time that I was given. No one can take that away from me and now I accept it. Now it's the time to do my part, and I'm doing it as one of your warriors."

My heart, however, was still in denial. I shouldn't treat him any differently. It was only fair to accept him merely as a Warrior.

"You're right, Julian, you're an American Immortal," I admitted, convinced that Julian spoke from his heart. "You did find your place. God's speed."

* * *

At the next moment we heard the loud engine of a motorcycle outside. It stopped in front of the restaurant and I saw Alex push Raluca into the back room. He locked the door and turned off the lights. With a finger on his lips signaling us to stay still and quiet, he pulled out his gun, reloaded it, and pointed it directly at the door.

Raluca followed his example and pulled her gun, too. I heard steps coming from inside the restaurant. None of us who stayed behind had bothered to lock the front door. Someone was walking around, stepping heavily on the wood floor and crunching all that debris.

At first, I wanted to go out and face the intruder, but Alex stopped me, pressing his hand on my shoulder.

"It could be the police," he whispered. "They might be just patrolling and they saw the lights on. This isn't good. I can't risk for us to be discovered here or to be arrested again."

"Police? What do you mean by being arrested again," I asked, astonished.

"One Amestec killed his Immortal father and was caught. He was judged in criminal court, found guilty, and sent to prison. I went after him to kill him in there—he was going to get out in thirty years and live as an Immortal. I hope I won't have to shoot the police officer but this door latch is very loose."

"There's another way *I* can handle this," I said, thinking about what else I could do with the mind of a mortal man.

"There's no time," responded Alex coldly, waiting for the door to open.

The sound of the footsteps seemed to come in our direction so Alex released the safety on his gun. The intruder stopped by the door and I could imagine that I saw his hand ready to press the door latch.

I closed my eyes and forced my mind to seize the latch. The hand on the other side tried unsuccessfully to turn it and a second later it gave up and moved away.

I remembered that I had left the Vortex on the table and again I tried to see with my mind his movements in his attempt to leave, but I realized that the mind of the stranger on the other side of the door was out of my reach. I heard him pause for another moment and then he rushed outside, got on his motorcycle, and sped off with a loud report from his muffler.

"How did you do that?" asked Alex, as he tried to open the still locked door.

"How do you know that it was me?" I asked as I easily released the latch. The restaurant was empty and in semi-darkness.

"Somehow I have no doubt that it was you," answered Alex as he followed me, but his tone of voice sounded different.

Something didn't seem right. The place was a mess—chairs and tables were upside down as they had been when they were used for shields, and there were hundreds of bullet casings on the floor with the walls riddled with holes. Still, the police officer didn't call for back-up or try to investigate the shooting. He wasn't there for more than two minutes, and the time he was there, he spent just walking around carefully. I was suspicious of his motives and I looked around to see if something was missing.

I walked to first table by the bar and my spirit froze. The stranger had left, but he had taken something with him—my Vortex had disappeared.

"That wasn't the police!" I exclaimed, running out into the street, but it was too late. I glowed my eyes and looked both directions but the street was empty. I stood outside, wondering if what I had just witnessed was possible. No one besides its master could handle that weapon.

"He took the Vortex," I said to Alex, who ran outside with me.

"That could only have been the Transylvanian. He's its master." Alex was puzzled, but at the same time he was positive. He made his eyes glow, too, but I knew he couldn't see in what direction the motorcycle went when it left the restaurant.

I returned inside and this time I felt anger, and a bit of fear.

Fear.

That couldn't be. I'm fearless! I could no longer be defied, at least by any other Immortal or any hybrid ever created. I was fully restored for this purpose. I was sure I felt no fear of being destroyed but I feared being forced to accept governance. At that moment I knew in my spirit that this person who stole the Vortex (or just took back what was his) was a force I had never encountered before.

He was coming for me—but not as an enemy—although I felt he was one.

Julian and Raluca watched me discretely because they could feel my concern. It wasn't the emotion I wanted them to see reflecting from me, but I was powerless to go against it. Julian stepped towards me and touched my shoulder in an attempt to show his support.

"Well, I'm glad that you two made peace," interfered Alex, and I sensed irritation in his voice. "We need to leave for now. The police may still patrol this area at this late hour. We live in Boca, if you care to accompany us there."

"No, but thanks," I responded. "Raluca and I'll return to Wellington."

"Sure, if that's what you want," agreed Alex, but his demeanor was hesitant.

"All right, Alex, what are you not telling me? Spit it out." I had started to speak like them, dropping somewhat my old fashioned style of speaking English.

The young man stood there smiling at me, still shirtless, handsome, but composed—yet he couldn't control a feeling of surprise.

"I was hoping to keep my discoveries for myself for a while, and maybe try my luck to encourage you to linger longer, but only around me. I can see, now, that you won't allow that. But what I know is for your ears only."

Raluca and Julian went outside in the street before they were even asked.

"I told you that I ran DNA on you because Serban wanted to make sure you're not an impostor," Alex began, locking the door behind Julian. Then he walked straight to me with a determined look. "Well, from the results, I can say that that you *are* an impostor."

"What are you talking about," I mumbled, surprised by Alex's accusations.

"You aren't Serban's sister."

Alex's vibrant eyes were locked on me and I sensed that despite his tough demeanor, his heart was soft and jubilant. He wasn't a threat to me, but this secret was too much for him to bear any longer.

"It's true, you are the real Healer, but Prince Gavril was not your father. That makes you not related to Serban in any possible way."

"Are you certain?" I asked him, still in denial.

I needed my brother, Serban, in my life. I needed clarity in my path. I needed all the devotion from my Warriors for the new war against the Amestec. How would they follow me if I wasn't the daughter of a Prince?

"I'm positive. Thanks to Serban, I have here the DNA of all the existing Immortal Warriors, with the exception of Gallbor's and yours—until the last samples arrived this morning. None of those males is your father or is related to you as a sibling. None."

"Alex, that's impossible. This means that you don't have everybody in your data base or the results are faulty."

"I ran them twice, Safira, and I'm almost positive about this. And even if there is a very small chance that I don't have everyone's DNA, the truth remains unchanged. For now, only Octavian, *may* be your only brother. I'm sorry to break this news to you, but personally, I'm glad that Serban has no superiority over us anymore."

"This is very hard to accept," I said, but I instantly detected a passing light in the man's eyes.

"You're a born leader, Lady Safira. It's very hard for me to get used to calling you that, but you deserve it. You're born to lead. You came here unarmed, a soft spoken woman, but everything you say or do is so powerful. I had to fight hard to build a reputation for myself, to gain trust and power over my peers. To you, all this comes easy and natural."

"What is it, Alex? Just say it!"

"I have a good idea who your father is."

"You just said that I'm not related to anyone in your data base," I said, annoyed by his little game.

"Yes, and that's why your father could undeniably be only one Immortal."

"Who is he?"

"Gallbor."

11

THE BLACK EAGLE PALACE was now my residence as well as my prison. With each day, with each nightmare, with each year that passed, I was on the path of insanity. Nothing could satisfy me anymore, not even the delightful naked body of Francesca in my bed every night.

I desperately loved the dead girl.

Mr. Lutz watched me in suffering silence, not understanding my unsettled torment. The good old man's health was in jeopardy and the realization that I would probably lose him one day was painful. He was my only family, the only person in the whole world that cared enough about me to bring me home— a home that now was my torture chamber. And all because of a girl who had died there many years ago.

Perhaps her spirit had never left—I didn't know—but her sudden death was a curse. My unqualified and superstitious conclusion was that a judgment had been released upon her death. The first to pay for it was my own father, who loved her and who was murdered in his own bed. It has been said that a curse will affect three generations, and that only meant one thing—I was next.

I loved her, too!

* * *

Mr. Lutz died early one morning in June while I was beside him. I stood by the edge of his bed and I held his hand. His eyes were sincere and affectionate. I thanked him for five years of devotion and service to me. He smiled, turned his head towards the ceiling, and said something in a language I didn't understand: ea miroase ca florile de liliac.

I had never cried in my life, but I broke down and cried for losing Mr. Lutz—the only grandfather I ever had.

There was a lady who was residing in my palace, Mrs. Flora Gunter, who spoke Romanian and translated Mr. Lutz's last word to me: she smells like lilac flowers. *I will never know what he meant to tell me or to whom he was referring.*

Perhaps he saw a ghost when he died—my ghost; everyone's ghost.

"Did you happen to know a young lady named Safira?" I continued to ask Mrs. Flora, who I had invited for tea to thank her for helping so generously with Mr. Lutz's funeral arrangements. She raised her eyebrows, sincerely surprised by my question.

"Yes, I had the pleasure to meet Lady Safira, very long ago, here at a ball given by your father in her honor. She was a very beautiful girl – I believe that your father was engaged to marry her."

I was astounded!

It was my turn to choke on my wine. That was a detail of which I was not made aware by Mr. Lutz. He had only said that my father was in love with her.

"I suppose this comes as a surprise for you," remarked the lady. "If you were not told of it, it was simply because your father married your mother after Lady Safira's death. Such information sometimes comes across as unwelcome."

I nodded in agreement with her, but my father's and mother's sentiments were unimportant to me at that moment. I thanked my guest again for her help and company.

"Come to think about it," she said before she left, *"this is something remarkable I remember about Safira—she always smelled like lilac flowers."*

* * *

That night I took a late stroll along the Crisu River. My soul was as empty as a deserted island. I had thought about drowning many times before, but now seemed to be the right moment for it. Why would I want to go through this life hoping for a time of healing from her love when I didn't want to live without her?

If I could not find peace in my soul, at least I could find the woman I loved in death—or so I thought.

The sky was dark and overcast, with no stars or moon light. After midnight, the gas lamps that illuminated the bridge were extinguished. I stopped in the middle of the bridge, where I thought the water would be the deepest. I climbed up and crossed over the other side the railing, ready to let go. I was firmly convinced that I was doing the right thing. The water was flowing quietly, but its blackness was threatening to me, and I had no doubt that I would not survive the jump.

"I would not advise you to do that," I heard a voice from behind me, speaking in German. The man was not far from where I was standing, but I could not see him at all. His presence irritated me, but I was very curious about his identity.

"Why would you care?" I asked without looking at him. But then I had a sudden and peculiar change of mind. Rather than the water taking my life, perhaps a deranged stranger would take upon himself the task of terminating my misery.

"Well, I do care about my friends," he answered, still remaining hidden.

"Friends? I don't know you, sir. Who are you?"

"Look at me," he said, and this time his voice was a bit demanding.

"I can't see you in this dark," I answered, after I turned in his direction.

"Yes, you can," he said again. *"Just open your eyes and* look. *"*

I wanted to reply something inappropriate, but at that moment everything around me started to illuminate and the night turned into day. To my surprise I could see the stranger very well—it was a man I had met on the train to Berlin five years ago—John Gallbor. My eyes were burning and I quickly closed them, believing that I was hallucinating.

"I can let you do that, not that jumping in the water would affect you in any way. You would not die."

"How would you know that?" I asked, laughing.

"I told you that I came for you. I am the Master of your kind," Gallbor responded seriously.

"And what kind is that? What kind of freak am I?" I turned my back on him, convinced that he was not going to be of any help to me.

"You are an Immortal," he said. I felt that something like a powerful and invisible force was holding me, and it stopped the beating of my heart.

"You are insane, Gallbor," I said to him, trying to turn around— but I couldn't. *"You are worse than me, and I thought I was the craziest person in the whole world."*

"Oh, you mean that your love for Safira is driving you to madness?" he asked, and at that moment his words provoked a sudden spasm in my body and freed me to move again. I jumped on his back.

"How do you know about her?"

"Because I was the one who placed her in your consciousness," Gallbor answered, grabbing me and roughly pushing me off of him.

His force was like something I had never encountered before. I actually floated in the air for a moment before I crashed to the ground, quite a distance away. Strangely, though, I did not feel any pain, although my body left a mark on the pavement.

"Stop right there," I begged him while I was still down. "Please make me understand."

"It was me who put her into your mind and made you fall in love with her."

"Why would you do that?" I screamed hatefully. "Do you know that I cannot make love with any woman without seeing her in my mind? I am doomed to desperately love only her. I don't want to live anymore. If she is dead, I want to die too. So, please do something about it. Help me die!"

"Would you like to stay alive and encounter the woman you love?"

"Safira? You are totally insane, sir. Why would I want to do that when the girl died before I was born?"

"Because she is not dead."

I stood up and with a force I did not know I was capable of, I hit Gallbor in his face. The man didn't move or appear to be surprised by my reaction. He opened his coat and pulled out two swords. One he handed to me.

"If you want to know the whole truth about her, then fight me for it," he said, and took a defensive position.

But I was angry. I had come here to die and end my days – not to hear all this nonsense from a stranger I had met on the train, even though he had knowledge about my ghost-love, Safira. He had declared her to be responsible for my insanity, and then he told me she is alive. And more, that supposedly he was my Master and I was an Immortal, whatever that might be.

I attacked him with the sword. I had never fought with such a weapon before, but I didn't seem to be incapable of maneuvering it or afraid to use it. The more I attacked, though, the less damage I was doing to Gallbor. He didn't seem to move at all—he just simply parried my swings. At that moment I hated using the sword.

"Try harder," he said, sounding amused by my clumsiness.

"Show me how," I provoked him, with a different intent in my mind. I had no doubt that he knew how to fight quite well, that he was very strong, and I would never win. Then, why not have him kill me as I had intended all along?

When Gallbor lifted up his sword and swung it my direction, I did nothing but stand still. His sword came directly and precisely towards my head. At that moment I thought I might be killed. I felt peace and no regrets.

But the metal hit my neck with power—and nothing happened. I was still standing! I saw and felt the cold sharp metal of the sword on my skin, but I was not cut.

"Interesting," said Gallbor, coming closer to me. *"I thought all along that this would happen."*

"You tried to kill me!" I exclaimed, more indignant than surprised that I didn't die.

"I have the power to bring you back to life," he said nonchalantly. *"Artamian, it's time for you to understand and accept what you are and who you are. You are an Immortal who can live forever. Only one thing can kill our kind—the blade of a sword—by decapitation. When this happens, our spirit leaves our body and flows into our killer's body. You are an Immortal, but one that is very powerful and indestructible. Unlike the old Order of Immortals, those who can get hurt and require a Healer, I allowed a certain gift and powers for you that are unique. Only a certain sword, the Silver Sword's Invisible blade, will destroy you, and it is lost."*

"Why would you do this for me?" I asked, sincerely astonished.

"To bring some sort of balance among us. There are only two more Immortals who are very powerful, but with different gifts from yours. One day you will unite with them and save our kind. And one of them is her—Lady Safira."

"Please, tell me the truth about Lady Safira," I pleaded, and my heart melted at the sound of her name. *"All I care about is her."*

"Well, you may not like what you are about to hear, but only the truth will make it right in your mind. Lady Safira is an Immortal Healer and your

Queen. Long ago she was raised in your father's palace because she was left behind by her mother. Her mother, Lady Amara, was also the only Immortal Healer and the mistress of your grandfather, Fers Martuzon. He managed to kill an Immortal and he received immortality. After that, Amara killed him too."

"What?" I said, extremely confused.

"Never mind," Gallbor continued, "you will have plenty of time to digest all of this. Just listen. Fers had a child, your father Milos, who was only half-immortal or Amestec. Amestec stay young in appearances and they are very powerful, but they do die of old age or from being wounded. Milos knew that he was not immortal like his Father, so he needed Lady Safira to touch him and give him immortality.

"The Amestec are forbidden to receive the gift of everlasting life. With the help of her brothers, the Transylvanian Immortal Warriors, Safira escaped Milos' palace. But he found her and brought her back to the Black Eagle Palace. Down in the cellars, he decapitated her. Through her death, he received immortality and some of Safira's powers."

"Wait a moment," I screamed in disbelief, "this cannot be the truth, I was told that my father loved her. How could he kill her?"

"I warned you that you wouldn't like this story," responded Gallbor and for a moment he was silent.

"Please continue," I begged him, even though my soul was in more torment than ever.

"The Amestec would do anything for immortality," continued Gallbor, collecting his swords and storing them back into his coat. "We are their creators because of our lust for mortal women, and they became our hunters for the gift. Children will kill parents; wives will kill husbands. This happened with your mother and father.

"Indeed, Milos loved Safira and after he married your mother, he would often confess his love for her, believing that she might still be alive. He wanted her back with him. Your mother was angry and hurt that she was not

Milos' only love.. One night she took a sword and decapitated your father. Unknowingly, she received immortality from your father. When she ran away, she was already pregnant with you. So, that is why you were born Immortal."

I knelt on the pavement and held my head in my hands. I was sure Gallbor was not lying to me. Everyone else had lied to me, but the truth was more dangerous than my past ignorance. The cruel reality of my past was made very clear to me. My father killed the woman he loved to gain what he could not obtain otherwise. I could fully understand my childhood with its frantic flights through the countryside and my mother's denial of me, as I grew up to resemble the man she had killed, her own husband.

"I am the son of killers," I concluded, and Gallbor moved over to stand beside me. "You are telling me that my father killed the woman he loved and my mother killed my father because of the same woman? It is worse that I could ever imagine. If you are our Master, why would you care about someone like me? What if I turned into a menace and became like them?"

"This is not what you are, Artamian. You are not responsible for what they did. You must make your own legacy and I am certain that you will not disappoint me. Safira was brought back to life. She is alive, powerful and as beautiful as you have come to know of her. She has embarked for a new land, now; she recently left for America, along with her brother, Octavian."

"Wonderful," I said, a bit frustrated. "I am glad that she lives. Why did you choose to bring her into my life and torment me with loving her, if I am not responsible for my father's murderous actions? Why do I love her so much?"

"Because, at some time in the future, your destinies will cross paths. You will become her Warrior and she will honor you. I love her, too, and I chose you to love and protect her."

"You must be completely mad," I laughed, but my spirit grew lighter with hope and happiness. "That would be impossible, especially when she learns that I am the son of her killer. You are wrong—she is not ever going to choose me."

"Perhaps, but by that time, you will be wise enough to impress her. However, it will not be your choice the matter. She will find you."

"How will she even know to look for me?" I asked, perplexed.

"Trust me—she will come looking for you."

"Could you at least make me handsome?"

Gallbor smiled.

Then he suddenly disappeared into the air.

12

I TOOK A DEEP breath, gripping the steering wheel tightly. My lungs filled with air and expanded under the pressure until I felt dizzy. I held my breath in as long as I could, then I let it go in a long exhale.

Many things had happened since this morning, when I woke up in a strange place, in a strange bed, naked, and in the arms of my former lover. Then everything else came my way like a storm, and the climactic stroke was Alex's theory that none other than Gallbor was my real father. I struggled not think about that revelation and to keep my mind neutral for the moment.

A whole new world of Immortals opened up to me—suddenly I wasn't alone anymore. My Transylvanians—Serban, Andreas, Codrin and Raluca; the Germans—Lars, Ditmar; and the Americans—Alex, Luke, Kyle, Cedric, even Julian. Above all, *the Transylvanian*, the master of the Vortex, whose powers and identity were a mystery, was bound to me.

And I couldn't forget Nagoshi, and the sad truth that Serban was not my brother. How could I return into his presence and admit to it myself? But how could I justify keeping it a secret?

Raluca didn't ask anything or try to make unnecessary conversation as we were driving back to Wellington, but her imagination of things was clearly reflected on her face and it was apparently focused on only one person. I hoped she wouldn't pay any attention to Alex's remarks, but the mention of my brother didn't escape her attention. She was my ticket to clear my own mind—I could entertain her thoughts instead of dealing with my new reality.

"You're going to like Octavian," I said to her, and she turned to me astonished as her large eyes blinked fast.

"How did you know I was thinking about him?"

"Somehow that comes easy for me. My brother is a great Warrior and a bit of ladies man."

Raluca smiled innocently and I could sense her delightful curiosity about Octavian. She already had a certain image in her mind of him. She brushed her hand through her hair and laid her head on the passenger side window.

"I just thought that how wonderful it is for you to have a male copy, someone with the same powers as you. I'll bet he's very handsome, too. Lady Safira, the powers you displayed to us are incomparable with any other Immortal. If this Octavian does things like you—it must be awesome. Yes, I would love to meet him."

"Slow down on thinking about him—I can tell that you're attracted to him already," I laughed. A gorgeous girl like Raluca would immediately be an object of interest to my brother. But at last, this time would be different—she was an Immortal and the hurt of unrequited love would not be as severe.

"I'm hesitant to ask you this," she started slowly, "but I couldn't help observing the resemblance between Julian and Andreas. Is it true that we Immortal women are only capable of loving the same type of man?"

The girl seemed worried about this notion that sounded silly to me, but it *was* true. My lovers both resembled each other, and at one point I wasn't sure who I truly loved. What would be the chance that my future master would resemble them?

Crazy thought...

Impossible? No. However, that would make him easier to love.

"The truth is that we do like a certain type, but it's not a set rule. Are you worried about it?"

"I thought that I loved Valli, but I couldn't bear to love someone who resembles him. I hate him now."

"Until you have closure, your future lover could potentially resemble him."

"No," said Raluca vehemently. "I hate him and my heart's broken. I'm sorry to whine like a teenager, but the whole time I watched Artamian and Julian I could see how deep their love is for you. I want that kind of love. Of all things, I had to encounter the wrong man."

"It's not easy to be at the other end of the rope, either. My heart is broken too—a year ago I had to let go of Julian. I can't keep the man I love because of what I am. I'm the Healer who is destined to accept a master and to not choose one. More than a century ago I loved Andreas—I have loved him all my life. Now he's back, but he's not my master either. None of the males around me are stronger than me. You, though, can still choose who to love and be happy."

"That's why the Transylvanian worries you?"

The girl paused and restrained her thinking as her soul felt the negative energy coming from me, and she kept quiet for a moment.

"Sorry," she whispered and her eyes shined, but not because they glowed.

"I don't regret anything," I answered, remembering the same response I got earlier from Julian.

But I did regret that my past was blended and ambiguous. It tore at my spirit and I strived vainly to overcome its power over me. But I couldn't deny the possibility of accepting this truth. And if I by accepting it, I must act on it.

"Raluca," I said to my warrior girl, "Octavian and I were once a team. Now that I don't have him here with me, can I count on you to fight with me?"

"I thought you would never ask," she answered, smiling, but sincerely serious about the offer.

"Fighting with me will be tough," I warned her.

"It's all right," said Raluca proudly, "I've got a resume that says I'm a better fighter than some of these guys!"

*   *   *

We finally arrived—home sweet home.

Everyone was still awake and waiting for us when we got to the house. The lights were off but they were all gathered in the dining room, sitting at the table and playing cards. Andreas got up quickly and came directly to me. Before I could step into the dining room, he put his arm against the door and positioned himself in my way. Raluca joined the others at the game, allowing Andreas to be alone with me.

"Is everything alright?" he asked with a worried voice. He leaned his face toward mine, but I avoided the temptation to kiss him and looked down at the floor. I was tired and not in the mood for more complications.

"Everything's fine, Andreas. It was a very long and unsettling day for me and it seems that it's not over yet."

"The thought of leaving you behind again, even with the Americans, was incredibly unbearable. But the fact that *he* was there…"

"Andreas, what is that you want to know that you don't know already?" I asked him impatiently. Settling things with one lover and repeating the same with another was not appealing to me at all at that late hour.

"Are you back with him?"

I lifted my head and looked into his eyes and at his loving features. I touched his lips with the tip of my fingers.

Crazy love! I no longer feared that he would awaken my heart, but his gentle presence would be hard to dismiss.

"No," I answered firmly. "I'm not back with him but I can't be with you either. Andreas, you must understand that regardless of our past together, you are obviously not my master, even though I wish it could be so."

"This isn't what I had hoped, after looking for you and loving you for more than a century," he replied solemnly, still holding me in the doorway.

"When I first met you, I fell in love with you—it was a passion like fire. When I met Julian, I was still missing you. I wanted to be loved and end my lingering pain, and Julian filled the void at that time. But things have changed once again. We all have to move on, even if it hurts. Being alive hurts—we can learn this from the mortals."

"I can still hope that your master will never come," said Andreas, and I kissed his lips quickly.

"You can hope if you wish to," I said, gazing at the other Immortals as I passed by Andreas. "Right now I need a word with Serban, and then I have to bring hell to earth."

I went straight to them and I slammed my fist on the table, scattering Serban's hand of cards. The noise and my unexpected reaction frightened them and made them feel uncomfortable. With the exception of Serban and Raluca, they all rose from their chairs and left.

"Bad news?" asked Serban, still sitting and gathering his cards, trying to ignore my unusual behavior.

"I need all my phones, immediately," I said, and I glowed my eyes on him. I hated to act like that, but they also must accept my rule if they choose to recognize me as their Queen. However, handling a few Immortal males would be a bit different from the SEALs I fought with in my first war.

Andreas had followed me into the room. "If you power them up, they will find you," he disagreed. "They burned your home in Georgia because they had found you. Are you sure this is what you want?"

"I'm not here to hide," I answered with an aggressive tone of voice. "I have a war to fight and a whole nation of Amestec to kill, not to mention that I must take back a certain sword and make sure I haven't lost the one I already found."

"Safira," argued Andreas, "we were just trying to protect you."

"Does it look like I need your protection?"

The two men looked at each other and then shook their heads, but inside their souls a new war was started—and that war was against the option of being forced or ordered by me to stay behind. My outburst was not welcomed and it was quite displeasing to them.

"We're your warriors, Safira. We were sent here to fight alongside you and not to watch you doing battle from a distance."

"Yes, Serban, you'll get your chance to fight, as soon as Alex finds the Amestec headquarters. But you must understand that I need the freedom to act upon my own findings and instincts. I need my phone to use the way I see fit and I need to get my own clothes, a place to stay, and weapons.

I lost the Vortex tonight! Apparently its rightful owner came and claimed it and I couldn't even track him. Phones now, please!"

Without waiting for Serban's approval, Andreas disappeared into one of the back rooms and came back with my mobile phone and the radio ear phone. I turned on my mobile and dialed Octavian's number. The phone rang a long time but he didn't answer. I left my mobile on my brother's number and I put in the ear phone. All I had to do was to wait for him to find my sequence and respond, or come and find me.

I couldn't leave him behind. If Nagoshi was here with the Silver Sword, I needed Octavian's help. Then we would wage war against all the Amestec under Nagoshi's command—he would *not* become our Master.

Suddenly, I realized the reason behind Octavian's failure to find me. It was the fact that our home in Peachtree City had burned to the ground. He had no monitors or satellites to track me down.

Stupid me! I had to go back for him.

"What's changed in you," asked Serban, getting up and turning on the light over the table. His facial expression was severe and I could read in it a bit of suspicion toward me. "What did Alex do to you? I am going to kill that bastard."

"Don't you trust him, Serban? Obviously you did this morning when you sent him my coffee cup."

"It was his idea; he wanted to know for sure. Didn't he tell you?"

"Tell me what?" I hated riddles and secrets—it was evident that the new course of my life was so rich in new developments, shrouded in small fragments of the truth, and as distorted as ever.

"He's our brother too. That's what he meant by having equal rights to have you."

"What are you saying Serban," I asked, suddenly amused by the direction of our conversation. But my efforts to keep a straight face seemed ineffectual – I laughed nervously for a few seconds.

Another brother? I just lost one that I had had until this evening, and now, with Alex in the picture, there was no way I could keep it a secret from Serban any longer. He lost the distant look on his face and laid his hand on my shoulder.

"He's just three hundred years younger than me," he said with an ironic smile, "but it's true. My father had mastered many women and his mother was one of them."

"Lovely," I answered calmly, but I became serious again. "Now you two can stop trying to kill each other. According to Alex's DNA matches, none of you are my brothers."

In the next moment no one was breathing, and there was total silence, like we were all in a grave. The corners of Serban's mouth drooped. His lips pursed and his eyes turned to me in an angry glow. I slowly backed away from all of them until I found myself leaning against a wall and I glowed my eyes back at him.

Raluca posted herself between us while Andreas just stood there with his hands hanging helplessly along his body. But he and Serban understood the gravity of my words. News of this magnitude could crush their souls and spirits deeply.

"That's a lie," Serban growled deeply in his chest and the sound of his voice shook the windows. I heard rapid steps moving on the stairs. The other Immortals had come down, intrigued by the commotion.

"What did you expect from him, Serban? If you two are brothers, then you'd better get along. Nevertheless, I am still the Healer."

I closed my eyes to calm the glow. Lars, Ditmar and Codrin were watching me quietly with anxious expectation. I could only presume that each of them including, Serban and Andreas, had detected something unusual in my behavior since the first time I was brought into their midst. They knew what a Healer was all about, but they didn't know *me*.

"I am Gallbor's daughter and I have only one real brother," I continued, and I crossed my hands over my chest. "His name is Octavian. When I was killed by Milos Martuzon, it was he who brought my spirit back to life. I can do the same for Immortals, but only if the spirit is still present. Octavian can revive a spirit that has gone, even into the shadows. That is a powerful gift because he is also Gallbor's son."

13

GALLBOR MADE IT VERY CLEAR TO ME. He has linked my destiny with this female Immortal that my father had murdered and who had stolen her immortal spirit.

The palace's library was vast and I found old manuscripts about the existence of powerful beings. Warriors of God, they were called, Immortals who had been exiled to our lands, protecting and fighting alongside mortals. I understood now many things about me and the Amestec, our enemy. They, too, were hunting us, the ones who were born immortal, and they were hunting Safira.

Now, I was a lone Immortal, but there were others out there, all fighting a war for a legacy. I needed the companionship and the security of my own kind.

Safira's room was my favorite place to hide from everything. I sensed that she was still there, just underneath my level of consciousness, and I didn't have those nightmares anymore. I was so in love with her. For hours I would stare at her picture and crave her love and her body. I dreamed of holding her in my arms and caressing her beautiful face, kissing her lips, and then making love with her. My soul and body were immersed in lust and desire. After those moments, I would find Francesca and make love with her instead.

I would not keep my eyes closed anymore—I wanted to see Safira's eyes looking back at me. I wanted to pretend that I was with her. Those feelings were so real, and perhaps that increased my prowess, because Francesca would beg for me to stop. Many times when this happened, she would run away from my bed.

But soon all this alternative reality took a toll on my spirit and well-being. Tired and mentally exhausted, I realized that I had to bury my past along with hers and live for the future—and our future and would not be this old place, where she had died. It was time to start the journey to find the woman I loved.

* * *

I sold my precious palace to Mr. Gunter, Flora's husband, and in 1914 I left for Paris. I do not know why I chose to go back there. I suppose it was because I was rich, now, and I could afford the life of luxury that I had always desired. Only Paris could give that to me. Yes, being apart from Francesca saddened me a little, but as I did with Renate, I buried her memory from my mind. She wanted to follow me in my traveling, but I refused to take her along. Safira's image was the one that I couldn't forget, and that troubled me.

I stayed in the best hotels, ate at the best restaurants, and entertained myself with beautiful women. But all those women could not tempt me enough to even take them to my bed, and they certainly could not satisfy my soul.

Also, my mother, Anda, was still there in Paris, perhaps still living in the same place. She was raising her children, the Amestec, the ones that were not supposed to exist. But I held no judgment for her—I made every attempt to love her. Her legacy was only for her to bear—she had killed my father because of jealousy and she had inherited immortal life.

Life in Paris was sublime for a while. While I was there, I developed a strange habit—I would go to funerals. I felt curious to know where that particular man's soul was going and how it was like to be dead, since I was going to live forever. But I was quite disturbed to feel that the spirits of every person who died were still around, in a kind of suspension or limbo. Tuesday was the last funeral that I decided to attend before focusing only on the living.

* * *

It was cold and it had rained for the past three days of the end of that September. The soil was soft, almost soupy, but obviously the funeral had not been postponed. I felt sorry for the deceased man to have such a ceremony as this. Because of the rain, there were only a few attendees, perhaps only the family—his wife and children. Because I could not blend into the crowd, I stood well behind the ceremony, pretending to mourn at another grave, so I would not become visible to the family or bring any attention to myself.

I watched them all. The wife seemed to be quite young and the boys, two of them, perhaps were adolescents. The priest completed a modified version of the requiem mass, and all was done very fast and quietly.

I was about to leave the cemetery, but my attention was caught by the name on the headstone by which I was standing: Jean Gutierre. The name was familiar. Could he be...?

"A very dreadful event," I heard a voice speaking to me in French, interrupting my thoughts. "Did you know the deceased?"

I turned to the young man. He was perhaps barely eighteen, also tall, with large brown eyes and fair skin. His hair was long, a rusty blonde, and it was covered by a black hat. I sensed immediately who he might be.

"Not well at all, but at one time in the past he was very helpful to me."

"Oh," smiled the young man, "he was my father."

"Please accept my condolences," I said, now certain that my mother's husband was dead and buried there. The tall young man was none other than my half-brother, Pierre, the Amestec.

"Thank you," he answered, quite jovially. "But the other funeral was for my younger brother, Luc. He was only fifteen."

I turned to him, surprised. I had been told that Amestec could die either of old age or by being killed by decapitation.

"Yes, he died," said the woman from the funeral, removing her scarf and revealing her face to me. Indeed it was her, Anda Kovack, still young and beautiful—of course. But now I knew clearly who she really was.

"Mrs. Gutierre," I saluted her bowing but not calling her as my mother.

"*My seeing you here is an unsettling surprise,*" *my mother continued in a very sad tone of voice.*

"*My apologies, madam,*" *I responded, a bit irritated that she was still unhappy with my presence,* "*but our encounter was not deliberate. I come here to the cemetery all the time. How did your son die?*"

"*He was very sick—there was not a cure for him,*" *she whispered into my ear.*

"*That was unfortunate, indeed,*" *I responded politely, not wanting to sound insensitive, but still wondering why she was lying to me. At this point, however, she thought that I was ignorant about my own origins.*

"*You have matured a little,*" *she added, this time in a softer voice.*

I bowed again, ready to depart, but she took one more step closer to me. And then another, until we were standing face to face. Her nostrils opened a little more, like she had inhaled something unpleasant in the air.

Then she looked into my eyes with a frightened expression on her face. I caught her look, but a moment later her face become friendly again.

"*Would you care to accept a dinner invitation? I know this is long overdue, but there is no need to pretend that we are complete strangers anymore.*"

"*I am not certain that would be wise,*" *I responded coldly over her allusion about my last visit.*

"*I apologize for my past behavior,*" *she insisted, holding my arm. Pierre and Luis exchanged a quick look as they observed their mother's controversial behavior.* "*Boys, this is your older brother, Artamian, the one who left us when he was very young.*"

The young men bowed politely to me, but again, their dark eyes sparkled. To my surprise, not even the talkative Pierre addressed me with even a single word on the way to their house. I had no clue what else she must have told them about me, but these two didn't seem to be curious about me or try to talk to me about our sudden reunion.

The house was still there, on 1220 Rochelle Avenue, looking the same with the three-story high facade made from red brick. The same massive entrance was there as well, dark and unwelcoming, as I remembered it from last time I stared at its closed doors. It smelled good inside, as I entered the foyer, like baked apples. A small fire was burning in the fireplace and I proceeded to it happily to warm up a little.

Mother left me there with my half-brothers and went to give orders for dinner. They asked me politely to sit and asked if I wished for any refreshments. I refused the refreshment offer and I took a seat by the window.

But the way they were looking at me, I felt as if I was inside a snake pit.

Mother came back to escort us to dinner and insisted that I would sit across from her, in Mr. Gutierre's former place. She had changed from her black dress into one of a lighter color, purple. Perhaps the most awkward moment for me was not her unusual requests or her nervousness, but that my mother actually looked exactly my age and my half-brothers looked like her younger siblings.

"So, my dear Artamian," she said, smiling as soon as the dessert was served, "where have you been for the past few years?"

"Home, back at the Black Eagle Castle," I answered, with my mouth full of cake. "Mr. Lutz came and looked for me in Berlin. It was very fortunate timing, considering that I didn't have a place to live anymore. Unfortunately, I lost him to death in the spring."

Mother's face turned a bit red and her eyes to a darker blue. Her hand dropped the wine glass and the burgundy liquid spilled all over on the table cloth, but she had the will power to continue to smile.

"It was only logical that you would inherit your father's palace," she said, and I thought her voice trembled a little. "I am surprised that you left Transylvania and came back here."

"I sold the palace three months ago," I said, understanding her subtle inquiry about my presence in Paris. "Do you remember Flora Cristea? She married Johan Gunter. I sold him the palace. I came to Paris because I had to, not because I desired to come here at all."

"You sold the Palace?" Mother's voice sounded a bit relieved.

"Yes, Madam, it was quite a dreadful place."

"I understand." Our eyes interacted for that moment, and we both knew that the whole truth was known by me and there was no need to hide it anymore.

"You look so much like your father," she continued, and I sensed that she intended to make me angry. "Except that you are so tall and muscular, and you don't have his eyes."

"I inherited your eyes, mother," I responded, accentuating the word 'mother'. As a matter fact, I inherited everything else from you."

"Great," said Pierre, standing up, agitated. "I am glad everything ended well for you, my brother, but please excuse me if I cannot continue to take part in this memory fest with you and Mother. May I retire to my room?"

Luis followed his brother and they both left the dining room, upset and in bad mood.

"What have you told them about me?" I asked curiously. "What did you tell them about themselves?"

"About you—the truth—which is that I hated your father and I could not bear to look at you."

"I regret that, but be at peace—at least Safira is alive and well."

"How do you know about her?" Mother's voice turned diabolically low and angry.

"Some things you cannot bury, even if you run away from them. You know that too. What you don't know is that Safira is destined to be mine."

"We shall see about that. Good bye, Artamian. I suppose we should never meet again in future."

With those words, she left me again with an almost threatening promise that if our paths would cross in the future, it would not be pleasant for either of us. She considered me to be a menace to her.

Out in the street, I took a deep breath, happy to end something that resembled a bad dream. My encounter with my estranged mother and brothers, however was not a terrible waste of time. In spite of not being able to pour out my anger to her for her terrible deeds of the past, I felt satisfied that I left her with the knowledge that I was an Immortal and she had not succeeded in destroying me.

"Do you care for some company?" The moment I turned the corner of the street, Luis and Pierre were waiting for me. They were dressed for town with long trench coats and tall hats.

"I apologize, but your company is not desired at this moment in time," I responded sincerely, since solace was what I needed, and not another useless dialog with my potential enemies.

"I thought you wanted to know the truth," said Pierre calmly.

"The truth about what?"

"About how Luc died," answered Luis impatiently. "She killed him."

The boy's faces were severe and sad. My feeling was that something very bad was about to happen.

"You mean that your mother killed your younger brother? But why?"

This was perplexing, even for me. I was aware of her violent past. But to kill her own child? On the other hand, she was heartless when she abandoned me.

"Because he found out the truth about her. She is an immortal being, but if we kill her, we became immortals too." Pierre sounded calm but ruthless saying these words. "You should know that, since you are her first born, that you are the only one of her offspring who inherited this particular gift from her. Is this not true?"

"What do you know about yourselves?" I asked him straightforwardly.

"That we are not like her, that we die, and we don't want to die. Unless we kill the ones like her and you, our deaths are certain!*"*

He accented his last word, but the boys held no threat to me. He was about to find out that not every Immortal dies.

"That is absolutely true," I agreed, watching as their actions became more restless. The street was empty and a confrontation at this late hour would not alert any witnesses.

"So, you admit to being like her, an immortal, right?" Luis' left hand slowly pulled a sword from under his trench coat, but he didn't lift it up for an attack.

"True again," I said, not doubting their intention for me anymore. "But in case math is hard for you, my dear brothers, I am only one person, so only one of you can kill me and properly become immortal. What you do after that? Will one of you will kill the other?"

"No," answered Pierre, "after we kill you, we will go back and kill her."

"Well, I wish you the best," I said, and I turned my back to them and walked away in the opposite direction.

"Artamian," yelled Luis, "draw your sword and fight me."

"I'm sorry to disappoint you, but I don't carry a sword," I said and I turned to him, irritated.

"Why not?" the boy asked, sincerely astonished.

"You will see – I have no need for one. But I am warning you boys, if you continue your threats, you will die today. So, Luis, it would be better for you to take your toy and go back home while you still can."

But my threat did nothing to scare him. My brother was determined to kill me, to cut off my head and take over my spirit. Gallbor was right—there was no allegiance between brothers or parents and children, when the prize of eternal life was at stake.

Luis lifted his sword and hit me hard. Then two more times, but nothing after that. When Pierre realized that Luis would never be successful, he lifted his sword and hit my neck with it. I think I counted seventeen blows. The blade refused to cut my neck and slice off my head. I watched them as they became frightened when I reached and grabbed the sword from Pierre's hand. He was the first one to fall headless.

Luis ran down the street and I was surprised at his unusually fast speed; however, I hate to run. I threw the sword in his direction but when the blade reached him, it only penetrated his back. Luis fell to the ground for a moment, but then he got up and started to run again.

I chased him until he reached the entrance to his house. I caught up with him, held him down and I pulled the blade from his back. I killed him there on the steps, but not before seeing Mother's eyes watching me in agony. She stood still in the door and remained silent.

"Pierre is down the street, headless," I said to her. "You will need to prepare more funerals. But don't worry, I will not attend those."

I handed her Pierre's sword and left without looking back. I had just killed my brothers and I felt nothing.

Perhaps I was a monster after all—as she was.

* * *

Two days later I embarked for America. First I wanted to go to Berlin and visit Herbert and Renate, but the war between France and Germany had started—I would have not been welcome there anymore. When I left Europe, I felt liberated.

I lived for a while in New York City during the First World War. I knew I could enlist and do a lot of damage, but I was not interested in the whole world knowing how weird and unusual I was. Our existence and survival was possible only because we stayed in shadows.

But I was a Warrior, too, and I felt very happy being one. I fought in the Second World War and all the wars and conflicts that followed. I also needed to know what else I could do because my body was like steel. No weapon could destroy me, not even through decapitation, like the rest of the Immortals.

Even if Safira were to attempt to kill me she would not be able to.

But this detail would not impress her too much.

14

Gallbor's daughter!

What was I thinking, proclaiming this in front of everyone without any evidence other that Alex's stupid suspicion? No one could positively confirm this to me, and the fact that I was not Prince Gavril's daughter did not make me any less of what I was, either. Without any doubt Octavian was Gallbor's son—could feel it so clearly in my spirit.

But what about me?

My blood accelerated in my body, but a cold sweat developed on my skin. I couldn't deny the truth about me, either. I surprised myself at how quickly I accepted it; either it was the truth or it wasn't, and then I had boasted so openly about it.

* * *

Raluca's blue shorts and white t-shirt was my new night wardrobe once again. I put a pillow on the couch and covered myself with a blanket. I was comfortable enough to spend the rest of the night on the couch in the living room. Lord Arthur happily lay on his side and started to snore right away. The rest of my companions left me alone and they retired to their rooms, a bit agitated by my daring confession. I sensed their confusion, but strangely, they didn't doubt me at all.

But, like many other nights in my long life, sleep wasn't within my grasp.

At first I wept in silence: I had just told Julian and Andreas that I couldn't respond to their love anymore. I must shut down every feeling I had for them and harden my heart.

The Master would come, but he would be left out. I couldn't foresee any man conquering my soul and body more than these two men had done. Again, that dreadful taste of loneliness was overtaking me, and it gave me chills.

What I desired was passion and making love! Those two things would keep my senses and impulses alive.

I got up and reached for a napkin from the coffee table. The noise of blowing my nose made me laugh. Actually, I was laughing at the thought that Serban and Alex were brothers. I could only imagine Serban's reaction when Alex told him about their uncommon connection. *Surprise—we are now a big and happy family.*

Unfortunately, they weren't my brothers and that saddened me a bit. I stood up, stepped over the dog, and headed to the patio. I opened the glass door and walked outside. Cooling air was all that I needed. The lawn was wet; one of Florida's ceaseless rains had just swept through the   area—a typical storm, short but wild. I had forgotten to put on my slippers and the moisture from the grass felt good.

* * *

My intention was to walk to the back gate and to venture into the cemetery. I didn't know why, but the cemetery intrigued me. Reading the names of the people who had lived but who were no more always filled my soul with compassion for them. After I passed through the gate, my senses detected something that appeared to be following me. Perhaps it was Lord Arthur, or perhaps the place was haunted. But that wouldn't terrify me. Mortals' spirits remain with the corpse for the first seven days; then, they slowly pass through the tunnel.

Sometimes there was light and sometimes there was dark at the other end.

Sometimes, some spirits stayed behind, refusing to leave.

The Immortal's spirit doesn't linger for more than a few minutes, perhaps ten or fifteen. Its destination is either another body or the shadows. When I died, part of me entered into Milos Martuzon, transforming him into an Immortal. But most of my spirit went into the shadows. There was nothing there. Nothing. That was when Octavian came fighting through the dark emptiness, snatching me out and bringing me back.

My follower caught up with me and I turned to glow my eyes. I recognized the "ghost" as Codrin, Raluca's older brother. I assumed that he was the one who had been entrusted to guard me that night. He smiled and bowed to me, as charming as always, and he took my hand into his.

I allowed it. I was curious.

"I thought I had lost you," he said, still gently grasping my hand. "It'll be daylight in an hour and you haven't slept at all."

"I can't sleep! I've got too much on my mind."

Codrin's soul was in perfect harmony with his spirit. Nothing bothered him. I assumed that was because of his perpetually joyful disposition, and that was the reason they had chosen him to accompany me. Serban and Andreas were, at this point, too emotionally charged and filled with despair.

Despite Codrin's outward calmness, I felt a strong anger in his spirit, like a hidden agony, and I waited for it to erupt. The young man curled his fingers around mine and he placed my hand on his chest. His shirt was open and I rubbed my fingers against his skin. I felt something there, like a large piece of metal just below the skin's surface. I was surprised—how did I miss it earlier in the day?

I freed my other hand from his and I touched his chest with all my fingers. The object was round in shape, with no jagged edges. It was covering a large portion of his heart and it seemed to me that was deliberately inserted in there.

"Codrin, are you hurt? What's this thing I'm touching?"

"Raluca told me that you've chosen her to be your right arm," he said, a bit hesitant and changing the subject. "Good choice. My sister's a feisty girl, very devoted and very honorable."

"Are you worried especially about something in her regard?"

My question took him by surprise. He nodded his head in agreement.

"May I show you something?"

Carefully avoiding stepping on the flower arrangements lying on the ground, we made our way around many inscribed headstones until we stopped at a particular one.

"Here lies baby Corey," he said, pointing to the small stone marker, and I glowed my eyes to see his name written on it. "I carried him here all by myself. I held his little coffin to my chest. He was only six months old—a beautiful boy with blue eyes."

Codrin squeezed my hand without feeling it, sincerely affected. I stretched my other hand and touched his forehead.

"He didn't even know what life was about; he didn't even know his name. Look here," he continued, dragging me to another stone, two rows down. "Here lies Mr. Bromolow—sixty one. A single man with a good situation, but uncommitted to a relationship with a woman or anyone else. He didn't have close family—just distant relatives. No one came to the service. It was only us, a few strangers, to take him to his eternal rest."

"Codrin what's your point here?"

"My point is that the baby didn't have a chance to live at all, while the other one wasted his life and ended up alone. They both died without purpose, not realizing their dreams in life."

"This is sad, indeed," I added, tolerant of Codrin's introspective, although fascinating, philosophical moment. "I have lost many mortals who I loved in my life."

"In a few hours we'll have to go to work—we'll be having a new funeral service. The viewing is tonight and the funeral's tomorrow. Her name is Johanna. She was only twenty seven, and she leaves two children behind. She was murdered by her husband because she had cheated on him. He was mean to her, abusive. It's no wonder she turned to someone who cherished her. Of course, I don't have all the understanding of the ugliness of human nature in marriage. I'm only ninety seven, but I have truly fallen in love. Yet, we don't seem to connect like the mortals, and we don't form those kinds of sentiments, do we?"

"We're no better, Codrin. Long ago the man who declared to love and protect me cut off my head because I dared to leave him and fall in love with another man."

"True, your story is well known to us," nodded Codrin, and his fists clenched. "However, Johanna's life is over. She doesn't have another chance to start over, to see if a new man is better, to go back and correct her past mistakes. She is, or I should say, she was a beautiful woman and just like that—everything stopped for her, and no one could help. I wish the Defenders still existed. They would have intervened before this tragedy happened."

"The Defenders?"

"Serban told us that they were an old Order of Immortals, sent to mortals to bring justice to the ones who couldn't have it otherwise. But there are none left. I guess they are just a legend now. Johanna needed a Defender; she didn't deserve to die like that."

"I am truly sorry for Johanna," I said, almost embarrassed for my own pettiness I was feeling earlier. I couldn't compare my own struggles with a mortal's loss of life.

"Good," he said suddenly, changing his disposition as he kissed my hand. "Because you should never cry again, Lady Safira; you have life eternal, the chance to love as many times you wish, and to fight many wars."

"Were you spying on me," I asked, impressed by his care and not offended that he was seeing me in such vulnerable moment. They saw my powers and they are well aware of my capabilities as a Warrior, but I felt as if I was nothing but a human soul and I wanted them to discover my delicate side.

"Not spying, just surveying my area of work, the place I was supposed to guard and protect, and you were in it."

"You haven't witnessed anything special. I just had a deep conversation with myself. Tears bring relief and comfort to me; I'm just a girl, after all."

"A girl? Yes, but one that is powerful and unconquerable. The truth is that earlier today we all wanted Alex to fight with you, so we could see you in action again."

"That wouldn't have been pleasing to your eyes."

* * *

The patio door of the house opened and I heard voices and movement coming towards us. It was just a matter of time until all the others had found us—they had hardly any distance at all to cover. Serban's eyes still looked severe, but his demeanor had softened a bit. Andreas looked tired, but content. They were all standing around me, with their eyes half glowed and a look of deferment on their faces. I took a seat on the stone bench near the graves and the others quietly followed my example, sitting down on the grass.

Our little meeting was well attended, but not everyone was present. Although the cemetery was an awkward place to gather, perhaps it was necessary. But the only one missing was the girl.

"Where is Raluca," I asked, making them understand that I was not dismissing their need to meet with me in such an unusual place.

"She doesn't need to be here," responded Codrin. "My sister's clean."

"Clean? What are you talking about?"

"Honorability." One by one, Serban, Andreas, Codrin, Lars and Ditmar took their shirts off for the second time since I had met them and pointed to their chests, exactly at the location of their hearts.

"All of us have it," said Serban, looking up at me from where he was sitting, "all but Raluca. We knew that the Amestec play dirty. They are aware that we withstand bullets and wounds, but if they aim for our hearts to wound them, their chances to immobilize and behead us are greater. Some time ago we found a doctor who we paid to insert these bullet proof shields under our skin to protect our hearts. Now we need to have these plates removed."

"Why now?"

"We aren't proud of them." responded Serban. "We were always afraid that the Americans would find out about them and laugh at us. Indeed, the shields have saved us numerous times, but this is not the way that a proud warrior fights."

"So you all want me to take them out?" Five heads nodded in agreement.

"Why here and not in the house?"

"We're not sure that Alex hasn't placed some sort of listening device in our house," responded Andreas, and I smiled at the fact that the new found brothers didn't trust each other.

"I know that we have placed a huge burden on you since you returned to us," said Serban, "but we are your warriors, and we want to fight this next war with honor and courage."

"I'm proud of you, no matter what," I said, and this was very true.

I didn't find it insulting or less honorable that they had chosen this method for their defense, but I understood. Earlier I had to force Alex to save his heart also, but he wouldn't admit his hurt to the others in order to save his pride. Times had changed, however, and our enemies were cruel and deceiving. Courage and honor were essential to win our war.

"But why not keep them? I have nothing against your shields. As a matter fact, I'm so happy you're all still alive. This is twenty-first century! Honorability has a different meaning for me."

I got down on the grass, squeezing in between Serban and Ditmar. The warriors welcomed me into their midst.

"You all must forgive me, too," I said slowly, accentuating every word. "I rushed to proclaim myself Gallbor's daughter only because Alex has a hunch. I'm not certain that this is possible. All my life I've believed that I was Prince Gavril's daughter, and I had Serban and Rares as brothers."

"Alex is obnoxious, but he's never wrong," said Serban, and he shook his head sadly. "Lady Safira, you are our Queen. I knew Gallbor and I see the resemblance between the two of you. I see that you are his daughter—you have his eyes and his powers—but at the same time you have a tender soul. I deeply regret losing you as a sister. My heart is really broken. But now, we all want to know about your brother."

"His name is Octavian—the one who raised me from death. Without a doubt he is Gallbor's son, and Lady Amara is also his mother. Over a year ago, we made war against a powerful Amestec named Prince Albert—you all heard about it. My brother fought him and won the Fire Sword back from him. We were very close to finding the Silver Sword, also known as the invisible blade, when I was taken away from my home by Gallbor. I must recapture the Silver Sword and eliminate its terrible threat. Octavian is the only one who can help me. Our bodies are indestructible and we can resist fire and explosions. He has always been my protector and I was pledged to keep his existence as a secret."

"It was a secret, all right," admitted Andreas. "We hadn't heard about him before now. Lady Safira, we do believe that you are Gallbor's daughter."

"It's true," I continued, embracing my knees with my arms. "Will you still accept me without any hard feelings?"

Serban turned and gazed at me as if from an immeasurable distance. His face was as pale as marble shining in the night, and I recognized instantly that he had a moment of reminiscence.

"We don't hold children responsible for their parent's mistakes," he said with a melancholy voice, plucking grass spears from the ground. "It wouldn't be fair. But sometimes it doesn't work that way."

He paused again, gathering more courage to relieve the burden of his soul.

"All of you are still very young, except for Andreas. However, I am very old. Seven hundred years ago, I married a mortal woman, a princess. We had a child together, a girl. I wanted so ardently to stay with them, to enjoy my lady and my daughter. But if I had done so, they would have found out who I was and that would have endangered their lives. So I left and suffered the loss."

"I'm so sorry," I whispered, touched by his confession. I had always wondered about Serban's history, but I had never dared to ask. However, just presuming that he had never conceived children was a bit unrealistic.

"I am, too," he continued. "That should have been a lesson for me, but two hundred years ago I fathered another child with a mortal, a son. Like any other Immortal, I thought that perhaps my offspring wouldn't rise against us and he would be safe. I don't know what happened to that child. I've often thought about it. I've killed so many Amestec—someone else's son or daughter. What if someone's killed mine?"

"I also had a son," said Andreas, avoiding my eyes. "It happened long ago. Mine died in battle, so I could say that I was lucky with him. None of us are without fault, Safira. We all did wrong."

"This doesn't change what you are and what we need to do," I said firmly. "The Amestec we are fighting now have the choice to not to rise against us, but they are doing it anyway. Does anyone have anything more to say to me?"

My eyes turned to Codrin, but he looked at the ground. I felt that his soul was in pain, and regardless of his sweet nature and his sincere smile to me, he had an agony in his heart and soul. I could sense it, but I couldn't remove it.

"Let your protective shields remain," I said, and I stood up. "There's nothing wrong with being cautious. I don't want to lose any of you. And that's an order!"

They rose and stood, forming a straight line to salute me, but I did something that my heart desired— hugged each one. I held each of them in my arms for a second.

I started with Serban, who was tight and nervous at first— I wasn't his sister anymore. Ditmar, Lars and Codrin were daring enough to kiss my cheeks in the European style. Last was Andreas. He kissed me on my lips and he wanted to kiss me longer, but Serban cleared his throat behind us.

We returned to the house. The rain started again.

15

I COULDN'T FOCUS ON ANYTHING else for the next fifty years, just waiting for Safira to find me.

My appearance didn't change at all and I liked that. But there was something about me that I couldn't see that made the Amestec recognize and hunt me. Finally, it proved to be nothing more than the fact that I was able to detect other Immortals, if I were to encounter one. Not that I was too anxious to meet one. But I did. Three in Boston, seven in Columbus, and only one in Detroit.

I couldn't help but realize that their number was shrinking and I didn't like that, but I didn't ask them about it. We acknowledged each other and we continued separately in our quests. I didn't know what they might think about me—truth be said – I was not part of their clan. I was born from former mortals who had turned out to be killers.

But I couldn't help noticing that I was taller and had a bigger build than they, and that was to my satisfaction.

* * *

It was at the turn of the new century, the summer of 2001, when I met him— Sum Nagoshi. The Amestec were searching for me and their new weapons intrigued me a lot. They were like nothing that I was familiar with in my past experience. They were not only trying to shoot me down, but they attacked me with some things that were much faster than a sword. They threw these objects at me, rather than attacking me in hand-to-hand combat.

Of course, there was no harm done. I just turned around and terminated them with their own weapons, but I liked the idea behind using those flying weapons. Researching the manufacturer brought me to him, back in New York.

* * *

The moment I entered his store I noticed his unusual collection of martial arts weapons. But most unusual was him—he was an Immortal. A bit too tall for a young Japanese man, he had very dark hair pulled back nicely into a ponytail, and dark penetrating eyes. His smile froze on his face at my appearance—I could tell immediately that he was an impostor.

"It's been quite a while since I've seen an original Immortal," were his first words, after he had stared at me for a few seconds. He had recognized me, too.

"Well, you're a surprise for me, too," I responded as I started walking around his store with confidence. I was not afraid of him, even though he was not authentic. I knew with certainty that he had killed someone like me for his immortality.

"Interesting place you have here."

I picked up a sword with a very short blade, but wide and sharp. Something like this would be easy to carry, but it was not what I was seeking.

"Are you interested in anything in particular?" he asked, coming towards me, but not before pressing a button under the counter. "I have all kinds of weapons, and even more swords. In my professional opinion, that one is too small—it doesn't suit you."

"I don't care too much for swords," I said, placing the weapon back on the counter. His eyebrows rose in confusion.

"I'm not sure I understand that—no Immortal is without one. How do you fight against them?"

"Not very long ago, you were one of them too, right? Who did you kill? Never mind, I don't care. However, you still can be killed—you know that."

Nagoshi was not too willing to answer that particular remark and perhaps this entire conversation was uncomfortable to him. I wasn't welcome in his store, but instinctively I knew that I had to dig deeper and that I was not here by coincidence.

"To answer to your question, I killed them with their own weapons," I said, moving deeper inside the store.

"So, you aren't interested in a sword," he repeated, avoiding me by walking to the other end of the counter. In the corner of my eye I saw a shifting motion, like two shadows trying to get behind me. Nagoshi blinked, undisturbed.

"Call off your dogs if you want your head to remain attached to your body," I threatened him, and I turned to the men behind me who were holding swords in their hands, ready for an attack. "I'm not here to harm you."

"Then, what do you want?" he said signaling to his men to back off. "What's your name?"

"My name is Artamian. I need new weapons that are faster and better than a sword. I saw what the Amestec bought from you, but I want something even more damaging."

Something told me that in a place crawling with Amestec, Nagoshi had to have a better weapon to defend himself.

"Well, look around," he invited, as he made himself comfortable behind the counter.

"Now I see why they let you live—they like your collection. You combined the tradition of your people with a little modern day ingenuity. These Shurikens are bigger and sharper. Simple, but made with genius."

Many of the weapons I had seen before, in the hands of the nineteen Amestec I had killed so far, by turning their weapons on them. I knew that each one I eliminated was one less that would hunt for Safira. They all wanted her

139

for her gift, to kill her or force her to make them immortal. I wanted her for my soul. My spirit was attached to hers and I wanted that day to come sooner, rather than later. Until then, I was doing my part.

"These are a little too soft for me," I said, rejecting all of them like an unhappy customer. "I'm sure you can do better than this, you of all people, since you are still alive."

"For your information, they're all heading down south lately. They're seeking something much more meaningful than you or me."

"How so?" I asked, knowing that he was referring to Safira. So now I knew—she is in the southern United States. "What do you mean?"

"They are after the Queen," he responded, a bit irritated by my seeming lack of knowledge. "Everyone wants to find her. Anyway, you're right, they let me live because of what I can do for them. Come with me."

I followed him to the back of the store, to a room that turned out to be a training facility. Like any gym, it was spacious with much room in which to move around. He opened a trunk and showed me something lying on the bottom—a disc apparently made from stainless steel, but shining like was just freshly sharpened.

"This is a Vortex Shuriken, a weapon no one can handle so far, not even me. I made it for myself, but I made it like this by mistake. It has no place to hold a grip and it cuts through any flesh. It cut off three of my fingers." He showed me his right hand and for the first time I noticed the missing digits. "Are you a daring person?"

His question made me laugh. I knew he wasn't serious about his offer, primarily because he was convinced that all that would happen was for me to lose my hand. I bent down slowly and gingerly touched it. It was indeed sharp. If my flesh had been normal, the skin of my fingers would have been rapidly removed. But any metal, no matter how sharp, couldn't hurt me. I held it in my hand like was rubber.

"That's impossible" Nagoshi exclaimed, and his eyes suddenly became bigger. I saw fear in them too, and his self-protective instinct took over. Incredibly

fast, he opened another trunk and he pulled out a sword, taking the traditional defensive position.

But his sword was somewhat strange, made with a light colored metal that gleamed like silver. It had a wide blade, but the blade was very thin, almost like paper. Was that the secret weapon he kept for his defense? A shiny, fragile sword? Where was his traditional and magical Ninja sword? Surely he must have one.

"Nagoshi, I thought you were a businessman. I'm not going to leave without paying you for this "thing". Back off and lay that little toothpick aside."

"I'm sure you will pay for it," he mumbled. "What kind of devil are you? How can you do that?"

"Do what?" I played with him. I saw his forehead sweating and his eyes checked the exit door. I threw the Vortex in his direction and he ducked under the counter. Although larger in size and weight that the common small Shuriken, this weapon made a circle around the room and returned into my hand.

"This is great," I exclaimed. quite excited, "I could get used to something like this. With a little practice, I could have found your head wherever you might hide."

"This weapon is mind controlled," Nagoshi replied and I could tell that he was extremely nervous. "You aren't the kind of Immortal who can do that."

"Try me," I said, furious that he was not impressed by my one unprecedented quality and was willing to discount me. "You lied to me—this weapon wasn't made like this by accident. You thought you could control it with your mind—you bastard. But that was the one power you couldn't acquire, wasn't it? You know why? Because it's a natural gift—not for impostors."

Again I swung it and released the weapon in his direction. This time he stood up and parried it. When the blade of the sword encountered the metal, the noise of the clash was like an explosion. But the blade was strong enough to stop the fury of the rotating Shuriken. Little tongues of fire filled the room and fell to the floor. The Vortex returned to me, but Nagoshi's sword became invisible.

"I want you to allow me to leave and I want you to stay away from me forever!" Nagoshi exclaimed, and he quickly passed by me to leave the room.

But as he passed, I saw him lifting his hand towards me. At first I didn't see anything but then I felt a searing pain in my left hand. I had never felt this kind of physical pain before. I opened my left palm and looked at it. What I saw made me freeze in amazement, and perhaps fear, too. My palm had a deep cut in the middle, just below my fingers. I didn't bleed—it seemed that the blood coagulated before it exited my skin.

Did Nagoshi's sword cut me? How was that possible?

I turned to look for him, but he was gone. His store was empty and there was no one around.

I dropped the Shuriken and I lay down on the floor. After more than a century, another extraordinary moment had happened to me. I remembered that Gallbor had mentioned something about one weapon that could harm me. I wasn't invincible after all. There was a weapon in existence that could destroy me and I believed with certainty in its powers.

Still puzzled and confused, I saw myself exposed to the possibility that I might become more vulnerable, even to a plain blade. With my uninjured hand I picked up the Vortex and pushed it against my neck.

No, I didn't want to go through this long life in fear of death; that was unacceptable. I had to know what was wrong with me.

I sliced hard but nothing happened—the shuriken did not cut my neck. So it all came down to that particular weapon, that invisible sword. I had just found my enemy.

No, actually I had just lost my enemy. I must find that invisible blade again and it must be destroyed. I could only imagine how dangerous it was, not only for me but for all of my Immortal kind. Even to Safira.

Nagoshi knew about Safira. He called her the Queen.

What if he was looking for her, too?

As I left the store, I took a small sword and the Vortex with me.

16

THE MALL EXHAUSTED ME. We walked around for a couple of miles, it seemed, but it felt more like twenty miles in my new shoes. I could feel the blisters blossoming and destroying my feet.

At one point I twisted my ankle and I landed in someone's' arms, but my shopping bags were still intact. The young man grabbed me by my shoulder and I felt his fingernail scratching my skin as he raised me up to a standing position. I was too embarrassed to look at him, but we both apologized to each other.

Raluca had taken me to her favorite shops and my ATM card was hot from running it through all the scanners. I wasn't a fan of prolonged shopping, but it made my companion happy.

My purse contained all of my identification documents, so my fortune was safe at the bank ⌐I was still a rich woman. I bought some of my favorite clothes and accessories, but I couldn't make up my mind about stopping to eat out. I had always cooked at home for Octavian and me, and I really wasn't sure about all the menus of the fast food places in the mall.

So Raluca decided for me. She wanted Starbucks—muffins and coffee.

"You guys had a party last night without me," said Raluca, returning with our order. I quickly grabbed the coffee cup, ignoring the muffin for now.

"Yes, it was just the guys," I said, trying to make it sound unimportant. "You wouldn't have liked it. By the way, I got the chance to know your brother a bit more intimately—he's very pleasant. He's very protective of you, and he taught me a bit of history."

"Let me guess! About the legendary *Justitiari* or *Aparatori*? In modern English, they are better known as Enforcers and Defenders."

"Exactly—although Serban mentioned very little about them."

"They aren't very well known among the Americans, but they were quite real for Europeans. As a matter fact, they were the subject of one of our great bedtime story heroes as we were growing up. The legends said that after the great separation, they were also sent to protect mortals. Serban and Andreas had a chance encounter with them centuries later."

"Interesting. Well, I must confess that I grew up isolated. I knew nothing of Immortals until Andreas took me away from the Black Eagle Castle."

"One story said that Serban was in love once with a Defender girl. He saw her manipulating fire, but he refuses to talk much about her."

"But there's a reason Codrin mentioned them. He's hiding something, isn't he?"

"Indeed," agreed Raluca, and her smiled disappeared. "He won't tell anyone but me. He thinks he has blood on his hands."

"What do you mean by that?" I asked, pausing my cup halfway to my lips.

"Johanna. Codrin was in love with her and she was in love with him. He's afraid that he caused her death. Her husband is a crazy person and a tyrant."

The fear of a man was unknown to me, but I understood it by the visible signs of mental anguish that I recognized in the tormented soul of a woman.

"And are you sure that Codrin's affair with Johanna was the reason her husband killed her?"

"It wasn't like a true affair; they didn't meet in hiding or make love. She would take her children to the park every day and my brother would go, sit on a bench, and just stare at her. I think he was in love, but he didn't want to get involved with a mortal. He wanted to stay clean."

It was the second time in a few hours that I had heard the word "clean". Perhaps they meant to say *be virtuous and respect our law*—a very commendable thing to do, since we all had broken our laws at one time or another, including me. And all for love.

"Then, Codrin isn't guilty of anything," I said, convinced that just an innocent flirt in the park couldn't produce such an effect on a husband, to be pushed to the limits and kill his wife. Unless the man was indeed crazy and paranoid.

"Tell it to Codrin," said Raluca, and her large blue eyes widened a little with grief. "He believes otherwise, and he suffers. Codrin is my only brother and I care about him very much."

I was very worried about my brother, too. My ear piece and phone were still on and they were continually dialing his number, but there was no response.

That afternoon, the only call I received was from Alex. He called to make sure he had me in his contact list, and he told me that he had detected some Amestec activity in the mall area—to be aware of danger.

"We need to leave," I said to Raluca, but not before I grabbed the muffin and stored it in my purse. A moment later, Raluca halted and turned around to look behind us in the crowd of people, like she recognized someone.

"What is it?" I asked, trying to look in the same direction, but I couldn't see anyone in particular. Amestec should be easy to spot because of their long hair, styling it as the Immortals do.

"Nothing," she answered quickly, and she turned to me and smiled, but her face said otherwise. "I thought I had seen a ghost."

"A ghost? Was it Valli?" I asked, and my nerves grew taut.

"No, he's not dead…yet," she answered slowly, looking disturbed. "This one looked like Rares."

"Rares?"

The effect of her words troubled my mind as much as Raluca's. I was certain that who she saw wasn't Rares, but perhaps someone that resembled him—if indeed someone was there. However, that was close to impossible. Raluca wouldn't purposely make such an error. Her complexion turned pale and she appeared to be confused.

"Raluca, we're both tired. Let's go home."

"What about hunting the Amestec?" she insisted, perhaps disappointed to cut short our time together. "It'll be fun!"

"I am sure it *would* be fun, but we don't have any weapons and there' no one to back us up."

"There are a couple of swords in your Land Rover, and some guns," she said stubbornly. "All I have to do is make them follow me to the car while you go and get the weapons. I have done this many times."

"I am sure you're an excellent bait, but this isn't the right time for it," I said, pushing her forward. We left the mall holding our bags, and it wasn't until we exited the elevator to the parking garage that we realized we had been followed.

"Well," I said, "it seems to me that we may not have any choice."

There were five men behind us who we had spotted earlier in the Nike store. We appeared to be young girls and we probably looked like easy prey for them.

"I told you this would be easy," said Raluca, walking calmly towards our vehicle.

"Maybe they don't know what we are," I said, having trouble believing that finding Amestec was so easy. "We shouldn't harm them if they aren't after a kill."

"Oh, they've detected our aroma already. They know who we are and they were sent to find us. All right then—I'll strike up a stupid conversation with them while you slip away and get the weapons."

We stopped and waited for them to come closer. Raluca smiled at them, but then she dropped her bags to the ground, ready for a fight. The guys slowed down their pace, hesitating, trying to decide the best way to approach us. The lighting in the garage was pretty good, so I could see them without the need to glow my eyes. One was Immortal impostor, two were Amestec, and two were Hybrids. They were all armed.

An SUV was slowly approaching us at the same time. Someone leaned half way through the passenger window and started shooting at the quintet. The gun had a silencer, but I was familiar with that specific sound. In a few seconds our stalkers were on the ground before they could counter-attack.

It was Alex, Luke, and another Immortal female that I didn't recognize who had rescued us.

"Good job, Sabrina," Alex said to the female, who lowered her Springfield XD gun and put it away in her belt. The tall, beautiful brunette was the lone shooter.

Then, Alex and Luke pulled out their swords and quickly decapitated the five without remorse. They didn't bleed.

I was disappointed. I was accustomed to fighting my enemies myself and making good use of my powers. This was an easy kill, shock and awe—probably the American style.

"This is a public location, and we have no time for anything fancy to draw attention to us," commented Alex to my unasked question. "We find them and kill them, and Serban buries them."

"Alex, what are you doing here?"

"I was looking for you," he answered, as they loaded the bodies in their car. "We caught your signal along with theirs—Nagoshi sent them. I have a hunch about where he'll be tomorrow."

17

THE PARK WAS EMPTY—or so I thought. I heard the sound of steps slowly approaching behind me, crunching on the gravel walkway. There were four of them. Amestec. I held my weapon tight, ready to charge. My Vortex had never let me down.

I had gotten as far south as Atlanta, killing as many Amestec as I could. Sometimes I encountered one of them, and sometimes they were in groups. It was unusual for me to see more than one or two of them at first, but then I knew that they were preparing something.

The most I killed at once were ten. It was a massacre, but it allowed me to be unemotional. A few were girls—all stimulated by the same supreme desire—to kill us and inherit life everlasting. I used myself as a trap—my scent drew them to me so easily.

As I was about to battle the four Amestec, another sound to my right made me spin around. A young girl was heading my way, still at some distance from me, walking a German shepherd. She was tall and slim wearing a long coat, a windbreaker with a hood over her head that masked her face. She turned left and then right, looking around as if she were worried, and a few times she stopped like she was in need of a rest. I thought she might be either sick or lost. The dog behaved very nicely, however, walking close to her side, protecting his master.

I hid behind a tree. Now I had to wait for this mortal to go away and not endanger her life with my actions. Suddenly, the Amestec stopped and imitated me, jumping behind a long row of bushes.

The girl suddenly stopped walking and unexpectedly got on her knees, as if she were praying. The dog started to bark loudly and nervously. I hoped that she wouldn't see me or the four men. Perhaps she was visually impaired and that was why she acted so unusual. I was worried for her safety, too. If the Amestec were hunting me, getting into a fight with a mortal in the vicinity would be a frightening thing for this fragile young lady to witness.

She stayed on her knees for a few moments, then rose and walked past me. I couldn't see her face, but something coming from her presence awakened my senses. A shadow from the past, a scent, a figure, and a loving face were the memories that overwhelmed me at that moment. I held my head with my palms, pressing hard. The weakness that I was feeling gradually disappeared.

I waited patiently—but to my surprise, the Amestec forgot about me and slowly started to follow the strange girl without bothering to acknowledge my presence. Why would they do that? She was just a mortal, wasn't she? Something wasn't right.

I stepped from behind the tree and released my Vortex. The weapon rotated in the air and caught up with the two of them who were bringing up the rear of their group. Their heads and bodies fell on the ground as the weapon returned to me. I needed to be faster, before the girl heard us.

The remaining two Amestec stopped and turned around to look. As they faced me, two Shurikens flew my way. The Vortex sliced through them as the weapons met in the air. Their eyes looked at me with anger and they started to run towards me. I was very fortunate to not encounter more of them. I recognized who the two of them were. Without a doubt they were my half-brothers— Anda's sons. They knew it too, because they became confused.

I jumped to the left, away from them. The Vortex returned to its master and once more I threw it hard. I wanted to get them both at once. One of them dropped fast, completely decapitated, but the other's neck wasn't completely sliced. I picked my Vortex, and walked toward him. He wasn't dead, yet, but his face was a picture of anger and sadness. I didn't care—it was too late for regrets. I knelt down to finish him off with my sword.

I heard the sound of a golf cart speeding my way and I saw a shadow of a man with a raised sword over his head. A sword? He couldn't be Amestec! Or could he? I slowly turned, ready for one more action.

"That's quite an amazing weapon," said the stranger, and his eyes focused on my Vortex. "Thank you for your assistance."

"Gallbor," I exclaimed, thinking that I recognized the young man in front of me as my Master.

"I am not Gallbor," he answered, a bit confused, but once he saw my face he stepped back. "Are you Milos Martuzon or his ghost?"

"I am not Milos. My name is Artamian."

"I apologize, Artamian, but you and Milos have similar features," he said very politely. "Why did you call me Gallbor?"

"Because I thought that you were him. You two look very much alike. Gallbor and I met long ago, and we're friends."

"My name is Octavian," he responded, bowing slightly to me. I did the same. Suddenly my face flushed.

"Octavian, Lady Safira's brother?" I asked, astonished. I couldn't believe that I was in the presence of Safira's brother. That meant only one thing— Safira was here, somewhere close by. How lucky could I be?

"Yes. Why is that important to you?"

"Gallbor made me promise that I would find her one day and protect her," I mumbled, concerned that Octavian would treat me as an enemy and force me to leave.

"What took you so long?" he asked in a very friendly manner.

"There were a few little bumps in the road," I said, pointing to the Amestec. "Besides, I am Milos's son. I'm not certain I could just show myself to your sister and expect to be welcomed."

"Milos's son—and born Immortal," murmured Octavian, and he came closer to stare at me. He asked for permission to hold my Vortex – and he did it exactly like me—he didn't get hurt.

"You are quite powerful to possess a weapon such as this. What can you tell me about yourself?"

"I can't be killed by a regular sword or anything sharp," I answered, somewhat proudly. Here in front of me was another very powerful Immortal who looked like Gallbor, and who had quite a few of his abilities. I didn't know what to make of him, but perhaps Safira's brother was Gallbor's son. And Safira too? That would explain Gallbor's love for her.

"Interesting," nodded Octavian. "So, you are untouchable?"

"I wish I were. I am seeking the one sword that could kill me—the Silver Sword. A few years back I encountered Nagoshi, an impostor Immortal, who is its master. I got this Shuriken from him."

"My sister and I are bound to find the Silver Sword and bring it back to the Order. What do you know about Nagoshi and his sword?"

"The blade turns invisible when it is in contact with another metal. It almost sliced my hand off. It is a dangerous weapon, and for Safira's sake, I want to find it and destroy it.

I've been hunting Nagoshi since he escaped from me. He is heading south—I'm following him. I thought I would do a little clean up here, first—less of them—better for Safira."

Octavian raised his eyes from my weapon to my face, analyzing and evaluating me. Then he shook his head and handed my Vortex back to me.

"Was that her?" I asked, and my voice trembled in anticipation. "The girl who was being followed by Amestec. Was that Lady Safira?"

"Yes, and I'm grateful to you for saving her. A month ago, my sister and I fought in Greece against Prince Albert. We recaptured the Fire Sword and won the war."

Saying that, Octavian proudly swung his sword in the air. Immediately, flames blazed out from the blade.

"I've heard of Prince Albert," I replied. "Perhaps he's one of my siblings."

"He was. How many more do you have?"

"I don't know, but I've killed as many as I could," I said, pointing to the two headless ones. "Please tell me more about Safira."

"She's not well these days, but it's just temporary," he answered, hesitantly bending down to take a closer look at my so called brothers. "Her powers are depleted and she's very vulnerable. I will mention to her that you saved her."

"No, please. She doesn't need to know. Allow me to look after her, but to stay anonymous."

"As long she's with me, I can protect her."

"I don't take my oath lightly—my allegiance is to be her guardian."

"Let me give you a bit of advice about my sister," said Octavian, hiding his sword in the back of the cart. "Be careful—she likes to be in control. She's stubborn, but she changes her mind easily if you ae patient. Saying that, I mean that she's unpredictable. So never back away. Keep it cool at all times—she doesn't go for the mushy kind of relationship. Stand your ground—looking like that, you've got a lot to overcome."

"Thanks," I said, a little puzzled, "but why are you telling me these things?"

"I can read your feelings for her and she'll sense them, too, right away. However, if you want her not to hate you, just be yourself."

"What about her master?" I must to admit that many times I wondered if Gallbor had allowed me to be strong enough to become her master. I wished it so ardently, but he was never clear about that. He simply chose me exclusively to love and guard her.

Octavian gazed at me one more time. Then he did something amazing. He took the head of the first Amestec I killed and sat it on its neck. Then he touched the skin all around the severed wound with the tip of his fingers. The skin of the head and neck reattached itself like it never been apart. He did the same thing with the other three.

"Who knows," he responded, lifting one of the Amestec and carrying him to his golf cart.

I helped him with the other three. "Don't worry about them—they'll be gone forever. In the meantime, be free to hunt Nagoshi and Safira will eventually come to you. Take care of my sister."

Saying that, Octavian finished sitting the Amestec in the golf cart, saluted me, bowed deeply, and drove away in a hurry, in the same direction that Safira had walked.

*   *   *

I had no other reason to linger around. Safira was here in this suburb of Atlanta, but my time had not yet come. I must hunt down Nagoshi and Safira would find me. That evening, I got on my motorcycle and headed to south Florida, near the tip of the peninsula.

Six months after I got there, I lost my Vortex.

I had chased down an Amestec in Miami, but I wasn't the only hunter. They were my brothers, the Transylvanians. I let them keep the Vortex, for now. I bought two guns, instead, and I started carrying the small sword I took from Nagoshi's collection.

It would not be the same as wielding my Vortex but there is a purpose in everything—I had started to believe in that philosophy more and more.

I was also pursued by the American Immortals. I couldn't join them—I had to stay apart from them all. But one evening, six months later, as I passed by their headquarters, I regained control of my weapon. There was only one way the Vortex could have been there, and only one person who could handle it—or maybe two.

I lingered around, waiting. Soon, the Americans had a lead on Nagoshi's whereabouts.

I went after him.

So did she.

18

IT WAS LATE IN THE AFTERNOON on Saturday when I arrived at Casa Marina Hotel in Key West. Although it was the middle of June, the weather was perfect—just about an average temperature, with a cooling sea breeze and not a cloud in the sky.

Alex had predicted that I might find Nagoshi here. His half-immortal daughter was getting married this day. The chances were small that he would come to the wedding, but again—miracles could happen.

The Warriors wanted to follow me and capture Nagoshi, but I convinced them that their presence there would raise his suspicion and he wouldn't be there. I could deal with him alone if I encountered him and track the location of his army.

I regretted leaving Raluca without resolving the matter of her spirit after she believed that she saw Rares at the mall, but I *had* to take this opportunity to find the Silver Sword.

The valet took my Rover, and I asked him to leave my driver's side window open a couple of inches. He took his tip, puzzled over my request, but he didn't make any unnecessary remark about it. I was making sure that one of the Dragon Shuriken could find its way out of the car if I needed it. It made me angry to be without my old sword, and I was most frustrated to lose the Vortex.

Determined, I went straight through the open doors of the hotel and I didn't stop walking until I reached the bar. The wedding reception hadn't started yet, but the hotel's hospitality room was already full of guests.

"Hi," said a young man who was sitting beside me. "I see you aren't drinking yet."

"Hi," I responded back. I wouldn't allow him to disturb me too long. "What would you recommend?"

"Their Pina Colada is the best in the world," he responded with a big smile. He was in his late twenties, with red hair and green eyes, small in stature, but with a daring attitude. I read him quickly— there was nothing malicious about him, but he wasn't very smart, either. He was just a silly boy who was looking for a good time and perhaps a little casual sex.

"OK, I'll try one," I said, and I asked the bartender for it.

"My name's Bruce," he said jovially. "I'm a friend of the groom."

"Megan," I answered quickly. "I'm here for the bride." I smiled again because there wasn't a shred of truth in anything I'd said since I arrived here.

The drink was very tasty, indeed. It had a lot of whipped cream on top and that had always been a pleasure to my mouth.

"It's good," I said, sipping small amounts and holding them in my mouth before I swallowed.

"I am glad you like it. I've already had four so far. So, are you staying overnight?"

"No, I'm just here for the wedding. I couldn't get a room here," I said with a sad face. "Unfortunately, I'll have to drive back to Boca tonight."

"Oh, that's a bummer," he exclaimed. "It's not safe to drive late at night. If you want to crash somewhere later on, I'm in room 3016. I'll be more than happy to share it you."

"Thanks Bruce, that's so nice of you."

"You're so pretty," he continued as he became more daring, leaning towards me. But I didn't hear the rest of his mumbling. In the corner of my eye I saw someone standing near the dance floor, a tall young man with long dark hair and luminous eyes. He watched me intensely. I couldn't make myself move and I didn't turn around right away so he wouldn't see that he had gotten my attention.

I had inhaled a certain scent that was well known to me and I held my breath for a moment, breathing it deeply into my lungs. I knew *what* he was, but *who* he was, was a mystery. I watched him moving around. My eyes followed all his movements and I became a little frustrated that he wouldn't fully turn my direction.

"So, Annika is very upset," I heard Bruce continuing to talk to me. "Her father didn't show up to give her away. I had told her not to expect him. Her mother hasn't seen him in more than twenty years, either."

I assumed he was talking about Mr. Nagoshi's daughter, and his comment reminded me that I came here to find him. Alex was pessimistic that he would attempt to come to her wedding, but I had a little more faith.

"Bruce, would you mind if I used your room to freshen up?" I asked the young man. "I'll be right back. You just stay here and wait for me, OK?"

He happily gave me the key card and winked at the bartender, who seemed to be interested in this development. I slipped a hundred dollar bill into his palm when he brought me the second drink. "Do you have something stronger for my friend?" I asked him in a whisper. He nodded. He clearly understood my request.

I walked around from table to table, from one group of guests to another, staring at every person of Asian descent. Finding one in particular was going to be a tremendous challenge. Since he was an Immortal, I focused on young looking Asian males.

I also wanted to find my mysterious Immortal who had momentarily disappeared from my view. The wedding ceremony was an hour away so I had time to seek out those two.

The mysterious Immortal I was seeking was real, not an impostor; he was armed, but he wasn't a danger to me. It was funny—I always thought that my first reaction would be to run away from unknown Immortals since they all wanted was me, but I was wrong. This one intrigued me so much with his game of hide and seek.

A few people cleared the way from the dance floor and I spotted him again. He was wearing a black suit and a white shirt, simple but elegant. I saw his profile but not much of his face: a bold forehead and a Roman nose, with a full lower lip. His hair was dark and wavy, but not pulled back in a ponytail, so it covered a good portion of his face. He was sitting alone at a table in a corner of the room near the bandstand, sipping his drink. I don't know what was in my own drink, but my body felt light and aroused.

He suddenly stood up and turned to me. I turned my head to the left, but not before I saw a streak of blue light in his eyes when he looked at me. Then he moved to the bar, turning his back to me again.

I couldn't believe it. He had just cast a spell on me.

An incredible feeling of attraction made me realize that I was in trouble and I couldn't resist him. Who was he that he could do that to me?

Something had happened to me. I wasn't that weak. I should be able to overcome his spell—lately, every Immortal male who took a wishful chance to glow their eyes on me were unsuccessful. I got closer to him and I tried to read his mind. What I felt coming from him astonished me—he knew who I was and this unknown Immortal man was in love with me. I put my drink down on a random table.

I slowly walked in his direction. He had large shoulders, and he was taller—much more fit and with more muscles than any of the other Immortals I knew. He was no one that I knew, but in a way, just standing a few feet away from him, he felt familiar. Perhaps it was just the effect of those feelings he had for me that I sensed in his heart. How could this be possible? Was I wrong and was it only my imagination? So far I clearly had been able to judge everyone, mortal or immortal, and be right about it.

He took one more step closer, but he turned to me only half way. His scent smelled fresh and my brain fought against him, but my body was stirred by his presence. I instantly knew that I wanted to have an adventure with this stranger—I wanted to have impulsive sex with a stranger—even though this was one notion I was so much against before now.

My eyes measured him again and I knew without a doubt that I was in for a treat.

His body heat rose. I felt it—he wanted me, too. He never turned in my direction but he stood there quietly, tense and ready. His simple presence seduced my mind and body, melting into nothingness every modicum of judgment and will power that I had remaining.

"Room 3016," I whispered to him, and he nodded in agreement.

I left the hospitality room, running to the elevator. The car was slow in arriving and I lost my patience as I was waiting for it, so I ran up the stairs. I wasn't concerned about Bruce; the bartender would take care of him, but I was afraid that I would change my mind.

What I was about to do wasn't me, not the logical Safira.

*   *   *

I left the door open a couple of inches and I collapsed on the bed. So there I was, tense with anticipation. I needed to let my inhibitions loose in abandonment. It truly felt like I was under a warlock's spell.

I rose from the bed to walk around the room, but I didn't bother to turn on the lights. I pulled the heavy drapes and covered the windows when I heard the sound of the door opening. He came in and locked the door. I didn't turn to look, but I was sure he had removed his clothes. I heard the rattle of pistols being laid on the table. A chill of nervousness passed through me, but I was determined to satisfy my body, and nothing else.

He walked slowly over the plush carpet so he wouldn't frighten me. He softly pulled my hair aside as he started to kiss my neck. His touch felt calming, but my pulse was accelerating. He pulled the shoulders of my dress down to my breasts as he continued to kiss my neck and shoulders. His breath was hot as his lips touched my skin.

My dress dropped a little more to my waist as he reached around my back to unclasp my bra. His hands gently cupped my breasts and massaged my nipples when the bra fell to the floor. Then he totally removed my dress and his fingers slipped inside the waistband of my panties.

I started to tremble. I had let him undress me, and the sensation was relaxing and soothing.

Throughout my long life I had doubted that I would ever feel like this in the arms of a stranger; however, here I was, in a room and naked with a man totally unknown to me.

"I've never done this with someone I didn't know," I said, a bit embarrassed, hesitating to turn and see his face. "I don't even know who you are."

"Who I am isn't important, Lady Safira," he said. His voice was soft, but deep. "You chose me and I'm all yours."

I attempted to turn around, but he quickly put his fingers over my eyes.

"Don't look, just keep your eyes closed the whole time and enjoy it. Promise me you won't open your eyes. Please."

"It's not fair," I said, puzzled by his silly request, but I did close my eyes. I liked the sound of his voice, and his accent was soothing, but masculine. The scent of his immortality smelled so good. "You know who I am, but I don't know you."

"You're my Queen," he whispered, "and I love you. I'll satisfy you Lady Safira."

"You love me?" I asked, but in the next moment he lifted me up in his arms and laid me on the bed, on my back. I kept my eyes closed as he lightly laid his body over mine and started kissing me.

His lips softly touched mine. I liked that. I returned his kisses, holding his face in my hands. I didn't want him to stop kissing me. His lips were curved and sensual, and it seemed that just his kisses alone could almost satisfy me.

"You are so amazing, my Queen," he answered softly. I had no idea why, but I believed him. His soft fingers circled around my breasts and nipples a few times, and then his palms kneaded them in an upward rotation.

The next part of me to enjoy his gentle kisses were my nipples as they disappeared into his mouth. My body convulsed for a moment and my torso lifted up in invitation.

I touched his chest. It was massive, soft and hairless; then my hands slipped down to his muscular abdomen. I knew what I was seeking and my hand rested on it. He was erect and ready for me, and I was ready for him. I couldn't wait any longer and I guided him in. As I felt him through my wetness, my insides vibrated and I screamed.

"I've desired you for so long," he whispered, pushing in further and increasing the speed of his movement.

I gasped for air. I attempted to raise my head, but he started to kiss me more aggressively and passionately. My climax was fast and wild as he continued his movements inside me, until I sensed that his eyes had started to illuminate. I opened my eyes, too. I could only see the glowing of his eyes.

Wave after wave of trembling continued for the longest time. He satisfied me over and over until I lost count. He eventually sensed my exhaustion and he finally withdrew from me, to my regret.

He rolled over on his back and lifted me as if I were a feather. He laid me on his chest and I collapsed in his arms. I tried to peek at his face, but all I could see was his strong jaw. I couldn't tell if he was handsome or not, but I didn't care. I lay motionless on top of him for a moment, but then the beauty of his body made me start caressing him.

My wandering hand slid down his abdomen and encountered his erection, up and ready again. I giggled with lust.

"You want more, my love?" he asked, and his words made me even more excited. I settled down on top of him while our bodies joined themselves again in a fiery encounter.

I started to kiss him again with fury and hunger—his lips and tongue were making love with mine, too, until our delirious moment came to an end with our delicious climaxes. I had lost track of time, but he gently lifted me and laid me beside him.

"I must leave you now," he said, as he rose from the bed and dressed. "Goodbye, my Queen."

"Wait," I said, rising from the bed. I was still naked as I tried to stop him. "Please, I must know who you are. Why are you talking to me like a lover if you aren't willing to become one?"

Why did he want to remain anonymous after we had made love so beautifully? He stopped and half way turned to me.

"Didn't you enjoy me?" I asked, trying my old fashioned word game on his mind.

His eyes glowed again as he came towards me. He glowed on purpose so I couldn't see clearly his face. It was exactly like in my old dream – he was going to disappear before I could see him. I tried glowing my eyes, but he held me tightly to his chest.

"Yes, my love," he replied, and started kissing me again— the power of his glow made me close my eyes. "I've loved you for the longest time and I have dreamed of making love with you every day of my life. This evening was a miracle and I was healed from my sufferings. But if you knew my identity, I'm afraid I would lose you. One day, my time will come and you will choose me freely."

"But you feel so familiar, like we have met before. Please, at least tell me where you come from. I deserve to know that much."

"I am also an Immortal Warrior."

He turned and left quickly, leaving me with only this cryptic answer. I wasn't sure what to believe. I wanted to keep him so badly; I wanted to have him close to me. I wanted him to be my lover, against my belief that I should wait for a master. But his fear of losing me was real. I could feel it.

I had denied Andreas' and Julian's affection and held back any temptation—even though I loved them. But now I had met a stranger and had fallen recklessly into his arms. I allowed myself to be loved by him and I savored his passion for me. Now, at least, I could give him a name. He had said "also", so I could call him The Transylvanian.

The Transylvanian? My mouth opened wide in astonishment. It was him! There was no doubt in my mind that I had just made love with the mysterious Immortal the Americans called *The Transylvanian*, the master of the Vortex.

The Transylvanian had become, in that instant, my lover and my enemy.

I hurriedly dressed and left the room.

19

TWO HOURS.

How could I have been gone for so long? Sweat dripped down my back—I was mad at myself and furious at *him*, The Transylvanian. But by the time I reached the elevator, I couldn't just blame him alone. I was the one who had made the invitation. A warm sensation suddenly passed through my whole body.

This wasn't over for me. The moments of passionate love we had together had fired up my soul. I liked it and I wanted more I ran down on the stairs, forcing myself to let go of my feelings and clear my mind.

* * *

The wedding was over by now. I had missed the ceremony and the possibility of finding Nagoshi. If by any chance he had appeared to maintain the tradition of giving her away to the groom, I had missed all that—I had been gone for two hours.

My eyes searched the room intensely. All the guests were sitting at their tables now and the dinner had already been served. Maybe I could find him if he was still there. My best chance was to find Bruce, who seemed to be a close friend of the groom and who had a little insight into the family drama. I spotted him at a table near the front entrance and I tried to get his attention. He saw me, and the first thing he did was to come weaving towards me and pull me to the dance floor for a slow dance. I reluctantly followed him.

"Beautiful Megan," he said, with a large smile and a strong aroma of alcohol. He was almost too drunk to stand up. "Where have you been for so long? I missed you."

"I'm sorry, Bruce," I responded, trying to keep him upright and balanced. "I was so tired, I'm afraid I fell asleep in your bed. How was the wedding? Who gave away the bride?"

Bruce didn't answer me right away. His left hand was around my waist and he was holding me tightly. I hated every second of his closeness and the way he slobbered on my dress—but I couldn't leave him, not yet.

"Too bad you weren't here," he responded, laying his head on my shoulder. "Annika was in tears. Her father still didn't come, but he sent his son."

"His son?" I asked, astonished and I stopped dancing.

"Apparently her father has another family, and it turns out that Annika has a brother. He introduced himself as that."

"How old is he?"

"He looked pretty young—I don't know. Will you spent the rest of the evening with me?" The song was over and I separated myself from Bruce's embrace.

"Sure," I answered, walking backwards, "but I need to find some friends first. I'll be right back."

I walked around again, looking for a young Nagoshi. Why did he sent his son and where was he hiding? Was his son an Amestec? I could be sure of that! If Nagoshi was an impostor Immortal, his children had to be Amestec. Annika was an Amestec, even if she had no knowledge of it.

Suddenly, I realized why The Transylvanian was here. Alex had told me that he was a loner who constantly chased the rogue Amestec. This time, if I encountered him again, there would be no love between us. But then what? I couldn't undo what had happened between us, but I could make sure he would never glow his eyes on me again.

I went outside in the courtyard and observed everyone who was sitting at their tables on the both sides of the two twin pools. If Nagoshi's son was here and The Transylvanian was here, I was on the right path. This Immortal Warrior was an unexpected aid I might or might not use. I couldn't help wondering if he had the Vortex with him—I certainly wanted to see him in action. But what if I was wrong about his identity?

I looked up and down the beach. There was no one lying on the sand, just a few people getting ready for some evening fishing and some Wave Runners that had been left behind. I turned around and went back inside the hotel. I passed through the lobby and went out to the parking lot.

I knew that The Transylvanian was known to ride a motorcycle and I wanted to see if I could spot one. The parking lot was on the right side of the hotel. It was full, but there wasn't a motorcycle or anything else interesting for me there. I passed by my own Rover and I looked inside. I saw my gun, and I wasn't comfortable looking for Nagoshi's son without one, but without a place on my body to hide it, I would have to leave it in the car.

The hotel had an additional parking area across the street, hidden behind an auxiliary building and backing up to the beach. I headed that way and I saw him on the second row.

He was standing in the middle of the row with his back toward me, facing the next row beyond him. I ran towards him, feeling even more frustrated. I realized at that moment that my focus had shifted so easily from finding Nagoshi's son, as I intended all along, to finding *him*.

"What are you doing here?" I asked, grabbing his arm. "Listen, we need to talk about what happened between us, and especially about your identity."

He turned only half way again, but in the evening light I could see his features better. Damn, he looked so familiar. But instead of talking to me, as I demanded, he stepped in front of me like he was offering me his protection.

"Are you armed, my Lady?" he asked, with his deep baritone voice.

"What?" I moved from behind him to see what he was staring at. A man was facing us a few feet away, apparently waiting for something or someone. He was a young Asian male, average height, with long dark hair that was gathered into a ponytail. I knew who he was and that we had both found him.

"No. Are you armed?" I asked The Transylvanian. My weapon could have been in Peachtree City, for all the good it was doing me here.

"Yes and no," he answered, placing himself in front of me again. "The problem is that my weapon's on my bike and our friend is standing between us and it."

I moved from behind him and I saw that the man stood beside an elegant black motorcycle with gray and maroon stripes.

"He doesn't seem to be armed," I said—I couldn't see any weapons in the man's hand.

"Trust me, he is," confirmed The Transylvanian. "He's the master and creator of all the modern Shurikens the Amestec use against us."

That would explain why so many Amestec were armed with these Japanese weapons and why Serban had a full trunk of them. "Do you know him?"

"His name is Sum Nagoshi," he answered with no hesitance. "We're old enemies. I've been chasing him for a long time."

"He's Nagoshi?" I asked, feeling even more confused as I stared at him. "He's not an Amestec anymore! What harm he could do to *you*?"

"He has the only weapon that could kill us both, my Lady." Saying this he turned his face fully to me.

I stepped back in astonishment. The man, who until a second ago was just an unknown warrior from Transylvania, a powerful warrior who had mastered the Vortex and the man who I had made love with, was the perfect image of Milos Martuzon.

I exhaled with fury and my face flushed with rage. I was in total denial.

No, that was impossible! My fierce enemy was dead—his wife had killed him and she had become Immortal. Milos was no longer alive; he couldn't be. But the man looking back at me had his features and the resemblance couldn't be a coincidence.

I backed away until I bumped into the car behind me. The Transylvanian moved towards me and his blue eyes were deep and grave.

"Stop right there!" I yelled at him. In fact, my voice was just a harsh whisper, but I was ready for a fist fight. "Who are you?"

"My name is Artamian," he said, coming closer to me in small steps. "I know what are you're thinking, but I'm not Milos Martuzon. However, I *am* his son. I'm not your enemy, no more than you want to make me be."

"Milos' son!"

And born Immortal, too.

My anger boiled rapidly inside me. My legs trembled and I felt like falling on my knees but surprisingly, I was still standing. No. This couldn't be happening to me. I was Gallbor's daughter, so powerful and gifted. I couldn't allow my emotions to overcome me and destroy my mission.

Nagoshi made the choice for me. As he approached us, I could see a sword in his left hand. By the look of the grip and blade, it looked like it was the Silver Sword. I would kill Artamian later; now, I had to fight and take back the relic.

"My weapon is in the saddle bag on the right," Artamian said, covering me with his body. "I'll keep Nagoshi away from you. Now, go and get it."

But I didn't move. The Transylvanian's words amazed me again and I was frozen in place. He was putting himself in harm way, unarmed and facing the weapon he feared would destroy him, just to protect me. I hated him that moment, as much as I was fascinated by his cool demeanor.

Nevertheless—he was my warrior and he *was* bound to serve me.

"Artamian, you're in my way," Nagoshi said to him with a smirking smile on his face. He swung the sword in the air a few times, but something in its sound as it whistled through the air didn't feel right to me. "Let me have Lady Safira."

"Please, go," he insisted, pushing me behind a car. I stood motionless for a second, puzzled that Nagoshi had recognized me or that he knew that I was here. How was that possible? Who was after whom?

"I see that you still carry my Vortex," continued Nagoshi, making small, careful steps towards us. You can't get to it, can you? You don't have the mental ability to master that weapon. So, what are you going to do? Just go away and let me take my Queen with me."

"Shut up, Nagoshi!" yelled Artamian. Then he bent over me again and I felt a stroke of heat in my heart from being so close to him. "I know you can handle the Vortex—go get it and save yourself."

"No," I answered firmly.

Artamian's face was closer to mine but my sudden aversion towards him stopped me from looking to him for protection anymore. I just couldn't. His scent was wonderful, but I didn't want to remember that only a few minutes ago I was in his arms and he had kissed me, held my naked body, and declared his love for me. As much as I desired him, he wasn't the same man in my mind and I refused to feel attracted to him.

"Why not?" he asked surprised.

"This is why," I answered. I stood up and caught the Vortex with my right hand. I had located the weapon and I brought it to me with the power of my mind. Artamian's eyes grew larger and he moved to my side. But not just his eyes grew bigger, he seemed to grow taller, too. Nagoshi's face lost its smirk and became serious; his gray eyes glimmered with spite.

"Lady Safira, what a surprise—you can master the Vortex! I'd heard many things about you. Apparently, all of them are true."

I spun the weapon with my two fingers and released it towards Nagoshi. He lifted his sword and parried the weapon's spin in the air. The two weapons collided, but mine returned to me. I twisted my body to the right to gain more speed and force. The sharp circle rotated faster, but my opponent was just as fast and he managed to stop it again.

I leaped to the hood of a car and somersaulted to get closer to him, trying again to overcome him. I aimed the Vortex for his head while I made an arc in the air with my right arm to hit his left hand—the one that was holding the sword. Nagoshi followed my movements and his body rotated in the air. His sword came downward very close to me, nearly cutting off my hand.

It was too dangerous to fight any closer like I was doing. At that moment I needed to use my mind to guide the Vortex, but it was too late.

Artamian grabbed the weapon from my hand and ran with it towards Nagoshi. The two men fought closer than I had, and Artamian attacked Nagoshi with a fury that was beyond my own. He used the Vortex like he was fighting with another sword, and his arm extended fully to hit hard.

The sword met the sharp disk closer to its hilt, but the blade held its own. Artamian bent down, swinging in a low arc for his opponents hands. Nagoshi sliced the sword's blade down with extreme power, forcing Artamian to back away. This fight was absolutely crazy—the Vortex wasn't a hand to hand weapon—it was made to be thrown.

What was he doing? For just a split second I wished that Nagoshi would eliminate Artamian. My enemy would be gone—at least, the son of the man who looked like him.

But my hate towards him didn't have time to flourish. From the corner of my eye, I saw a security guard on a golf cart who appeared from the left corner of the parking lot.

"Somebody's coming," I shouted. I didn't want anyone to witness a man fighting with a sword and take the chance of having a mortal being aware of our existence.

I turned my head for a moment. The last thing I saw was Nagoshi running towards the beach and Artamian running after him. I followed behind. Nagoshi jumped onto a Wave Runner that seemed to be waiting for him on the shore—perhaps his only means of transportation. He started the engine and drove towards the deep water without looking back.

The Transylvanian sailed the Vortex as rapidly as possible to intercept him, but it fell short. Then he drew his Smith and Wesson with the silencer from his suit coat and fired several shots, but they all missed.

"He's gone," said Artamian, as he caught the returning Vortex with his left hand. "Something's very wrong."

"What would that be, beside the fact that you let him get away."

"His sword didn't turn invisible. I fought him when he had the Silver Sword before—I know it very well."

He put his gun away in his belt behind his suit coat, switched hands with the Vortex, and showed me his left palm with a huge scar.

"This cut was made by Nagoshi's Silver Sword. It turned invisible the moment it came in contact with a metal object. He's moving fast, now, and I can't throw the Vortex that far. Maybe you should try."

I grabbed the shuriken from his hand, but I knew better. Nagoshi's little jet ski was too far in the ocean by now. My mind couldn't use the Vortex to catch up with him. I was angry and frustrated.

"Why did you interfere in my fight?" I asked Artamian, and I turned all my anger onto him. "My mind can master the Vortex! I could have terminated Nagoshi! What were you trying to prove to me? You know, I *could* kill you right now."

"You could try," he answered, lifting his hands in the air as if in surrender, "but with what? I can't be killed by any means other than Nagoshi's invisible blade."

I didn't believe him right away, but then I realized that he was the master of the Vortex. Perhaps he was right—he couldn't be cut by any traditional sword. He looked at me, trying to read into my soul. Without removing his eyes from mine, he took my hand holding the Vortex and forced the weapon on his neck. I could feel that he was pushing hard, but nothing happened—there was no cut.

"How is this possible?" I asked him, although I despised to be in his presence any longer. But I needed answers. "Milos' son, why are you an Immortal?"

"I don't know," he answered, remaining close to me. "I was told that I was supposed to be born like this, and…"

"And what?" I asked, irritated, but knowing that he was telling the truth. "Who told you that?"

"Someone named Gallbor."

I stood still, dumbfounded, too terrified to ask for more details.

I looked up at him, at his face that brought back all my terrible memories, and I wished for both of us to vanish—forever. I was troubled by the fact that he even existed and I was horrified by the meaning of his words. I wanted to let loose and to scream hysterically. But what would have been the sense of that? Would it relieve my pain and shame? No! Absolutely not! He wasn't the chosen one. Gallbor wouldn't do that to me.

I kept silent. This new information was churning in my brain, like a communication error message. I simply turned my back to him and still holding his Vortex, I walked to the other parking area to find my car, but Artamian followed me. When I reached my Land Rover, I dropped his weapon into my trunk, although he didn't seem to care.

"Stay away from me," I said, and my eyes glowed blue thunder on him. "I still can kill you if I want."

"Lady Safira," he said rapidly, grabbing both of my arms above the elbows. His grip was very strong and I felt his passion. "*I am not here to hurt you!*" He strongly emphasized each word.

"Then why are you looking for the Silver Sword?"

"So no one can use it against me…or you."

"Ha," I said and I pushed him away with disgust. "But *you* would use it against *me*! Your father did, and so will you!"

"I am not my father." His voice was deeper, and had calmed considerably. "I am very well aware of what my father did to you, of what my mother did to him, and how evil she was. Look into my eyes and see—I am not your enemy. I am bound to serve you."

There was a sweet smile on his lips and his eyes sparkled. He had great clear blue eyes, with a certain softness in them. I would be lying to say that I didn't care about what he was saying.

I read him, too. He was honest, strong, and sincere.

"I never want to see you again!" I said, accenting every word. "I despise you and nothing will ever change that." I turned my back on him and got in the Rover.

I drove away with his weapon.

I kept it as I kept Grant's car.

He would come for it.

20

DEERFIELD'S BEACH WAS QUITE BUSY in the early afternoon. Some of the people were enjoying the Sunday before getting back to work, but most of them were tourists on their last day of vacation before returning home.

The ocean has always captivated me. I stood with my toes deep in the sand, facing a big tidal pool. It calmed me and I needed that more than anything. I had one of Raluca's red bikinis on and I was tempted to go into the ocean, but just staying still comforted me.

The wind and the breeze caressed my face. I liked it. The sun was hot. It felt like a hot kiss on my lips. *His* lips were hot. *Forget him*, demanded my mind, but my heart wrestled. How could I forget him when we had made such passionate love?

My mind was telling me that making love with him was like drinking poison, but my heart argued back in denial.

I didn't seem to get a break, a moment of peace. Was this how my life was going to be from now on? Why could no one else take over and fight this war for me? My brother was still gone—I had no one else I could turn to who was strong enough. The rest of the Immortals had been cruelly hunted and slayed.

He could. The one called The Transylvanian could certainly fight my war, but I didn't want him. I hated him. I hated the fact that he was Milos' son, and more than that—he looked like Milos. I couldn't face him without remembering the man who killed me. I couldn't let go of that. And what kind of father was Gallbor to entrust Milos' son with such powers? Now I could be certain that Gallbor was not, in truth, my father.

"A penny for your thoughts," I heard Alex behind me. He was wearing a pair of red shorts, his hair was in a ponytail, and he was shirtless—dressed for lifeguard duty. I had sent Raluca to bring him to me. "I heard you were looking for me. What else happened in Key West?"

The question raised a chill down my spine. "What do you mean?"

"I mean, did you encounter any Amestec? I can't believe that Nagoshi would go there alone. We should have come with you."

"It's all right, he came alone," I assured him, and I assumed that he didn't know that I met Artamian there. There was something else, something more dangerous that worried him. "Unfortunately, he didn't have the Silver Sword with him, but he had a good copy of it. If he's in charge of the rest of Amestec, he must have a command post somewhere, far from visual contact with the mortals."

"Are you sure he still has the sword?"

"You can't gain this much power over others without anything to back up your claim. He still has it."

"I'm sorry your mission was a miss."

"It wasn't a miss because I was able to develop a good theory," I said, getting my feet out of the sand. "Nagoshi escaped me on water. Is it possible to find out if they could have something like a large boat for their headquarters? You said you couldn't locate anything on the land. Try that."

"That definitely sounds interesting." nodded Alex, but he blinked a little too fast. "You know, you could come to talk to me any time I'm in the lifeguard booth."

"I know," I said. But I didn't want go to talk with him because I had seen Julian up in his booth. I couldn't face him, either.

"I am glad you're back," he said, patting my shoulder. "I'll have Luke to start monitoring the surrounding waters right away."

*   *   *

"Would you care for a walk?" I asked Raluca, who seemed somewhat distracted. She had taken a seat randomly on someone's beach chair. The owner of the chair didn't seem to mind and he stood by her on the sand, enjoying his view of her. The girl was gorgeous in her pink bikini, the only kind of bathing suit she seemed to own. She reluctantly stood up and followed me down the beach. We waded in the water as the ocean rolled up on the shore.

"The sun feels so good," I started, since my companion was deep in thought.

"Indeed. The sun has a great effect on people, especially on males. I've already received a marriage proposal!"

"You're a very attractive girl. I am sorry I had to leave you before we talked about the man you saw on Friday, the one you thought was Rares. I was worried about you."

"I'm not easily disturbed, but I suppose I appeared to be a basket case," she said, trying to smile.

"Not at all. I want to assure you that it's nothing. People resemble each other—especially our kind. Trust me, it isn't uncommon to think you've recognized someone and it turns out to be somebody else."

I was the best witness to my own comments. Julian and Andreas. Artamian and Milos.

"You're right. Perhaps it's just my guilt feeling for being responsible for Rares' death. It's been a year, but it feels like yesterday."

"It *does* feel like yesterday," said a man behind us.

I turned immediately. He was a young man with dark long hair and intense dark eyes. He wore metallic green swim trunks with a white t-shirt. He was handsome with perfect features, although they were perhaps a bit to symmetric, but they reminded me of a very young James Dean. Raluca didn't turn to face him. She knew the stranger's identity by the sound of his voice.

"Valli!" The girl's face turned pale. It was obvious, from the frightened look in her eyes that her fear of this guy was enormous. My mind traveled to my car where I had left the Vortex, but was too far away—again.

So, my prediction was right—he came for her.

"Beautiful Raluca," he said as a large smile brightened his face. "Did you miss me?"

"What do you want, Valli," asked Raluca, forcing her face into a calm demeanor. "Do you have a death wish? What are you doing here?"

"Oh, I have a love wish," he responded ironically, "I came to take you with me. You could be my bride now—we're the same, now."

"I'm not going *anywhere* with you," she said, but her eyes looked at me, imploring me to not intervene.

"I don't think you have that choice," Valli responded, and I saw three men approaching from behind him dressed in similar outfits. Immortals, but former Amestec. But Valli was *her* son—Anda's son—Rares' killer, and more dangerous because of this.

"You brought an army to take me?" she asked, with an ironic smile.

"To take you without incident" he answered, touching her face with his fingers. Raluca stepped back.

"You're not going to get too far."

"I know that your dogs are close by, but in order to take you peacefully, I'm going to invite your friend to come along," he said, and he moved closer to look at me. "You're a pretty girl—how lucky can I get?"

"Get away from her!" yelled Raluca, and for the very first time since I had known her she was ready to attack. I realized that Valli had no idea who I was, but I needed to know where he was planning to take Raluca.

That wasn't what Raluca had in mind, but one of the men grabbed my arm and forced me to walk towards the dressing rooms. Valli did the same with Raluca.

"Leave her alone," she implored. "She's just a girl who I met on the beach. She had nothing to do with anything. Listen, let her go."

"Stop it," snapped Valli. "Just let me remind you that I've got no problem shooting one mortal on this beach for every time you attempt to get away—starting with your new friend."

I wasn't worried. Alex and Julian would see our movements and be alert to our disappearance. I took a quick look at their booth, but they weren't on it. The last thing I saw before I was pulled away was them heading toward a small crowd where someone was lying on the sand. With so many people gathered around, it was hard for me to detect what all the commotion was about.

They took us up the shore to the private side of Deerfield Beach. We crossed the street to the canal and they loaded us onto a yacht that was parked in one the slips.

"Don't dare speak," Raluca whispered to me as I was pushed into the boat where two more hybrids were waiting for us.

Her request was strange, and my mind raced to determine what her reasoning was. It would make more sense for me to scream for help, rather than to quietly follow them into the danger. That's what these guys would expect.

"I know what you're trying to do," Raluca said to Valli, once the boat's engine had started and we were sailing furiously into the deep water.

The boat was a forty foot long sailing Catamaran, with white leather benches on both sides of the hull, an entertainment booth in the middle of the deck, and stairs leading to the top main control cabin.

"Like what," he asked, forcing me to move to the other side of the boat. One of the Hybrids used plastic zip cuffs and tied my hands together behind my back. I didn't like that at all! I could break metal, but plastic wouldn't break easily and I risked cutting my wrists.

"You want to start a war," said Raluca, and without being asked, she offered her arms to be tied, too. I wished she hadn't done that.

"A war wouldn't get us anywhere without us getting *her*."

"Who are you talking about?"

"The Queen," responded Valli, as he cuffed Raluca's hands. "We know she's here in this area."

"You heard wrong—she isn't here. I would know!"

"My dear, please don't contradict me. She *is* here—one of us saw her yesterday in Key West. She's back here now with the rest of the Americans."

I knew he was talking about my encounter with Nagoshi. Raluca looked at me intensely, but I nodded to her to stay calm. There were only six of them—we could easily take them down.

When he turned, I saw that he had a gun. I could kill the hybrids with it—but I needed a sword or any kind of sharp object for the four impostors.

"There's no love between us any longer, Valli. Just let me go," Raluca continued to try to reason with Valli.

"I still love you. I truly want to be with you. We could have a great life together."

"I don't believe you."

"Then, why do you think I'm here? You think it's just to start a war? The war is already on, my dear, and we're going to win this time."

"So, what are you going to do with me? Sacrifice me for one of your brothers?"

Valli grimed. Far in the distance I saw a large ocean liner coming our direction. I wondered why the coast guard hadn't been alerted by now to come looking for us. It had been fifteen minutes since we left the slip.

"You've got a very low opinion of me," said Valli, texting on his cell phone, to connect with others in his army.

"You proved me exactly right when you killed Rares."

The young man's eyes narrowed and a deep line appeared between them. It was easy to guess that he was annoyed by Raluca. I needed for her to be quiet and to not aggravate him, for her own sake. I sensed that he was cruel and indifferent, a change in his attitude that contained much rage and anger. I couldn't sense if it was Rares that I felt, but I doubted it; however, it was impossible for me to be sure of that since Rares wasn't my brother.

"You are totally clueless," he replied and walked towards Raluca with a threatening move.

"Then enlighten me," she said, but this time in a softer tone of voice. "There was a time when you shared many things with me."

"That time belongs in the past. You can't expect me to open up and tell you all our secrets. Do you take me for a fool?"

"No. But you want me to be with you, right?"

"Yes, but only to make love with you—not for any other reason. I couldn't betray my people any more than you could betray yours."

"Your people? Valli, you're an Immortal now! Why are we enemies?"

Raluca's question didn't get an answer. Valli's attention suddenly turned to me as he read a text message on his phone.

"What's her name," he asked Raluca as he moved closer to me. But she hesitated to answer. The girl, who always called me Lady Safira, now couldn't open her mouth to give me a fake name. Her devotion to me was the beginning of a new episode of self-torment.

"Does she have a name and what is it?" Valli demanded as he continued to look at me suspiciously. Then he lifted my chin with his right hand while with the left he used his mobile to take a picture of me. "Tell me her name, Raluca, or I'll put a bullet in her head."

"Megan," I answered quickly. How much harm could I do just for saying this one word? At the same time, I realized something more about Raluca that I didn't previously know: she couldn't tell a lie. That's why Valli asked her my name.

"Megan? We'll see about that."

In a split second, our situation changed from unknown to eminent danger. Valli would know in a moment that I was the

Queen. I couldn't see if he received another text message, but he lifted up the seat of the bench and pulled out a sword.

My hands sweated. Of all the times I had the chance to kill some impostors, and especially the one who killed Rares, I was unarmed and in a bikini. Valli pointed the sword at Raluca.

"Tell me the truth. What's her name?"

Raluca looked down for a second—that second felt like an eternity before she answered.

"Her name is Megan, like she said."

"Then why did it take you so long to answer?"

"Because I couldn't remember it right away. I told you, I just met her on the beach."

That was a great answer, but Valli was still suspicious of his former lover. Raluca's whole demeanor then changed from calm to agitated. Her hands started to shake and her face flushed. Valli's eyes had a strange gleam in them and I could feel the danger. His sword swung towards Raluca's neck. I attempted to run to her aid, but three men grabbed me to hold me still.

"For the last time," he whispered, "is her real name Megan?"

She looked at me calmly. She knew what was about to happen and she accepted it.

"Yes, it is," she whispered, like she was saying goodbye.

My entire body felt as if it were covered in ice.

"Too bad, my love," he said. "You just bet your life on it."

Valli's blade sliced off her head.

Her eyes were still locked on me, large and beautiful.

21

THIS COULDN'T BE POSSIBLE. It was as if Milos Martuzon had killed me all over again.

What a hideous recollection. And how could I have let it happen to her?

Raluca's spirit was still around. It was likely that it didn't transfer to another body, since the only non-immortals with us were the two hybrids. Perhaps Valli wanted it that way. But I needed to reattach her head immediately and try to revive her.

That meant that I had to kill everyone on the boat in less than a minute. My hands were still tied behind my back and three men were holding me down on the deck. But my legs were free.

"You killed her," I screamed, trying to get up with three men on top of me. My anger won and I used my head to hit them randomly until I pushed them off of me. I kicked them in their groins and they doubled over in pain. As I got to my feet, Valli motioned for them to them to leave me alone.

"You are Lady Safira, the Queen," said Valli, coming towards me. "Raluca wouldn't sacrifice her life for a total stranger she'd just met on the beach. I killed her for you. You're the Healer and I've found you. How lucky can I be?"

He was right, but I didn't have time for this conversation. My right leg moved up and forward, into the jaw of one of the men standing behind me. He fell backward and hit the railing of the boat. Suspicious of my intention to put up a good fight and escape, Valli immediately took Raluca's body and threw it into the water, leaving her head behind. At that moment I lost all my presence of mind. Seeing her body afloat left me momentarily paralyzed.

I had a difficult decision to make: stay on board and kill everyone (although I was unarmed) or jump in the water and attend to Raluca. I didn't hesitate. I walked backwards, bent down, grabbed the girl's head with my hands tied behind my back, and jumped into the ocean. The water was warm and that was in my favor—to keep her body ready for the re-connection.

I released her head so it would float. I bent my legs together and brought my hands under them, to my front. I forced the plastic zip cuff to cut off my left hand and I set myself free. My right hand held my left hand and wrist together until they reattached and healed completely.

The wake from the boat had pushed Raluca's body away until it was already a good distance past me, and her head was rapidly floating in the opposite direction. I was wasting minutes, now.

Valli maneuvered his boat between me and the girl's head. I looked around, frustrated that of all the speed boats that were always running around, none came in our direction. I couldn't see the large liner, either. Anything would help, just to have Valli to stop the boat's motion for a minute.

I needed to get to Raluca. I knew that I couldn't expect any help from Alex. Whatever was happening on the beach, it was a diversion to keep him focused on that and lose track of me.

The hybrids aimed their guns at me. Valli stopped them from firing, perhaps because he didn't want any noise to bring unnecessary attention.

"Would you like to come back up on board, my Lady," Valli asked, laughing at my effort to swim around them. He would steer the boat in every direction I would try to swim. I had only one chance left—go under the boat. I could handle being able to swim in deep water, and considering the width of the boat, I could hold my breath for that long without any problem.

"She's dead! What the hell you want her for?" Valli's question was the last thing I heard.

I glowed my eyes and started swimming in a strange way, more like a mermaid. He revved up the engines to run over me, but I went deeper. To use such a large boat as a weapon didn't work on me.

I felt the motor's propeller pass over me and I kept going. The water had a certain sound and vibration that magnified the engine and I could hear them moving on the deck, too. I swam towards the other side of the boat, but when I got there, the hybrids were in the water, waiting for me.

One of them threw a fishing net in my path and he caught me. I waited for him to come closer. I partially floated and tread water so I wouldn't entangle myself even further in the net. When he attempted to pull me away, I extended my legs as much as I could and wrapped them around his neck. I twisted hard and his neck broke.

I pushed him up to surface, but not before another one could grab me. The hybrids came to the edge of the deck and pulled me up over the rail. The net was so tight around my body, I couldn't move.

"We've caught a great fish," smiled Valli with an evil look on his face, sitting on the bench and holding the sword he had used to kill Raluca.

"What are your plans for me," I asked, coughing out the water I had swallowed and fighting to keep my balance. My hair was entangled in the net and its silken threads cut into my face. "I'm warning you—I won't tolerate your crimes any longer. In a few minutes you'll be dead."

"Oh, what a beautiful accent," Valli replied, stepping closer while he placed the sword on top of the box. Now I realized why Raluca wanted me to stay quiet. "I was told about it. Your voice is magic, like a spell. I could just close my eyes and listen to you forever. I'm going to keep you as payment for killing my brothers and my mother."

"Have you heard I word I just said? You're an impostor, Valli! A criminal like them, who killed the woman he loved. You're nothing and you'll become only a sad memory. You'll die today! That's a promise!"

Raluca.

I gazed quickly to my left. Her body was still in my view, but it had drifted far away from the boat. This wasn't looking too good for me. I must get back into the water, but I had to have my body freed from this clinging net.

"I'm going to become famous by taking you to our kingdom," responded Valli, and he put his arms around me. "Did you hear that? We have a kingdom too, and with you, I'm going to be the Master."

"Are you going to show me off to everyone when I look like this?" I asked Valli, but that was a trap. "You'll be the laughing stock of your kingdom. I look like a drunken girl you picked up off the beach."

"What are you talking about?" he asked, and turned to fully look at me with his most ferocious glare.

"Safira is a mighty Immortal Queen, powerful and beautiful. Look at me. I'm all wet and wrapped up in a dirty fishing net. How can you prove who I am to them? I don't even look like her. She's got black hair, not red."

"Don't worry about that, my Lady. Someone just confirmed to me that our Queen has red hair now."

"Did you send them my picture?"

"Not yet," he answered, biting his lips. I was sure that he regretted saying that.

"Good. You haven't made a fool of yourself, yet. At least man up and clean me. Or are you afraid of me?"

"You can be sure that I'm not afraid of *you*," he said, and he came very close to me—but he didn't touch me. I felt his breath on my face and I smelled his halitosis, but I proudly kept my head up.

"I don't believe you," I continued my game of words. "How are you going to be a Master of Immortals and how will I be your Queen when you can't be in my presence unless I'm tied up? You're so fearful of me, and so weak, that all the others will take me away from you with no effort whatsoever."

Ruthlessness was in his nature, but my words struck him unexpectedly, like a wake-up call. I expected an explosion of anger, but there was something else I read in his spirit. He was, indeed, fearful of someone much more powerful than him. Perhaps it was Nagoshi, who had the sword that could destroy our entire kind, including me. He had felt panic, while I felt despair. By now, my Warrior girl's spirit must have crossed over into the shadows.

"We could figure this out together," I said impatiently, almost in tears. I was going to kill him for sure. But I was going to torture him before that. I wanted him to suffer like I was suffering right now.

"No, I can't untie you," he said, shaking his head. "You're too strong for me to set you free."

"Then it's all clear. You're going to have to give me to the one that's more powerful than you. The only question is, who's stronger, me or him? Who could win in a fight?"

Valli spat on the floor. He hesitantly signaled to one of the hybrid to come and remove the net. I saw that the hybrid's gun was pushed behind his belt. I didn't want to use it, but I had no other choice. When he turned his back on me, I immediately grabbed it and I emptied the gun's magazine into the hybrid. Valli ran to get his sword, as did the other three impostor Immortals.

"I knew not to trust you," he yelled furiously, coming towards me. "Now let's see just how strong you are."

They all surrounded me, but I didn't want to fight. I wanted to jump in the water and attend to Raluca, but four swords were pointed at me.

I took a deep breath. This display of power didn't particularly disturb me but I wasn't entirely confident that I wouldn't get hurt. My body would heal immediately from any kind of wound inflicted to my flesh; however, their swords were still dangerous if they slashed my neck.

Valli only wanted power over me—he didn't want to kill me. I could see that in his eyes. His spirit had dipped into a deep darkness when he killed Raluca. He fully experienced the pain of killing her, but the desire to rise in status above everyone else helped him to overcome the pain.

But rise above who?

"Do you fear Nagoshi?" I asked him, glowing my eyes on him.

"Nagoshi? Why I would fear him?" his question was a bit ironic. "I do *not* fear anyone."

"Yes you do! I can see it! Is he your leader? An impostor?"

Valli lowered the hand holding his sword and he moved his face close to mine. He was outraged! His mouth foamed as he spoke.

"Impostor? No my dear. The one *you* should fear is one of yours, a Warrior. He's seeking revenge and he'll rule over us all. His plan includes capturing you, Lady Safira, because he wants to be your Master. He's very powerful, more powerful than you."

"Can he heal," I asked, and my voice trembled.

"No, but he'll make sure you won't be in need of healing."

"I don't believe you. What's his mane?"

"I am sure you would like to know that, but it'll cost you." Saying that, he came closer, grabbed my face in his hands, and kissed me. I wanted to vomit.

"His name is Rex," continued Valli, licking his lips with pleasure. "He has many powers over minds and bodies. No weapon or Immortal Warrior can kill him. So, since you don't want to be my queen freely, I'm going to take you to him—he wants you so badly."

Words without any sense. I didn't want to believe him, but he wasn't lying—it was the truth. All Immortal men wished for my love. Who was Rex and why was he so powerful? Rex was sure that he was to be my Master.

My brain silenced my heart from entertaining unnecessary thoughts of self-pity.

To the men's surprise, I slowly knelt down. They looked at each other, not knowing what to do. But I knew.

I moved rapidly on my knees to the closest man to me. I anchored the palms of my hands on the deck while my right foot kicked up in the air.

My foot smashed the hand that was holding the sword and I grabbed the weapon before it reached the deck. I rotated my body in a full circle and I decapitated him. The other man's sword came furiously slashing down on mine. I jumped onto the bench and then over his head. I desperately needed to get back into the water.

Suddenly, to my left, I heard the roar of a boat. But the boat I thought I heard wasn't what I had hoped it would be—it was a Wave Runner. A moment later, something hit us hard and the impact almost threw Valli overboard.

Suddenly I realized that there was one more person aboard. Then, a head rolled to my feet and the body followed. It belonged to the man who had attacked me.

"Do you always fight unarmed, my sister," asked the intruder, and I immediately recognized the voice. "Need some help?" A large smiled filled my face.

Octavian had found me. The tears I had held for so long slid down on my face.

"You always make such a grand entrance, my dear brother," I said.

I raised my hands. It wasn't my fight anymore, and only my brother understood my gesture. Valli and the other man turned to Octavian, who was holding the Fire Sword in his right hand. He was wearing navy blue swim trunks and a white t-shirt.

"Can you finish them for me? I've got to go; I lost something in the water."

"My pleasure," answered Octavian, and his eyes glowed.

I took advantage of the commotion of his presence and I jumped overboard. I didn't look behind to see who he killed next; it wasn't as important to me anymore. They would all die, and Valli would be among them.

I swam forward to find Raluca. She had floated a good distance from the boat. The first thing I found was her body. It appeared to be like a mannequin bobbing on the ocean's surface. Her head was smaller, and it had floated even further away. I kept her body under my left arm and I swam to the right where I thought it should be, but I couldn't see anything. I needed to get to a higher position, but to turn back to the boat would make me lose even more precious time.

As I swam in what I thought was the right direction, I felt something touching my back. I turned with my fist clenched, ready to throw a punch at a hybrid that might have jumped in the water, but it was Raluca's head. My right hand retrieved the missing body part with care.

I had never done a healing in the water before, and I wasn't sure I could reattach her head to her body, because both were wet. I couldn't get to the boat and perform the reattachment because Octavian was there, still fighting Valli.

Octavian took his time, as always. I liked to be fast. His style was to toy with the enemy, like a lion torturing a gazelle, rather than swiftly conclude the fight. The Fire Sword was in flames, even in broad daylight. Valli wasn't a good fighter, but he wasn't bad, either.

The power of my brother's sword cut the railing in half, but Valli quickly got away from him. The flames were amazing and continuous, and destroyed every part of the vessel they touched.

I swam back with the girl's body and I went around to the opposite side of the boat. I put her head on the deck and shoved her body up to join her head. I dried my hands on a t-shirt I found hanging on a railing.

I re-attached Raluca's head to her body and she still looked so beautiful. Her face hadn't lost its color, but her body was cold. The deeper water of the ocean was colder than the shallow water at the beach. I held my hands around her forehead for several moments, longer than I normally would have done. I didn't feel her spirit—it was gone into the shadows.

"Octavian," I yelled to my brother and I pointed to Raluca. "I need your help! Now!"

My brother looked at me from the corner of his eye, but he didn't move his head. I hoped he understood. Valli turned his whole body to us instead, completely captivated by the sight of the girl he had decapitated, now with her head back in place. Octavian took advantage of Valli's inattention, swung the sword, and took off his head. That cut was definite. No one would ever put Valli back together.

Octavian came closer and bent down on one knee. His eyes rose with surprise as he looked at Raluca. Her blonde hair confused him for a moment, but he felt her, too.

"She's Immortal," he murmured, more to himself than to me.

"She was killed by Valli, the one you just terminated. I can't help her—she's in the shadows. Octavian, you must go after her."

"This will take me a moment," he said, placing one hand on her heart and the other on her forehead.

"Please bring her back," I implored. "She died for me."

My brother nodded. I watched him. I hadn't seen him in a week and I had missed him so much. A few soft lines were noticeable on his forehead and he appeared to be a little more mature to me. His sweet face was serious and grave, and I could feel the change in him. It wasn't just in his body, but in his spirit, too. He closed his eyes and began to concentrate.

"She's gone far," he said, shaking his head. "She went too far, too fast. I can't see her."

"I was gone in the shadows for three days. What's different about her? Valli was an impostor Immortal, like Milos Martuzon. He killed Rares, too."

"Hold on, I've found her—somehow she knows me."

Raluca's chest started to move up and down, a sign that her heart was beating normally and she was breathing.

"It wasn't Rares' spirit in Valli," said Octavian, standing up and turning to me, touching my forehead.

I heard his words, but I didn't understand them. His touch was like the effect of a sleeping pill. I slid down on the deck and rested my back against the cabin bulkhead. There was suddenly something like serenity in the air.

Everything was quiet, now. Four men were lying on the deck with no heads, and one was full of bullets. No one was bleeding—it would be an easy clean up. It had been thirty minutes of a small hell, but I had been through things like this before.

"She'll be awake in a few minutes," said Octavian. His hand softly caressed her face. The dead girl caught his attention. "I think we should clean this boat, don't you?"

"Yes. We need to leave this place before more of them come after us. Hide the bodies in the cabin. Serban will dispose of them later. For now, though, leave Valli out. I want Raluca to see him dead."

"OK. What's with your red hair and the bikini?" he asked as he lifted two bodies at once and threw them down stairs.

"It's a long, complicated story." I ran to him and fell into his arms. My brother held me tight.

I was so happy to see him. I laid my head on his shoulder. In a few seconds, as I basked in my brother's comfort, I sensed someone moving behind us. Raluca was up and she was staring in horror at Valli's head, separated from his body.

But when her eyes made contact with Octavian's, she smiled.

22

BY THE TIME WE RETURNED to the shore, the weather had changed drastically—it was pouring rain, and there was lightning popping all around us, answered by what sounded like the thunder of fifty orchestral timpani. We anchored the boat in an empty slip, even though the Fire Sword had done quite a lot of damage to it. We followed the opposite route back to Deerfield Beach that our kidnappers had forced us earlier in the day.

The beach was empty by now. The people had abandoned it, finding refuge from the storm inside hotels, restaurants, stores, or cars.

Alex and Julian were waiting for us by the lifeguard's area that had a canopy. They handed us dry towels and terrycloth robes. He was there too—The Transylvanian. He was still dressed in navy blue pants and a white polo shirt outside his pants, perhaps to mask the guns. The rain didn't seem to bother him at all. His wet shirt was tight, emphasizing his muscular chest.

My first instinct, albeit stupid, was to cover my body from his sight. What would that have accomplished? Our time in Key West nullified any modesty I might have felt. I just felt naked again in the two piece wet bikini I was wearing.

There wasn't much use for us to put our clothes back on—our bodies were soaking wet. I had been in the water for a good portion of the time and my skin was becoming wrinkled. But Artamian didn't appear to be interested in looking at me and that annoyed me a bit – without a concrete reason.

Raluca, Octavian, and I wrapped the towels over our hair and we put the robes on over our wet bathing suits. Julian, who recognized Octavian, called him by name and saluted him, but differently this time. My brother was holding Raluca's arm and she seemed to still be in somewhat of a trance.

"Great! You're back!" exclaimed Alex, staring with an amazed expression at Octavian, as if he seen a ghost. "What happened? Who took you away?"

"Valli, of course," answered Raluca, without releasing my brother's arm. "This Warrior is the one who killed Valli and rescued us."

"Alex, this is my brother, Octavian," I presented him. "Octavian, this is Alex, the leader of the Americans." The men simply acknowledged each other by bowing their heads. They both stood tall and respectful.

But I didn't introduce The Transylvanian. His presence there, although I anticipated that he would find me, almost sent me into shock. He was, at once, irritating and intriguing to me. I had so many questions to ask him, ones that I couldn't understand or readily accept, like his immortality and his chance encounter with Gallbor— my father. I hated that he resembled Milos so perfectly, but I would rather have that than have him looking like Anda. He was here—I couldn't remove this reality, so I had to deal with him until he had left me forever.

"What happened here?" I asked Alex. "Why didn't you come to our rescue?"

"My apologies," he said, touching his face with his right palm as if he were stopping water from dripping, "but it was *his* fault." Saying that, he turned his head to Artamian.

"What?" My eyes darkened in anger for a moment.

"He sounded the alarm that someone on the beach had passed out. It was an older man who had fallen into a diabetic coma. By the time we had figured it all out, you were out of our sight. I called Luke to trace your whereabouts, but your cell phone was in your car. I got in the speed boat and drove it east, looking for you."

"We were forced to go south," I said, walking toward The Transylvanian, and I positioned myself in his face and looked into his eyes. I hated his face, but it was his eyes that fascinated me.

"It was the only way you could have had the chance to find Nagoshi," he said, unimpressed by my frustration. "I knew they would take you somewhere close to their headquarters."

"You endangered her life," exclaimed Julian, moving towards him with his fists clinched. "Not only hers, but Raluca's, too. Who the hell are you, anyway?"

But Artamian didn't responded. He was much taller than Julian, and he looked over our heads, towards Octavian. To my surprise, my brother saluted him. Then without another word, The Transylvanian turned away from us and walked away.

"You're talking about two Warriors," replied Raluca, perhaps irritated by Julian's remark. "We breathe danger all the time."

"So Nagoshi is here?" Octavian asked me, ignoring my astonished look.

"Alex had a good lead on him. His information was that he would be at his daughter's wedding in Key West. I encountered him there, but he escaped me. I also met The Transylvanian there; his real name is Artamian Martuzon. I *don't* want him around us. Do you all hear me?"

My voice was full of rage. They all nodded in agreement, except for my brother.

"I'd like to go home now," we all heard Raluca's weak voice from behind the rest of the group.

She looked pale and tired—understandable, of course, for someone who had been headless and in the shadows for at least thirty minutes. Her hand was resting on her chest, touching her neck softly where her head had been severed. But nothing diminished this warrior girl's courage and skills.

Her death was the only proof to me of how honorable she was. Her brother, Codrin, had called her that and I agreed.

"We're going back to Wellington, to Serban," I said to Alex. "Let's meet late tonight at the Greek place. I have new information about our enemy and it's not good news."

* * *

I left for the parking area with Raluca and Octavian following me. I was quite anxious to hear what had happened to my brother after we became separated.

"How did you get here?" I asked, hugging him again.

"I flew in this morning," he responded, holding me by my shoulders. "Our plane was the only thing that escaped the fire. Everything else is gone."

"How did you find me?"

"I received an alert from your friend, Detective John. He called me late on that Wednesday evening to tell me that our house was on fire and that you had left for Florida with your former lover."

Raluca, who until then had walked by my side, cleared her throat and started to walk a step behind us.

"At first, what he was telling me didn't sound right," continued Octavian. "Who could destroy our home, and why? I tried to call you, but your phone was off. What happened with you?"

"My trip here wasn't by choice. It was Gallbor's will to relocate me here in the middle of the night, and naked. My phone was deliberately lost for a while. I was about to come back to look for you."

"I stayed in the Samson's house to try and find out who was behind the fire, but my computers were gone. I was able to detect your signal again only an hour ago, from the plane—I had saved a satellite receiver and a laptop in the cockpit. You were fighting on that boat."

"Good timing. We're at war again. According to Valli—who you just killed—a rogue Immortal Warrior named Rex is in control of an army of Amestec, Impostors, Hybrids, and the Silver Sword."

"I thought that Nagoshi had the Silver sword."

"Rex must have taken it from him. He's someone who wants to rule over us, to be my Master, and he's very powerful. The Americans have a great tech room, so we're back in business."

"You drove your old Rover here?" asked my brother when I got to the car.

"Andreas drove it while I was an unwilling traveling participant. Oh, please don't tell me that you brought your Jaguar with you."

"No, I left it behind. I bought this instead."

Two car spaces from me was a brand new copper colored Stingray. I smiled.

"Interesting color for a Corvette."

"It was the only one they had on the dealership's lot." My brother's eyes shifted innocently from me to Raluca. The rain had stopped by now, but I handed the girl another towel and her dress from the back seat.

"I have to make a stop," I said to her, "can you take my brother to your home?"

"Where do you need to stop," she worriedly asked me. "I'm coming with you."

"I don't need you, not this time. I'm only stopping to get something for dinner because I'll be cooking tonight. I can find my way back. I've got GPS."

It wasn't without pleasure that she bent down to take a seat beside my brother, and the Stingray sped away from the parking area. I had seen the spark and the attraction in their eyes. Whatever the outcome may have been with Nelda, my brother was quite impressed by the beautiful blonde Immortal girl.

Who knew? At that point they both were hurt, physically and emotionally, and they needed each other.

* * *

I sat down in my Land Rover, removed my robe, put on my dress, and started the engine. My Rover felt like an old home, familiar and comforting. I laid my head on the steering wheel like on a pillow for a moment. My head felt heavy, but my heart felt relief. My brother was here now. He would resolve many problems and I would get a break.

The knock on the Rover's door window startled me. I saw the gun first, and then the man. The face looking at me was to a hybrid—I saw the mark on his neck. But before I could react in any way and look down for my weapon, the same face, along with his body ended up smashed on my dashboard.

Someone held the hybrid's head in his arms and twisted, hard and fast. His neck broke, and the hybrid's body remained inert.

"Unlock the trunk," I heard someone yelling at me.

It was Artamian. I could feel heat blasting through my eyes and skin. I looked away, not willing to respond to him, but I had no choice.

A second hybrid came running towards the car, shooting at him. This time Artamian lifted his hand, and with a powerful down stroke, hit this one on the crown of his head. The man fell down like the wet towel on the floorboard of my car.

Artamian had killed those men as easily as he would kill a fly on the windshield. It was obvious that he had no need for his fancy guns.

Oh, I dreaded even the existence of this man so much!

"Stupid hybrids," he mumbled, checking the one on the ground for his vital signs.

"How did you know what they were?" I asked, surprised.

He ignored my question. "I would suggest you get another vehicle," he said, grabbing the hybrid.

"Why are you here? What part of *I don't want to see you anymore*, don't you understand? How did you find me?"

"All I did was to follow my instincts. It took me a hundred years to find you, and I'm not going away. We need to talk about you and me. "

He loaded the dead bodies in the trunk and stood there for a moment, staring at the Vortex—his weapon. But he didn't take it back into his possession.

"You and me? There's no "between us"! How did you even know that I exist?"

Artamian walked slowly to the passenger side of my car. I hesitated to let him in, but he continued to stand there, so I unlocked the door.

My heart didn't believe he would ever be my master. The fact that another Immortal male had risen, more powerful and an enemy to all of us, was a dark and heavy burden on my mind.

What if Valli was right? *He has powers over minds and bodies, and no weapon or Immortal man can kill him.* What if the Silver Sword *couldn't* kill him? And he was coming for me!

Who was Rex? That would be another riddle for me to solve, as I did before with Anda and Prince Albert. Could he be one of hers?

What if my fears became reality again? I would be captured and held in possession of a man I wouldn't love? My nerves struggled to shake off the bad energy from my thoughts.

"Do you have a brother named Rex?" I asked Artamian, once he got in and put the seat belt on. His clothes were dry by now, and his hair was even curlier.

"I don't know," he answered, calmly. "I killed the two Amestec brothers that came for me in Paris, and a few more I met randomly in my travels. I heard that you also killed two of them."

"I don't care about your life story." I said, backing out of the parking space. I searched for the nearest Publix; taking him with me seemed to be the only option. "Just tell me about Gallbor."

"I'll start with telling about you.

"I didn't know who I was until I met him—John Gallbor—on a train to Berlin. I had fallen asleep and he touched my forehead. Then he disappeared into thin air. All I knew was that after that, everything changed for me. The first time I kissed a girl with blonde hair and sparkling green eyes, I saw in my mind the image of a girl with dark hair and blue eyes. It was you I saw, not the blonde. It happened the same with every female in my life. In my mind I was kissing you, I was making love with you."

"Just tell me about Gallbor, please," I interrupted him, as my face flushed again. I tried so hard to accept him without recalling the fact that we had made love, but all I could think of was only that notion about him.

"He found me again, on a bridge in Oradea, after I had returned to the Black Eagle Castle to regain my rightful ownership."

The mention of that particular place made me nauseated. I hit my brakes and turned into a parking area. I was very close to throwing up. I got out of the car and breathed the hot, humid air deeply into my lungs.

"I'm sorry," he said, coming around to my side of the car, touching my shoulder. "Maybe you're too upset to listen to my story."

Oh, I hated him. I hated his presumption that I was just another sensitive soul who was so upset by bad memories, just like mortals. And I didn't care that he thought that about me. I pushed him away.

His touch only reminded me of how vulnerable I was to fall for his charms and give myself to a complete stranger. But his demeanor didn't seem to provoke feelings of repulsion in me. He was gentle, serious and he treated me like an equal. I wasn't used to being treated like that, not even by my brother, and I wasn't sure if I liked it.

"Continue," I said, grabbing my purse and walking towards the grocery store.

"I wanted to end my life at that moment, on the bridge, when Gallbor came to me," he said, following me. "After he persuaded me to not leap from the bridge, I went back to the castle. I found your room with your portrait, and Mr. Lutz told me your story. I fell desperately in love with you, even though I knew that you were dead. Then my nightmares started. I felt like it was me who killed you. So I didn't wanted to live anymore. You were my curse. I thought that perhaps we could meet after death and be together—

that was all that I wanted. However, it was Gallbor who ruined all my plans by telling me that I was born Immortal. He told me that I can't be killed by a regular sword, that you are still alive, and I would be found by you."

"Why you?" I asked while he held the entrance door open for me. I pretended to ignore his story and all the strange encounters of me in his life.

Why did the almighty Gallbor, the one who supposedly was my father, choose him to be sent to me? And for what reason, if he wasn't going to be my Master?

"Gallbor said that he loves you. I believed him about everything until I met Nagoshi and got a cut from his sword. I guess there *is* something out there capable of destroying me and I don't like that idea at all."

"All right then. You tell a good story. One way or the other I'll decide what's true."

"You don't believe me?"

I turned to him after I dropped two cans of Rotel tomatoes in my basket, along with two boxes of pasta and some red kidney beans.

"Who would believe you? How could you just fall in love like that, with someone you've never seen in your life, with only a picture? That's not love. The mortals would call it obsession, and that's dangerous."

"I'm not a danger to you. We already have great memories together."

"You glowed on me," I said, blushing, knowing he was reminding me about our time in Key West. "Those moments aren't important to me. I've never done that before."

"Done what?"

"Made love with a stranger," I responded, irritated at his persistence and all his silly questions. "I would have never made love with you, knowing who you are."

"Still, you chose me for a reason," he insisted, smiling at me. His scent was so enticing, and his presence so close to me agitated me and stirred my instincts at the same time.

"I had my one and only nervous breakdown in Key West."

"No, my Lady, you didn't. You may think that, but our spirits were connected."

"Well, they're disconnected now. I don't like you at all. I also can't believe that since you were young, Gallbor put me in your mind and you fell in love with me, and then you felt guilty for my death to the point that you wanted to terminate your own life."

"You don't believe me, only because I am *his* son. Isn't that right?"

"Yes," I admitted, a bit too loudly. A few ladies passed by, but they walked around us, suspecting that we were just a couple in the middle of a fight. "Your father was supposed to be my protector, but he was a liar. He knew who I was and he kept me captive for his own benefit."

"Yes, he was a despotic killer, but he loved you."

"He killed me," I said, raising my voice. Some curious heads popped up at the end of some aisles and looked at us. "I'm talking about cutting off my head."

"He loved you. He killed you because you left him, and he couldn't endure that. You wouldn't stay with him after you discovered who he was, an Amestec. You were born enemies. But he cried over you every night until his wife, my mother, killed him. He didn't want to live anymore, not without you."

"How do you even know that?"

"Because I felt it in my bones. I felt it in the castle. He loved you in the most horrible way."

"You are right, very horrible. And now you're here, his son. Do you *love* me too?"

Artamian's face changed in color, losing his softness and clarity.

"Tell me," he said in a deeper tone of voice, "the Immortal man who loved you in the past and lost your love, is he still alive?"

"Yes," I responded stopping at the cashier, puzzled by his unusual question.

"The mortal one doesn't count. He died for your cause, but he's also alive now. Immortals die too, and they could die for love. Well, I wished it for myself and I was ready for it, if it hadn't been for Gallbor. How do you reconcile that for my feelings?"

Before I got the chance to pay and respond to him, he calmly bowed to me in the old fashioned way and left through the exit door. He left me there, just like that. Speechless.

By the time I got outside, he had disappeared.

Whatever. I hated him even more.

But there wasn't anything calm about his passion for me. It was a storm inside his soul, and that made me believe him.

23

MY ENCOUNTER WITH ARTAMIAN didn't satisfy my spirit at all. I hadn't received the right answers from him. Secretly, however, I allowed myself to be impressed by his strange story and by his great powers. He had stripped away any possible motive for me to hate him, but I was happy to hate him anyway. Nothing made sense most of the time, but this was normal for me.

I was in the kitchen cooking. I needed to do something interesting, anytime I felt that I needed to feel like a mortal. It was not only me that needed that, but Raluca too.

She watched me quietly, or at least she tried to watch me, but her focus was on Octavian. He stood at the dining room table, talking intensely with Serban, while stroking Lord Arthur's coat as the dog laid his head on his lap. Codrin and the Germans were standing behind them listening. Only Andreas was absent; perhaps he had been sent away for some sort of guard duty.

I wished I had been here, to see their faces when Octavian walked into their midst. Serban said that he would recognize our future Master right away, and I knew it wasn't me. Serban also knew that my brother was Gallbor's son. I still wondered if Octavian knew it.

"Be patient with him," I whispered to Raluca. "He's still dealing with a hard breakup with a mortal girl."

Raluca nodded, but her eyes glowed for a short moment. She was smitten with him and with the fact that he brought her back to life, but she was holding something back.

"Did you tell them about what happened to you today?"

"No."

"Why not?" I was surprised that she hadn't rushed to tell them about her experience, but I hadn't told them about the bodies in my car, either. I hadn't told them about Rex, the Immortal enemy, yet. There was time for that and I hoped that they would know his identity.

"I'd rather have you tell them," responded Raluca, slowly chewing on a bite of an apple. "The fact is, I haven't done anything more than to fail to protect you. And right now, Serban is extremely mad at Alex for the same reason."

"Raluca," I said to her with a firm voice, "I've lived for one hundred and fifty years, and I did quite well without a guardian."

"You had Octavian," she said, smiling.

"Indeed. He did the same thing for me that he did for you. He brought back my spirit."

But my warrior girl had no comment in that regard, as I thought she would. What could been more traumatic than being killed without any regard by the man who had loved you at one time, and then being brought back to life? Her indifference and calmness was a clear sign to me that Raluca's spirit was clean and empty of every bad memory about that incident.

Was it possible that Octavian had cleared her spirit when I told him that she was killed by her former lover? It was so welcoming that she had returned to her sweet and relaxed demeanor. She was almost happy.

"Would you like to talk to me about it?" I insisted. "I'm a good listener."

"I'm OK, honestly. Just knowing that you went through the same thing makes me stronger."

"But you could have been lost forever."

"True. But now I'm back. It's called faith."

"Faith in what?"

"Destiny."

"Destiny! That's something I'm not looking forward to. Can we rely on it?"

"What are you cooking?" she asked, changing the subject, and her voice had the overtone of a giggle. "This is great—it'll be the first time we've used the stove."

I was right—she acted like she was happy.

"Just a little something, enough to feed all these guys," I responded, looking at them.

"Like what?"

"Chili pasta casserole. This is easy—nothing to it. All you need is two pounds of ground beef; two boxes of penne pasta, two cans of Rotel tomatoes, two cans of red kidney beans, some spaghetti sauce, some chili powder, and a big bag of shredded Monterey cheese, of course."

"It'll be lots of food."

"Left overs are great. All right. I'll brown the meat and you'll boil the pasta. Once the meat is done, I'll stir in the beans, the Rotel tomatoes, and a bit of spaghetti sauce. I'll need two casserole dishes. When the pasta's done, I'll pour the chili powder and the sauce over it, and sprinkle the cheese on top. Then we turn on the heat to 350 degrees and put it in the oven for 30 minutes."

"Wow! I've never put any thought about cooking before. You make it sound so easy."

*   *   *

The Germans were the first to the dinner table and then they came back for seconds. My dish was a success. Indeed, I wanted them all to experience a normal dinner time, where they gathered around as a group, eating and talking.

They all did just that. I watched them telling stories and laughing, and my spirit was at ease. They also accepted my brother as one of them so easily, with no reservations. In a way, they all looked to him as a leader—or the son of one.

No one asked me or Raluca about our encounter with Valli. Serban was told about Valli's termination, and I could sense relief in his spirit—he believed that Valli was the one who had slain Rares. However, if what my brother said was true, then Rares' spirit went to another Amestec, one that no one knew about.

I also observed him staring at Octavian. He was in a reflective mood and I had no intention of pressing him for any opinion. My brother's actions and demonstration of powers would be impressive enough for this old Immortal Warrior to decide what to believe.

*   *   *

"We're going out," said Serban, gallantly kissing my hand. "It was a wonderful dinner you prepared for us, my Lady. Thank you."

"You're very welcome."

"He looks so much like him," whispered Serban in my ear. "He looks like Gallbor. There's no doubt about it."

I nodded my head. Serban was happy and content, and it was the very first time I had seen him like that.

"I heard there's a boat in need of a clean-up," he said, signaling to Codrin, Ditmar, and Lars to be ready. Everyone rose from the table and collected their guns. "It's getting dark outside, a good time to take care of things. We'll be back soon. Andreas is there to keep an eye on things."

"Don't forget that Alex is having a meeting tonight."

"Are you ladies be going to be all right by yourselves?" Octavian's question wasn't for me, but Raluca seemed to be speechless.

She stopped in the middle of the kitchen floor with a load of dishes in her hands. Her face turned red and her eyes turned to me, imploring. Her panicked look made me understand that she was still so vulnerable, looking for love, but afraid that her pursuit of my brother could be deemed as forbidden.

"Sure, unless the ghosts from the cemetery would care for some leftovers," I joked, grabbing the dishes from Raluca's hands.

They all left, but Octavian turned once more to gaze at the girl before he closed the door. She was still standing in the same place in a trance, not looking and not paying attention to anything.

"What's wrong Raluca?" I asked, motioning for her to walk towards the couch. "Is my brother scaring you?"

"Yes," she said softly, sitting down hard on a cushion, "but not like you think. At first I thought that I would never be over Valli's love and his betrayal. I was so hurt, but I lived with it every day. But now, I feel like I'm falling in love with Octavian too fast, and I'm overwhelmed by what he did for me. I'm also terrified that he's out of reach for me."

"What makes you think that? I'm sure he likes you very much."

I started the dishwasher, thinking quickly of what advice I could give her. Me! I was the one who could never get it right, for me or for anyone else. I always deliberately freed myself from the men I loved, when in truth, I still desired their love so intensely.

"Right now, I'm trying to keep my heart in check. I don't want to fall in love with him, but that's extremely difficult. If he's going to become our new Master, love will the last thing in his future. Masters are untouchable—supreme—and he could never love me."

"That's not a rule at all. Gallbor did it."

"Indeed. But look at what happened to him. He gave up his powers and…"

At that moment, Lord Arthur growled. I knew my dog and I knew that he was familiar with all the Immortals living in the house. He wouldn't make that sound if he detected one of them. I sensed movement outside, around the perimeter of the house. Raluca's eyes followed the noise that stopped at the back door.

"We've got company," I whispered to her, turning off all the lights. "Where are the guns?"

She signaled me to follow her towards the stairs. Lord Arthur's impulse was to run to the back door and jump on it to protect us, but I knew that our visitors would have no mercy or no fear of my dog. I grabbed him by the leash and forced him to follow me upstairs.

"You're brave Lord Arthur, but not today," I said to the dog, running behind the Warrior girl. "I need to keep you safe. Raluca, where're you going?"

"Up on the roof," she answered, pulling down the attic staircase. "The guns are up there, too."

"Why on the roof?" I asked, astonished. "We're not running away."

"No, but I know what they are and we can attack them from there."

"What are you talking about?" Raluca made no sense to me, and I felt like we were trying to get away and avoid fighting the intruders. "Can the dog get up there? Isn't it too hot?"

"Throw me his leash. I'll pull him up, you push him from behind," said Raluca, getting in the attic and lying on her belly. "Our attic has air conditioning; we're in here a lot. Just don't try to stand up."

She pulled the leash, encouraging the dog to climb the ten narrow wooden steps. To my surprise, the dog didn't have a problem getting up. I pulled the staircase up and closed the trap door. I tied the dog's leash to a rafter, warned him not to bark, and I continued to crawl, followed the girl. On the other side of the attic was a dormer window.

Raluca opened a container that had been deliberately placed there. I looked inside, but instead of guns and ammunition, I saw bows made of aluminum, arrows, and Shurikens. I picked up the weapons I thought I'd need. I unlatched the window and raised it in its frame. I crawled out and the Warrior girl followed me closely.

"We need to be very fast and quiet," she whispered. "No loud guns. Our mortal neighbors are only a few feet away. These people are most likely Nagoshi's soldiers."

As I stepped out onto the roof, I took my sandals off and placed my foot hard on the ceramic shingles. This wasn't a flat surface like Greek homes, but keeping my balance wasn't a challenge for me.

"I'll be fast. Are they Amestec or hybrids?"

"Perhaps both."

"How do you know?"

"We've fought Nagoshi's army before. They found you somehow. Perhaps they bugged your car, or maybe they detected your scent."

The first black shadow attacked me from behind. He stabbed me hard in the back with a Cyclone. I had barely sensed him behind me. As I fell down, Raluca turned to me. In the next moment her arrow found the heart of another shadow. My attacker came over to me to assess my injuries, but I leaped forward before he could reach me. Rather than landing on my feet, I flew backwards in the air, kicking him in the temple with my right leg.

The man lost his balance and fell to his knees. I spun my body rapidly in the other direction and kicked him again in his jaw with my left foot. This time he fell forward, unconscious. He was armed with a long curved sword, like an Arabian scimitar or a Japanese Dragonfly. I took it from him, but I couldn't tell if he was Amestec or hybrid, so I threw him off the roof—we would do our decapitating later. He landed in the back yard near the pool.

By the time I picked up his sword, I heard another one come straight towards me. The man was dressed all in black and I could only see his eyes. I parried fast, but my commandeered sword was too shiny and narrow. I felt strange fighting with it because it rotated so easily in my hand. The man swung his sword towards me again, hard from my left to right. I parried strongly, forcing his blade down to the roof, and I stepped on it. While his body bent towards the sword, I beheaded him, quietly and efficiently.

I looked for Raluca, since I hadn't seen her on the roof for some time. From my front, another shadow ran towards me. His sword was held high, but I didn't have the patience for fighting him. I threw a Dragon and it hit him in his left eye. I struck his neck with a horizontal swing and his body fell on the roof, while his head bounced on the back yard grass.

I looked down from the edge of the roof, but I still didn't see Raluca. Just then, one shadow was climbing up the side wall. How they could do that, with no hand or foot holds?

I picked up the bow, notched an arrow in place, and I released it. It hit him in the back of his neck and he fell back to the ground.

I jumped down from the roof and I stepped over three bodies before I got to the patio door. The door was wide open and all the lights were still turned off. I walked slowly inside, trying not to glow my eyes, and holding the sword high. I could hear rapid steps coming towards me. It was Lord Arthur who ran around my legs, happily wagging his tail.

"I let him out of the attic. The inside's clear," said Raluca, from behind the kitchen island. She glowed her eyes and I did, too.

A man was on the floor, dressed in black, with an arrow in his chest. Three more men were in the living room with Shurikens in their foreheads and two were on the stairs, hit by more arrows. My Warrior girl knew how to handle that bow very well.

"We need to take off a couple of heads," she continued, pointing to the ones on the stairs. "Well, that was fast and quiet, wasn't it?"

"Yes," I agreed, checking the Amestec. "Great job, Raluca! You killed them all. I think the guys will have a lot of graves to dig tonight."

*   *   *

I heard the garage door opening. The men rushed inside with their guns drawn. Because of the dark, all of them glowed their eyes. When they encountered us, they lowered theirs weapons. Codrin turned on the kitchen lights.

"What happened here?" Serban was the first to ask.

"Just some late visitors," I said, holding the sword in the air and showing it to them.

"I recognize that sword by its shape," said Andreas. "It's Japanese—we've fought hybrids who used them, before."

"Most likely Nagoshi bugged your Land Rover in Key West," said Serban. "That's how they found you so easily. We need to ditch it."

"Are you all right?" asked Octavian, but again, the question was not for me.

Raluca didn't answer, but then I realized that she hadn't moved from behind the island since I came in.

"We're both OK," I answered.

I sensed that something was wrong with her, but she didn't want anyone to know.

"I need you guys to collect all these bodies. Beside the ones in here, there are three on the roof, a few in the back yard, and two hybrids in the trunk of my Rover."

Codrin, Lars and Ditmar left for the back yard while Andreas went to the roof. Serban and Octavian intended to ask more questions but the glow from my eyes made them hesitate. Serban left for the garage. My brother followed Serban, shaking his head. I rushed to Raluca who had collapsed on the floor. Her left leg was deeply cut above the knee and she had a Silver Spinner stuck in her lower back.

"Raluca, you should have told me sooner" I said, leaning down to her. "Stay still! I'm going to heal you. This is easy."

First I pulled out the Shuriken. The cut was deep but her spine was untouched. The electricity from my fingers made the flesh unite, quickly and painlessly.

Then I touched her leg. The bone was fractured, almost severed. I put pressure on it until the fracture became intact. I released the gray ash into her flesh. When the bone grew back in place, I touched her wound with my finger and the scar completely vanished.

"Thank you," she said gratefully, standing up and rubbing her leg, astonished.

"No need for thanking me—this is what I do."

"No. Thank you for understanding me."

She was referring to the fact that I saved her from Octavian finding out about her being hurt. But my brother knew it all along. What he didn't know was why the girl was avoiding him.

Under the cover of night, Serban took the hybrids, impostor immortals and Amestec, and buried them in the back cemetery. Them he took my Land Rover and sank it deep in the swamp.

I felt like I had lost my home again.

24

SABRINA HANDED ME a cup of coffee in a huge white porcelain cup. I poured lots of hazelnut creamer in the brew. The aroma made me feel good, calmer.

The Greek restaurant wasn't well lit, but there was enough light inside for us. Luke was setting up his monitors while Cedric continued to guard the door. Alex and Kyle were looking at some maps. Serban, Codrin, Lars and Ditmar found a seat at the table, apparently in an intense discussion, a little angry at each other for not protecting me.

Andreas just happened to stay closer to Julian. I still couldn't get over their resemblance. For now there was peace between them, but there was no peace between Alex and Serban. I had to witness the dirty glow from Serban's eyes to Alex for not saving me from Valli.

Only Raluca seemed to be mentally absent from our meeting, although she stood across from Octavian.

Love shouldn't be this complicated—but it always was.

"What's with your Warrior girl?" Octavian asked me as he joined me behind the bar. He pulled up a stool and sat on it, a bit distracted.

"What do you mean?" I asked, and I felt guilty for the question, but I needed to know his side of the story.

"I swear she's avoiding me. Have I done something wrong?"

"She was killed for my sake, Octavian—she has courage. Then, you saved her spirit and brought her back from the shadows; that was the scary thing."

"I think I'm very attracted to her. A blonde Immortal girl— she just took my breath away. I really hate for her to avoid me like she's doing."

"What happened to Nelda," I asked, without looking at him. I hadn't had the chance to ask him anything about the outcome with his mortal girlfriend. I needed to know the story before I could put his mind at rest.

"It's over. But it was harder that I thought. Her mother took her away on a book signing tour, so in a way, she knew that it was best for us to go our separate ways. She's safer without me."

"Raluca is falling in love with you" I said, and I caught a glimmer of satisfaction in his eyes. "However, I'll just warn you— she thinks you're unreachable."

"Why? Because I saved her life?"

"Because you're the undisputed leader of these Immortals," I said softly, sipping my coffee. "You may not be aware of that, but they all know about you and who you are."

Octavian smiled to me like I had said something funny. Our eyes met and I glowed on him for a short moment.

"Who I am? Safira, what are you trying to tell me?"

Instantly I knew that my brother had suspected something for a while now, and his intense conversation with Serban had brought his suspicions back to life.

"Your time has come, Octavian. Gallbor is no more. His disobedience cost him his Immortality. You're the one rising to take his place. You're his son. *You* are the image of him, and everyone in here knows it."

There was a quick awakening in his spirit, but then I couldn't sense anything more. My words sank into his soul first and that willed his mind to accept it. He raised his head and looked at everyone in the room. I was right—he not only looked more mature, but his handsome face was radiant with determination and confidence.

"Safira, I'm not like Gallbor. I don't have his powers. Just being his son doesn't make me a Master."

"You have the essence of his powers; he gave them to you at birth. This war will be starting soon and we need to find a battlefield for us as soon as possible, or we'll be doomed. Think about it, but think quickly. We've got a new generation who're becoming restless and an older one who're feeling despair."

"Where is Gallbor now?" His question was more polite, rather than inquisitive.

"I wish I knew the answer, but we lost him out there, somewhere in the mortal world."

Suddenly I felt that a strong wind brushed through my hair. Gallbor. *He* was in front of me the whole time. I just didn't see him that way. I saw the signs, but I didn't understand the old riddles that Nana Saveta used to ask me. My instincts had warned me about it, but I didn't pay attention.

"How would *he* know all this about me?"

"Who are you talking about?" asked Octavian, sincerely curious.

"I need to borrow your car. I'm going back to Atlanta to find him. I know who Gallbor is and I need to reach him right away."

"Are you sure about that?"

"Nothing's certain, but all the clues were in front of me. I need to be sure about the reason. I couldn't really understand any of them until now."

"I'll buddy up with Luke and use his tech room to keep you safe. And make sure your ear piece is on, at all times. Why is it important for you to find him?"

"Because I have so many questions to ask. I just need to see him. Are you coming?"

Octavian hesitated. "I'll just listen in."

*   *   *

"All right," shouted Alex, clapping his hands impatiently. "We're all here. Unfortunately, Luke isn't sure about what he's got so far. Go ahead, Luke."

"I scanned the area for all the boats from here to Miami, everything large enough to hold an army," started Luke, and the monitors displayed the images. "There're lot of little boats out there, more likely for vacationers, with six to ten people on board. Three of them are cruise liners, but they are all accounted for with their home offices. There's nothing out of place. Seven of the boats are large enough to carry twenty people or more, but those are owned by celebrities and other people who're mega-rich. I checked them out—the owners are all on board."

"They've got to be in something very big," I said firmly. "They aren't going to wage a war against us with jet skis."

Luke shook his head, held up his finger, and then pushed a button.

"Well, there is something else there but it can't be what we're looking for. A warship."

"A destroyer? Just one? Is it American?" Julian stood up and came closer to the bar area, looking at the image on the monitor's screen. We all turned to him.

"We may just have found what we're looking for," I said, and I went around the bar and stood by Julian. His former SEAL training was coming to the surface. "Do you recognize it?"

"Yes, I do. It's a DDJ class. Where exactly it is?" he asked.

"Seventy miles south of Miami Beach," responded Luke. "But the interesting thing is that it's very slowly sailing south."

"South? Heading towards Cuba?" asked Octavian.

"This ship is too close to land," said Julian, confidently. "The Key West Naval Air Station is known to hold war exercises and they could host warships, but just a single one doesn't make much sense."

"You mean to say that it's unusual to have a single warship so close to Miami?" I asked, looking straight at Alex's darkening eyes.

"I wouldn't call it unusual," Julian said hesitantly. "It could have come down from the naval station in Jacksonville, but it wouldn't be just one lone ship. Unless it was sent in a recon maneuver."

"The Navy's got no reason to go to Cuba," snapped Alex. "I hope I'm wrong but it looks like they're heading to Key West."

"Why would that be a problem?" asked Octavian. "You heard Julian—there *is* a Navy base there."

"Because Alex is paranoid most of the time," chuckled Serban. "And if by chance this could be the enemy's ship, how could they even gain control of it if it's assigned to the Navy?"

Serban's question was legitimate, so I answered him. I knew that mistakes could be made, even in the most secure places. While I was back in Germany, the then Commander Julian Grant never bothered to check my story out when I pretended to be a Red Cross nurse.

"They could keep the crew hostage in order not to raise any suspicion with the Air Station. I'm sure that a force like that could easily overwhelm the mortals."

"I'm just cautious," responded Alex to Serban. "We can't afford to be careless. Lady Safira is right—I'm sure they thoroughly studied this plan long before they executed it. That warship may be just a theory right now, but if it's not, and if it's run by a hundred Amestec, the American Immortals on the island could be their target."

"Continue," said Octavian who became very interested in this scenario. I remembered Alex's strange questions when I returned from Key West. At the time I thought he was referring to Artamian, but now those questions made sense.

"We were hunted down in our own homes, so last year I relocated everyone to an island just off Key West, to be safe. We've got children to protect. It's a small island, very well defended; we built a community on the beach."

"Did you just say that you were hunted specifically in your own homes?" I asked. This was the best time to tell them about our enemy.

"Yes. It was like they knew our addresses at all times, even though we moved often, from state to state. Why're you asking?"

"Before he was terminated, Valli told me that Rex, an Immortal Warrior, one of us, is the one in charge of the Amestec and the others—not Nagoshi, as we all thought. Rex has declared himself to be our future Master. He's also especially searching for me. Apparently he's very powerful and feared by his little army. They believe him to be invincible, and not even the Silver Sword can kill him. That changes the capabilities of our enemy somewhat. This is one Immortal to be feared and we need to better prepare ourselves for this war. Alex, are any of your men unaccounted for?"

"Absolutely not! I know them all, and I've never heard of Rex."

"What about the ones who died?"

A moment of silence followed my question and Alex's face became pale.

"I buried them myself, and I knew them by name. All the ones who were slayed are accounted for—they're in the ground, and some of their spirits transferred to impostors. I don't know who that Warrior could be. We had no one so powerful among us. By the way, I heard you had been found out and there was no one was around to protect you."

Serban hit the table with his fist and stood up, indignant.

"I had to recover Valli's body," he said furiously. "I needed to see him dead for myself. He *is* dead, no thanks to you."

The two brothers didn't miss a chance to get into a fight.

"That's enough," I demanded, calmly signaling to Serban to sit. "They came after me in Wellington. My car was bugged. That's an easy way to track someone. I wasn't alone; Raluca and I killed nine."

"But that doesn't mean that Rex had to be one of ours," denied Cedric.

"It has to be," Serban insisted. "They could only track you if they knew your identity, so he must have been an insider."

"Is not like we are hard to spot, we all look so distinctive," replied Alex, as he started to pace in a circle. "He's seeking Lady Safira, so he could be very well be a European. You think you have everyone under control, but you don't. I happen to think that Lady Safira may be right about this entire situation. If this destroyer is their headquarters, and this Rex guy is in charge, we're *all* in trouble."

"Julian, do you think that it could be possible for them to get close to the coast and the Naval Air Station wouldn't see them as a threat?" asked Octavian, and all eyes were on Julian.

"Yes. I don't see why they would consider another American military craft as an enemy, if their story checks out. Plus, they don't even need to get too close. They could fire from as much as sixty miles away and take out half the island."

"Well, it seems that we've found what we were looking for," I said, moving back behind the bar for another cup of coffee. "Theory or not, it's almost certain that's what our enemy has for its headquarters—a warship. It makes sense to me and it would for Rex. We need to have a plan to counter their plan."

"If they're heading for Key West, they could kill the entire American Immortal clan: seventy adults and sixteen children," said Kyle, looking at me agitated. "If we don't act, the American Immortals are doomed."

"Could we find a quick way to relocate them?" asked Sabrina, rubbing her chin nervously.

"Yes, let's do it right now," agreed Kyle. "There's not a moment to waste. You all need to help us."

"Relocate where?" asked Ditmar. "You're talking about finding a home for half of the island."

"No need for that," I replied, loud enough to cover all the commotion as they started to comment and give their opinions. "We're not going to allow that destroyer to get anywhere close to

Key West or to fire its guns. We're going to attack it and take it down. So get ready for battle."

"Attack a destroyer? That's close to impossible," exclaimed Julian surprised. "We don't have weapons with enough fire power for that and we can't get on board."

"You speak like a mortal," Andreas interrupted, and his eyes glowed with spite. "Of course it's possible. How do you think the Amestec took control of it?"

"We aren't going to attack the ship, just the people on it," I responded, a bit disappointed by Julian's remarks. He felt that disappointment in my voice and lowered his head.

"All right. Luke, you keep surveillance on the ship. Alex, you need to do a little recon—use your Coast Guard friends to get close to them and check their stories. Serban, we need as much ammunition as possible."

"We need more than heavy guns too," said Serban, with a bit of irritation in his voice. "We need a bigger army to use them."

"What we need, we can buy; those we need are here in this room," I responded firmly and everyone became quiet. I found myself in charge again, just because I was used to spitting out orders. "Octavian will help. We'll meet back here in two days and I expect everyone to do their part. Julian, help us understand the layout of the ship."

"Now?" Andreas was very irritated and in bad mood.

"Yes," I responded. "That destroyer will be our focus from now on. We need to get started *now!*"

25

THE CORVETTE WAS PARKED three houses down the street in my old subdivision. Before I knocked at Detective John's door, the sound of a basketball bouncing on the driveway in his back yard intrigued me.

Detective John Morris. John Gallbor. *Gallbor.*

For me, he was Detective John. For Artamian, he was John Gallbor. For everyone else, he was the mighty Gallbor. Detective John was continually around me. I remembered his ready smile, soft and gentle towards me. He looked like any regular mortal—he even managed to keep his hair short and light. And he was always there—around me.

Always.

*   *   *

I kept repeating his name all the way to Atlanta. I had left early in the morning, immediately following the meeting. The drive up the interstates, through Florida into Georgia, was only eight hours long in Octavian's fast Corvette Stingray. However, the time didn't pass fast enough for me. I tried to listen to the music on Sirius XM but I couldn't concentrate at all. A few times I thought I might be followed by someone, but it was only an eerie feeling that came bursting its way into my consciousness. I had no proof because I saw nothing out of the ordinary.

The Vortex was on the front passenger side of the car, on the floor. Artamian had had the opportunity to claim it, but he didn't. I could only guess his reason—he wanted to come back to me. I kept it for the same reason. Sometimes, what you hate is what you need to keep closer.

I might be chasing a shadow, but I had seen the light in Detective John's eyes and I have felt his soul. It was sincere and filled with true affection every time he looked at me. Why then, if not for the reason that he knew me? His actions were sometimes mysterious, as were his words.

Finding him gave me a fresh impulse and a renewal of my spirit.

Finding him meant finding my father. My thoughts were spinning rapidly in my mind. To see him would be like looking at your creator's face, the one who also possessed the secrets of your future life. Past, present, and future would be changed into a different light and a different dimension.

I knocked and waited. My emotions shook my body and I clenched my fists to stay calm. The man who opened the door didn't express any surprise to see me. Doubting him was legitimate; believing in him required some faith.

"So, you've come to me at last," he said calmly, inviting me in. I had no more doubts.

He appeared to be much older than he looked just a few days ago when he came to my house. He was aging too quickly. How was that possible?

"I possess a human body," he responded to my own thoughts. "This body is weak and fragile. I see genuine feelings of concern for me in your spirit and that is commendable. I welcome you, Lady Safira; make yourself at home. I've been waiting for you."

Saying that, he smiled at me as he always had in the past, warmly and affectionately. My legs felt weighted down, but I slowly walked further inside the house. It didn't appear to be the home of a single man.

From the hallway, I passed by the kitchen. It wasn't very large or elaborately decorated, but the natural oak cabinets, looked nice. It was neat, clean, and in order.

The living room was spacious, painted in a very light gray color—bright, simple, and comfortable. The baseboards, chair rails, and ceiling crowns were all stained to match the kitchen cabinets. The black leather couch and recliner seemed to be new, and the big screen TV was tuned to the Science Channel. The coffee table had two cell phones on it. Mechanically, I took a seat on the couch and he sat across from me in a comfortable looking arm chair.

"I don't even know where to start with my questions," I said, barely daring to look at him. "If you're Gallbor and you're my father, please don't let me wonder any longer. I have no actual proof that you are my father…"

"There's no need for that," he interrupted me, turning off the TV. "I'm the one who has a story for you. I'm certain you've heard many of our stories. But this one is even more amazing.

"I am, indeed, Gallbor."

* * *

"There were once six Orders in our Kingdom: Warriors, Defenders, Mavens, Titans, Transformers and Enforcers. Five thousand years ago we came to a major disagreement. The King was supposed to be elected every one hundred years, each time from a different Order, but the Titan King at that time abolished that law and declared his Order the eternal ruler.

"He forced the Warriors, Defenders and Enforcers into exile because we were the fighters. We had mighty weapons and we were considered dangerous. However, the dangerous ones were the one left behind. We were forever condemned to never return to the Kingdom of Kamara.

"Here in this realm where we were exiled, we created a Council made up of six representatives from each Order. My own father, Gaboor is part of the Council. We are bound to respect the Council's wishes and to follow its decisions.

"Then, to keep our existence safe, the Orders were separated, sent out into the world and given rules. One rule is known as the Supreme Law: *do not take the life of a mortal and do not harm the innocent ones*.

"The original generation of each Order was to stay behind and build a city. We were from the future, from an advanced society—the mortals had barely invented the wheel.

"Warriors are fighters, and only the Healer and the Spirit Master, possess gifts to empower the Order. We were stripped of our magical swords. The Council, knowing our powers, destroyed most of them. But each Order could retain only one, and those were given to the Enforcers—our new Police Force. Our ability to fight had no magic anymore.

"We also had the appearance to blend with the mortals. This world was our home now and we were all determined to share it and survive. We were sent to defend entire nations against invaders. We could only fight alongside the ones that we were defending, and not the attackers.

"The Defenders were creatures with great fire power who could destroy a life in an instant. They also look human, but they aren't as tall as Warriors. Their entire order is characterized by fiery red hair, olive skin and intense blue eyes. They, too, were bound by the rules of the Council. The Defenders were sent to defend the weak and the less fortunate against the evil ones. They would travel from place to place, looking for mortals in need of justice.

"The Enforcers became our police and the guardians of the Secret Mountain. No one can transit in and out without their permission. They have exceptionally long hair, so light that it's almost white, and a beautiful combination of blue and green eyes. They also have lethal weapons that are used by all of the Orders.

"The Titans, Transformers and the Mavens look different from mortals; however, as time passed I retained less and less memory of them. Through the centuries, even the memory of our beloved Kingdom of Kamara started to fade. One day you'll encounter the other Orders. You must tell the younger Warriors the whole truth about our origins."

"What you've told me is so interesting," I said, fascinated by his tale. "The young Warriors believe this to be just the stuff of legends. Father, how did we get into a war that will seemingly never end?"

"We, the Warriors, got too close to the ones we protected and created offspring with the mortals. The Council was indignant that we broke one of our laws and decided that those children weren't allowed to receive the gift of Immortality. But instead of sending the Enforcers to punish us, they banished us and forbade us from returning to the Mountain. They allowed us to solve our own problem, as long as we don't harm the ones who don't rise against us.

"However, the new rise of people, called the Amestec, discovered our weakness. Our immortal spirit could transfer into them. So, the war had started. For centuries, the law that forbids us to mate with the mortals no longer exists for any of the orders, but the Warriors were not informed of this law, and for a good reason."

"And the lost magical swords? What's their story?"

"The Silver Sword and the Fire Sword, were the only two of our weapons that the council didn't destroy. But they don't belong to us—they belong to the Enforcers. A specific weapon was kept so that every Order could be punished. The Silver Sword and the Fire Sword could destroy the Warriors and annihilate us for forever. I foresaw the danger of them being used against us, so I made them disappear. I was the one who stole them. But in traveling from one place to another, I lost them, too.

The Council allowed me to seek out the swords. When you have them both, the Enforcers will come for them."

"Please—tell me about *me*."

*   *   *

Gallbor smiled again, in that simple manner that made me feel loved by him, despite our peculiar situation.

"I was very powerful," he continued, but this time he looked down with his eyes focused on the carpet. "As a Master I had the power to travel in spirit and be omnipresent. That gift reduced my ability to stay in human form more than seven days at a time. In the secret Mountain I could safely return to my spirit and govern over my Order.

"But I was careless and arrogant. I was inclined to believe that I was invincible, that I was protected by my own power, so I deserved all I that I desired. And what I desired was your mother, Lady Amara. She was the Healer and she was our Queen, the one who kept the Warriors ready for battle. She would choose lovers from among the great men of our Order and I would just suffer in silence.

"As the Master, I was allowed to keep a woman, but the Healer was forbidden to me and I couldn't reproduce with her. The Council was concerned about the kind of powers that my offspring would inherit from me.

"Although I loved her in secret for centuries, I did nothing to save her from Fers Martuzon, her captor—the Prince of Transylvania. That was until one day my first commander, Prince Gavril, knowing of my love for her, offered to save her for me. It was the first time in over two thousand years that she was within my reach again, and I couldn't resist.

"When the rest of the clan had gone to a battle, I went in Gavril's place, to meet with her and declare my love. She returned my affection and I was thrilled and happy. I had never been that happy in my whole existence. She asked me to stay longer, but my time was limited in the human body I was using. But I didn't pay attention to this limitation. I couldn't stop loving her, making love with her."

I blushed and cleared my throat. Gallbor raised his head and turned his eyes in my direction. Our eyes met. I didn't pretend to understand, but I had seen that glow before.

"I knew then that I had rather be with her than to be alone, far from her sight. I didn't return to the Mountain anymore. But word came to me that the Irish Warriors needed my help, so I left her with Gavril. Fers Martuzon found her and took her back to his Palace. But she wasn't alone. She was pregnant with you—my daughter. You know the rest of the story.

"However, I didn't know at the time that Gavril was assumed to be your father, as everyone believed that he and Lady Amara were lovers. I didn't deny those allegations. With that knowledge, Gavril's sons thought you were their sister and they took it upon themselves to rescue and protect you. I released all my powers to you, my children. Now is the time for a new reign. That's all of the story. I told you that it would be a quick tale."

"This isn't all of the story," I said stubbornly. "Why haven't you ever showed yourself to me? Not as a Master, but as a father. I was longing to know you, the one who had unexpectedly placed all these duties on my shoulders, asked me to save both worlds, and find the relics. But you never gave me any guidance. Why?"

My attitude was fearless, but my voice was shaking. Either I had the right to ask this of him, or not, but without a doubt that he had acted like a coward.

"It's true," he rushed to answer me. "I *was* a coward. I couldn't come to you and tell you all these things without shaking your beliefs. And that's exactly what happened when you found out who you really are. But this time it was somewhat better; you're older and wiser."

"How could you know all these things about me," I asked, astonished.

"Because I feel you. I carry you in my spirit as you carry me. But one day, when this mortal body will perish, my spirit will still remain in you and in your brother."

"Mortal body? How did you get this mortal body? I suppose this is why I didn't see through you right away."

I stood up and came closer to him. I touched his shoulder and then I took his right hand and examined it. I saw the blood circulating through his veins and I felt that his flesh was soft, not hard like an immortal's flesh.

"Fifteen years ago, in a small town in Missouri, I happened to interrupt a fight between an Enforcer and a girl from the Defenders Order. She end up being frozen by the Enforcer's weapon, but she put up a great fight. I had never seen anything like that. Unfortunately, there wasn't much I could do for her—my healing gift didn't work on Defenders. But I couldn't let her perish. I brought her spirit back and guided it to the closest populated area to transfer into a human being—a new born baby girl. But before she was transformed into the mortal's life, her spirit warned me that I was also in danger and I must save myself the same way. She was a clairvoyant, and she released her gift to me. But I didn't believe her.

"Five months later, an Immortal turned against me. A small clan of Warriors called for my help, but one of them attacked me from behind. I had sensed the danger, but I was too proud, and that was my downfall. Although I wasn't a Spirit anymore, I was still Gallbor—the invincible—and I let my body's shield down. He cut off my head, and my powers transferred to him."

"What?" I murmured, in shock. I slowly slid down to the floor at his knees. How was that possible? Anger invaded my soul, along with the sudden need for revenge.

"My body was left headless on a bridge, in St. Charles, Missouri. I remembered what the Defender girl had told me. With the last of my strength, I guided my lingering spirit five miles down the road to find a new host—a St. Louis Police officer who was shot and in danger of dying. You know that my Spirit also multiplies, as yours does, so what went into my killer wasn't all of me. I entered into this new body and brought it back to life."

"As Detective John Morris."

"Yes," he responded, forcing me to get up. "When I learned that you were in the Atlanta area, I transferred there, keeping my mortal job, so I could be closer to you and your brother. Imagine my heart's delight when I met you and your brother, face to face. Now, I might have twenty or thirty years left on this earth, and then I'll taste the eternal shadow as a mortal."

"I could make you Immortal again," I whispered, but my eyes were painfully holding back heavy tears. "Even as a mortal, you still have some powers left."

"That was once true, but now I'm empty. I know about the mortal man to whom you gave eternal life, but that is not to be done again—at least, not for me. It doesn't work that way. Every gift you have won't work merely on your command. You only have it as your need for it arises."

"I don't understand," I said, a bit confused. "Don't you want me to try to save you?"

"Not this time, Safira. I'm eleven thousand years old. I'm tired and outdated, and it's time for me to go.

"Now, you must be aware that this Warrior traitor will come seeking you because he wants you, and he did all this because he wishes to become your Master. He's very powerful, now, and I can't stop him. He was the one who found your home and set it on fire. I saved you by having Andreas take you to your clan. It was time for you to return to your Order and rule as a true Healer and Queen."

"Is his name Rex?" I asked, not without bitterness. "Please tell me his name. Will he be my Master?"

"I didn't see my killer's face. But he's the man who dared to rise against me in order to have you. If you don't want him as a Master, I want you to rise against him with your own powers and with no doubts."

"I have doubts all the time," I said laughing nervously, and I shrugged my shoulders and raised my hands in the air. I was frustrated, too, and I shed tears that were less of anger and more of indecision. "Father, I doubt myself, you, and everything I'm able to do."

"You doubt with your mind," he said, as he stood up with me. "Your powers are in your heart and your spirit."

"Father, Octavian was born to rule, wasn't he?"

"I told you that you are wise. Yes, he's the Warrior Order's new Master, and the Council is aware of it. I'm proud of my legacy. Your brother will unite the Warriors and lead them to greatness while he learns to develop his powers."

"What about Artamian?" I asked, and I couldn't hold my rain of tears inside me any longer. "Why would you choose *him*?" Gallbor came closer to me and started to wipe my tears away.

"Your tears are also a weapon," he said calmly, caressing my face. "I did it because I love you. Artamian is my gift for you, a devoted warrior. In time you will appreciate his powers and his heart. Trust me, you'll need him. Forget the past and look at the future."

"But all the stupid things I did, the rules I broke..." I started to say, but Gallbor shook his head and gently touched my forehead.

"Everything you've done so far, every foolish thing or mistake you've made, is for you to use in the future. The new powers are also yours—you earned them. Octavian will earn his powers, too."

At that moment the back door opened and a teenage boy holding a basketball entered the house. His face was flushed, with sweat dripping from his hair to his shoulders. I was stunned by his appearance. The youth was tall, had long dark hair, and blue eyes. If I hadn't known better, I would have thought that it was Octavian, only a bit younger.

"Dacian," said Gallbor, "this is Safira, the guest I mentioned to you earlier. We're almost done, so please give us a few more minutes."

The boy turned and waved to me. His eyes looked at me curiously for a few seconds, and he smiled. Then he opened the refrigerator, grabbed a bottle of water, and headed back outside. I didn't dare to ask about the young man. I was astonished and mute. Instantly, I remembered the two cell phones on the table. I followed Dacian to the door and I looked at him through the glass.

"He's your younger brother," explained Gallbor, standing behind me. Dacian started to shoot long shots and free throws, and the ball stripped the net every time. "He's just turned seventeen. Lady Amara is his mother, too. I asked your mother to let me raise him. She had you for a while, but then she had Octavian until he was Dacian's age and you two united. I wanted him to be mine, in my care; it was my last chance to redeem myself. He wasn't told what he is, about his immortality. He went to the mortal's school and did everything just as they did."

"And you named him Dacian?" I touched my ear quickly to make sure that my phone was on and opened for Octavian to hear all this. If his satellite was following me, he should be able to see the boy in the back yard.

"What is he?" I asked, watching him, fascinated.

"Everything he wants to be. But for now, he's just a teenager. I want him to appear to be normal for as long as possible."

26

I STEPPED INTO THE STREET and stood still for a moment. I wasn't sure what I wanted to do. My new brother had captured my heart and my soul's desire was to linger around him longer. He was like me at that age—clueless and innocent of what I was and what I would become. But now it wasn't for me to change that part of him.

Nothing was conclusive to me, so far. After such a long time of longing to meet Gallbor, I was happy to know my father, but I was unsatisfied with the outcome. It wasn't reassuring and it didn't bring peace to my spirit. One of our own had turned against my father and killed him, for the whole purpose of becoming my Master.

My own father had chosen to give the son of a man I had hated in the past great powers, and sent him to help me. These weren't the answers I was looking for. I didn't like any of them, not what I had learned about the traitor and even less about Artamian's "help". Still, I had been crazy enough to make love with the one my father had assigned to be my bodyguard.

And there he was—Artamian—standing beside the driver's side of the Corvette.

His presence infuriated me as much it raised my body's heat. It was a feeling I couldn't grasp and it disconnected any control I had over my logic.

"What are you doing here," I snapped at him, getting closer to the car but not unlocking the doors. Artamian had on leather pants with a matching jacket, a sign for me that he had driven his motorcycle here. His hair was pulled back into a pony tail—he had no reason to hide his face.

"Where's your ride?"

"In his garage," he said, pointing to Gallbor's home. "I was sent to guard you."

"To guard me?" I laughed. "No one sent you to guard me. You just keep showing up like a ghost. Go away."

"I took an oath to protect you," he said, and his face was very serious. "It's an order from the Master."

"Gallbor isn't our master anymore," I said, and I got in his face and pushed him away to get to the driver's side door. "You have no such oath!"

"My orders aren't from Gallbor alone," he replied without moving. I lifted my head and looked into his face. He wasn't lying. So, if Gallbor hadn't sent him, it must have been Octavian. That explained my suspicion that the two acted like they knew each other, that day on the beach in Deerfield. But when did they meet?

"You're wrong," I said, without backing away.

We were so close. I inhaled his scent, and that was a bad idea. Without warning, he did the same. His nostrils enlarged, his eyes closed, and his face lifted. It was like we were charging our powers from each other's bodies.

"I'm not easily killed," I said, rapidly stepping back from his sphere of influence. "Fire and bullets can't kill me. Not even your Vortex."

"What about the Fire Sword and Silver Sword," he asked, grabbing my arm. "They could kill you, couldn't they?"

"They could kill you too," I responded, allowing him to walk me to the car's passenger side.

"That's why I'm here," he said, opening the door for me and moving the Vortex back into the trunk. "I'm driving tonight."

I was furious, but I understood what he meant. He impressed me again. I hated that about him. I hated the fact that he was always reminding me that he was there to sacrifice his immortal life for me. There was a time when I detested the fact that he could be my Master—now, I was looking at him with regret, almost wishing that it were so.

"Safira," I heard my brother's voice in my ear, "you need to find shelter for tonight. You've been followed—they've found you again."

"Are you sure?" I asked, though my question sounded ridiculous. I looked around me, up and down the street, but I couldn't see anything suspicious.

"How can this be possible? I don't have the Land Rover anymore."

"I don't know, but they're in the air, in a helicopter. They followed you all the time you drove up from Florida. You need to stay somewhere in Atlanta overnight and leave tomorrow morning."

"Well, I'm not alone," I responded, gazing at Artamian, who got behind the wheel. "The two of us could take them down."

"Negative. They may try to snatch you, and we don't need any unwanted attention. I need you to be at the Grecian house tomorrow night. Everyone's ready."

This wasn't an appealing request at all. The last thing I wanted was to spend a night in a hotel with a man who I didn't want around me.

"Safira," continued my brother, "stay away from hotels or any place where they could surround you."

"What about Gallbor and Dacian?"

"I'll keep an eye on them. Leave now!"

Artamian stepped hard on the accelerator and the Stingray took off fast up the street, turning left onto the main highway.

"Where to," he asked, changing lanes and passing cars.

"We've got to find a place to spend the night, but we can't use a hotel or motel. So, we may just sleep in the car, somewhere under a bridge," I answered, feeling extremely frustrated.

"Not necessarily," he said, and he made a sharp right turn into a subdivision. The homes there appeared to be brand new, and most of them weren't finished. "I'm sure we can find a house to accommodate us."

"Try the model home," I said. "They usually have furniture, and sometimes the power is connected."

"That would put us too close to the entrance," he said, slowing down and looking at the homes we passed for one that seemed to be finished. "I think this one will do."

We turned left into the driveway of a two story home. The house was quite imposing, with red brick and a gray stone entrance. Artamian got out of the car and after two tries, he lifted the garage door. He signaled for me to bring the car inside. That was very clever, I had to admit. When I had the car inside, I heard the garage door coming down with a bit of a squeaking noise.

There was no furniture or appliances inside the house. It smelled new. The walls were painted in a dark burgundy color, with a light colored contrasting carpet—not quite to my taste.

"Well, you can take the couch and I'll take the master bedroom," I joked, walking around in an attempt to find us something to sleep on.

"We need to go to the lower level," responded Artamian, opening the door to the basement. "You need to turn off your phone, too."

The room was illuminated by the glow from my eyes. Artamian felt my hesitation and shook his head, walking down the stairs. Reluctantly, I followed him.

"Octavian," I signaled my brother, "we've found a safe house. I'll shut down the mobile phone devices and I'll contact you the first thing in the morning. We'll be OK."

"I see your position, and I'll keep you monitored."

* * *

The basement was one room, completely empty and totally dark, with no windows to allow some light from the street. The heat pump hadn't been turned on and it was cold. The carpet and the paint, of course, smelled new. My instincts were assuring me that I was safe with Artamian in this place. But he wasn't safe with me.

At the same time it felt like a setup. He and I were alone here, in a cold room, far away from everything and anyone—it was reminiscent of something I was trying to forget—my old dream.

No. Nothing was going to happen. If it was a trap, I wouldn't fall for it.

I lightened my eyes, and I lost sight of Artamian for a moment. He came out of a side room that I could see was a bathroom, holding a large piece of carpet, a remnant from the upstairs floor. He didn't say a word, but he motioned for me to lie down and try it. I continued to stand. He removed his jacket, rolled it, making it into a pillow for me. I saw his two pistols, Smith and Wesson, on both sides of his belt. He took off the guns and his t-shirt, and put the shirt underneath his head. I closed my eyes—the sight of his muscular abdomen was disturbing.

"I'm sorry," he said, with his deep voice, "but this is all I could do for you, my Lady. So, please make the best of it. Good night."

Saying that, he laid on the carpet piece and turned to his left with his back toward me. I was still standing. Was I angry? Upset? No. It was just having to admit that he took his role to guard me so seriously.

I lay down, put my head on his jacket, and turned on my right side. We were back to back. I could feel heat coming from his body and I moved a bit closer to him. Although it was summer, this room had been built deep underground, so it was too cold for my short shorts and tank top. I disliked cold rooms like this—they reminded me of my time at Black Eagle Castle. He sensed my movement and turned my way. I thought he was going to embrace me, so I turned my body to face him. His eyes were on me, shining in the dark, calm and reassuring.

I wanted to be a simple Warrior girl, like Raluca or Sabrina, to just love someone and be happy. But I wasn't. *Make the best of it* were Artamian's words to me earlier. Not me. I was too emotional. I grew up among mortals, and I was too emotionally charged, as they would say. I was a mortal at heart and my nerves were as taut as a cable on a suspension bridge. Here I was, in this basement with a man I couldn't stand, but who I desired at the same time. That made me laugh.

"What is it?" asked Artamian, and he lifted his head, bending over me.

"I was thinking about the fact that for someone who an entire Order calls the Queen, I am quite unfit for the duty."

"You're too charged, emotionally" he said, smiling. "What you just said takes a lot of courage to admit."

"How do you know this?" I asked in dismay. "What else do you know?"

"It was just a guess," he answered simply. "I'm the same way. You should have seen me a hundred years ago. But I really don't want to change. Do you?"

"Sometimes I'd like to. Losing mortal friends was the hardest thing for me. I tend to cry a lot. I cry when I watch the mortal's movies and I cry when I lose someone I love—a mortal."

"But you saved one," he said, and his words were quite considerate as he referred to Julian. I glowed my eyes on him again. His right arm was lying over his chest, beside mine, like a divider between us. I passed my fingers over it.

"You've got strong hands," I said, remembering how he killed the hybrid just with his bare fists. I had the idea that he could be stronger than me, but I wasn't about to try my theory. I didn't need it to know—I was sure of it.

"Surely you won't mistake me for a gentle giant. I spent most of my younger years in Berlin, in a school for boys. I fought a lot. I had the reputation as being quite a villain."

He said the last sentence with a bitter sadness, but I was sure that allegation was only half true. That dreaded cold and unpleasant room gradually disappeared. The place was warming up.

"Tell me more," I asked, trying not to sound too interested. At that moment I realized that I had become more comfortable with him. When I looked at him, now, I didn't see Milos. Gallbor wanted me to forget the past, and I had known revenge. Milos could never have me, but his son could and did. I had made love with his son and I liked it. All I saw now was Artamian, and he was taking over my will power without even trying. It could have been Gallbor that was behind this, or just the simple fact that I was in this place with him—vulnerable to affectionate contact.

"My life moments are not great or worth mentioning," he said, "but I could tell you some things about you." I nodded for him to continue.

"I was nineteen when I first saw your face. I had never seen anyone or anything more beautiful. Imagine—to be desperately in love with someone who had died before you were born. Gallbor had a strange sense of humor. I felt some wild emotions there, at the Black Eagle Castle. I sobbed for years over your death, not knowing how my life was going to continue without you…"

"Hold on," I interrupted him. I rose half way, passed my tank top over my head, and took off my bra. Then I put my top back on.

"I am sorry," I said seriously, "I couldn't get comfortable with that thing on."

Artamian remained quiet and still. I stretched out my hand and touched his face.

"Why have you never wanted to fight me?" I asked. "Aren't you even curious to find out if you could be my Master?"

"I don't try or hope for anything because I know how odious I may appear to you," he said, and he turned face up, looking toward the ceiling in the dark. "What would be the meaning of that? Perhaps you would still hate me."

"But you glowed and cast a spell on me."

"Making love with you healed my soul and my body from my curse, a curse that condemned me to love you, more and more with the passing of the time. My love for you is an eternal flame burning in my soul, without rest. It will never change. But you're a wonderful person, Safira. You don't think of yourself as a Warrior or a Healer. Look back at your life and you'll see that your emotions kept you strong."

"Those are beautiful words, Artamian. Are you trying to charm me?"

"How could I," he whispered with no expression on his face.

"I don't hate you Artamian. Not anymore. Just don't glow your eyes on me."

I smiled, but I spoke the truth. An unprecedented connection was forming between us and I fought against it. He was like me, strong and independent, equal to me in some sort of way. I wouldn't want him to stop loving me.

"I'm a little chilly," I said, and my hands made their way over his shoulders.

I feared I would create a disaster, but that was my nature. I was passionate and impulsive with the men I loved and who I was attracted to. With me, the pattern was always falling in love first, then making love. With Artamian, I had no choice.

I leaned my head on his chest and rolled my body onto him. I could feel him, skin to skin. His body was hot, like an explosion of passion. At first he didn't move and he seemed to be puzzled. When his face turned to look at me, I was amazed. His eyes were deep, sad and fiery, dripping with love. I stared at him, frightened and charmed at the same time.

"I think I'll check the upper floor," he said, and he attempted to get up.

"No, I want you to stay," I whispered. I leaned to him and kissed his lips softly.

"Safira," he started to say, but I silenced him with another kiss. I couldn't separate my spirit from my flesh. In a perfect world, he would have been my safe haven and everything I had hoped for.

Meeting my eyes, he understood. No more words were needed from him—just making love. This time he took control.

He put his hands on my waist and lifted me up, laying me gently beside him. Then he lay on top of me. He claimed my body, and I wanted his body in return. I took the time to look into his face, trying to find something to make me hate him again, but all I could see was that fire in his eyes.

It thrilled and imprisoned my soul in the same time.

My soul wanted to find pleasure in loving him but my spirit was merciless in denying my heart. The reality was that I could easily fall in love with him—but that was the one thing that stood against me.

His hands undressed me slowly, first my top and then my shorts and panties. He followed every movement with touching, and he caressed my body inch by inch. His lips were smooth and so hot, while they moved from my lips to my nipples.

My skin trembled with desire. But my patience had ended. I held his back, pulling him towards me. I didn't want to rush through this moment, I wanted to savor it and enjoy its pleasure, but the energy I felt coming from him was like an electric shock.

His eyes glowed wildly as my hand found him fully erect and I guided him into my steaming wetness. He slowly made his way inside me, millimeter by millimeter. When my body fully engulfed him, it was a delirious burst, perfect and intense this time, elevated by our own feelings for each other. My body crashed as waves of pleasure flowed through it, and I was satisfied.

"The simple truth is that I want you to be mine, only mine," he said, rolling to the side, as he lifted me over him and held me tightly to his chest. "I desire you with such intensity that I could kill anyone in my way. I would die for you Safira! Never forget it."

His embrace was a delicious passion to my soul. I crossed my arms around his neck, wanting more.

He whispered in my ear, "You made love with me the second time because you actually like me, don't you?"

27

"I GOT MY HANDS ON as many weapons as I could," reported Serban, after I arrived at the Greek restaurant and filled my large cup with coffee.

Octavian seemed preoccupied and I had had no chance to talk to him since my return. Perhaps words were unnecessary at this moment. Everything he needed to know about our true origins was said and he had listened to Gallbor.

I didn't blame him for not wanting to come to see our father. He was stronger than me and much more wise. However, knowing the truth about Gallbor's having been betrayed, and his killer, was still a dark shadow that lingered without an end in our minds.

*   *   *

"Where's the warship," I asked Luke, who was ready to put on a show. Soon a gallery of images appeared on the monitor's screen, and they all showed the interior of a destroyer.

"Bad news—it's moved quickly to south—it's gone past Key Largo. Now it's about sixty miles away from Key West. It's happening—they're going to attack the Americans!"

"The Coast Guard told me that they're legit," said Alex, turning his back on me, heading to the tech room. I tried to discern his feelings, but he was torn about something other than this battle. I didn't know what else would conflict his mind. Everyone was present and waiting in anticipation, except for Artamian. He had left us again.

"It's worse than I thought," said Julian, staring at the images of our enemy's vessel on the four monitors. "I was wrong about this particular class of destroyer—it's newer and better than the one I'm familiar with. From the inside, it's built to be an operational anti-aircraft, anti-submarine and anti-surface ship. It has the capability of seeing every ship in the area, which means we can't get close to them in any way without them blowing us out of the water. And that's not all—they have four other boats linked to it—maybe it's how they mean to get to land. As I said before, it'll be nearly impossible for us to attack it, even if our intent is to kill *only* the enemy on board."

"There *are* people who could get on board," I answered stubbornly.

Everyone's eyes looked at me in dismay. That look was definitely hard to swallow. Only my brother nodded in agreement.

"Octavian and I could get on it from the air," I continued, a bit annoyed by their lack of confidence. "We could use our own plane, or rent a helicopter and jump aboard."

My people were confused and uneasy. They didn't dare to doubt me, but I sensed their dilemma. Octavian, who until that moment had stood by my side, walked away to the tech room to answer the phone. Alex was back in the group again, and listening.

"Once we're on board, we'll blow up their radar control room and their weapons room; that will blind them and leave the way open for the rest of you to come on board. We'll have to be fast and precise, but it's not impossible."

"They're going to shut you down any way they can," commented Serban.

"Possibly," I answered gently, "but my brother and I are fireproof."

"It's true," confirmed Julian," I saw her escape from a barn explosion alive. Lady Safira is also a brilliant war strategist."

"We need a diversion—something to allow us to get closer to the ship," I said, while I could hear many murmurs talking about my plan. "They're using a military craft to hide and deceive us—so we need a counterplan. Since they won't consider the Coast Guard to be a threat, we could use their helicopters or boats."

"I'll work on that," responded Alex from behind me. He was holding a sword tightly in his hand—perhaps his old weapon.

"So, we'll have to split up," I continued, encouraged by Alex's comment. "Some of us will be on the Coast Guard boat, and others will attack from the air."

"We'll go on the boat," volunteered Serban, and in his spirit was determined not to be denied.

His eyes opened large because they wanted to send me a message. I understood why. They felt guilty because of the protective armor over their hearts, and that didn't relieve their conscience. They were firmly convinced that with that advantage, they had the right to claim the most dangerous part of the mission.

"All right then. The Europeans will take the boats while the Americans will fly. Do you agree, Alex?"

But Alex didn't answer me. I turned to face him and I read his thoughts. I sensed that he felt some doubt in my judgment, but his mind was more agitated regarding the safety of his people. It was the same feeling I had felt when I first met him—the fear of failure, but with a courageous heart.

I walked around the room, hoping that Octavian would take over and come up with a different plan. But he didn't. He stood over to the side of the group, quiet and deep in thought.

I became a little aggravated about this. I wanted him to say something, to get involved, and to bring a little more enthusiasm into our little war room. I had to say something that would raise their spirits even more.

"Listen, all of you! Fifteen years ago, Warrior Rex convinced my father, Gallbor, to meet with him and then viciously attacked him from behind. Rex killed him and took over his power. That's why he's so powerful. His whole intention is to be my Master and then to reign over all of us. We either win this battle or be prepared to perish. Luke, we need you to stay here at all times to monitor their movements and to keep us informed. The rest of you—pack up the guns and let's get on the road."

"No," snapped Alex. "We'll all go by boats. That destroyer has to remain sixty miles away from shore, or we all die to keep it there."

"I agree," said Sabrina, boldly, "there aren't enough of us to split up, and we could do better together. We need to keep them away from the island. If Octavian and Safira could pave the way for us, we'll get on board and fight."

Serban crossed his arms over his chest and shook his head, although it wasn't his choice. He wanted his part of the glory and he didn't want to share it with Alex.

"If we divide into two groups, we'll have a better chance to destroy them all," he argued, going for the most efficient plan. "Some of us will have to come from the air."

"Then, someone has to take charge and decide the plan of action," I said harshly. "We can't be divided in this."

"Well, apparently we *are* divided," said Andreas hitting the table with his fist. "So what's it going to be?"

Octavian turned to me, looking for an intervention on my part, but I shook my head. His whole existence would defy its purpose if I accepted this challenge.

I had been in charge of everything between us for so long, and Octavian had always followed my lead because he pictured me as the leader.

But not this time—not anymore.

"We're going for the boats," he said loudly. "Even using the Coast Guard as a cover, the chances are they'll become aggressive. Safira and I can get on the ship first, from the helicopter. We'll destroy their weapons room and help you all to come aboard."

Serban and Andreas pursed their lips, disappointed. Lars, Ditmar and Codrin stood up to disagree. Only Raluca remained seated and quiet, but I sensed that her spirit was at peace with whatever the outcome would be.

"We don't have enough people to carry out such a mission," commented Serban.

"We do now," responded Octavian, turning to the door.

*   *   *

At that moment I heard the sound of a car pulling up to the front of the restaurant. A moment later, three boys and two girls, all teenagers, entered, accompanied by Artamian. One boy with loose dreadlocks and one girl were African-American. It wasn't hard to see that they were Immortals.

All were very young, but they carried themselves very boldly. It was quite an amazing display of modern fashion, especially with their long dark hair and sparking blue eyes.

"Our children," murmured Cedric, and I suspected that a girl and a boy in the group were his. "What're they doing here?"

"We're not children anymore," responded the one that stood to the right of Artamian. He had clear eyes and a proud smile. "We're Americans and we're here to fight. We're very good at maneuvering the Shurikens and we're sharpshooters. My name is Wesley, and I'm seventeen. Beside me are Calvin and Sylvan, and the ladies are Phillia and Gianna. We've been training for the past five years and we're ready to prove what we can do."

Their presence left everyone else dumbfounded and somewhat unsettled. All they could see in our new additions was their young age, but not their abilities. I realized, sadly, that even in our world, we could become outdated.

The new generation knew how to fight better in the modern world and they were fearless about it, and these young people were ready to show us what they could do.

"We'll see about that," I answered, and in a fraction of second, my mind ordered the Vortex to come to me.

The weapon flew straight from the bar in my direction. Half way on its course I stopped it high in the air. From the other side of the room, five Shurikens came my way in the same time. I saw them in slow motion and I raised my left hand, effortlessly catching the first one.

But I didn't hold it—I threw it back to the sender with all the speed with which I was capable. I did the same with the rest.

All five youths drew their pistols and shot down the flying objects before they reached their targets. The Shurikens fell to the floor, shattered beyond repair.

Wesley smiled proudly during the entire exhibition. I gazed at my brother from the corner of my eye.

Without a word, Octavian lifted his hand towards the Vortex. The weapon rotated away from me and toward the youngsters, flying very close over their heads. But none of them ducked away in fear. He laid the Vortex back on the table without touching it, continuing to guide it with his mind. Their eyes glowed with exuberance—they loved that.

I placed a red glass on the shelf in the middle of some clear ones. I nodded my head to Wesley in an invitation to only shoot the red glass. The young man, who was still standing in the back and across the room, narrowed his eyes as he measured the distance to his target.

He closed his eyes tightly, slowly raised his hand holding the gun, and pulled the trigger. Only the red glass that shattered.

I stepped toward them and I touched their foreheads. One by one they bowed to me as they sensed my powers. I turned to the rest of the Warriors and I nodded. It was my way of confirming that the youths were ready to fight alongside us. But as I looked at them, my mind traveled in different direction.

"We need a better strategy," I said, and I went to stand aside Luke. "We have to get on that boat unseen and unheard, and keep the mortals on the ship safe."

"What are you talking about," asked Alex. "For all we know, we'll have a huge advantage just by the destruction of their communication and weapons rooms."

"But all that firepower will cause the Navy to send their jets and open fire on all of us," said Octavian, and his eyes narrowed as he suspected what I was up to.

"So what's going to be?" asked Andreas, his favorite phrase.

"Cyber war," I said, and my face broke into a smile.

"The ship can't be controlled remotely from a distance. It wasn't built that way," interrupted Julian, exasperated. "This is the modern Navy. No one can just take over our most secret defenses."

"Understood! But we have the best tech room here, with the best capacity. There must be a way to breach their system and freeze their monitors just for a few minutes, to give us time to get closer and board the ship. Luke, isn't that possible?"

"Of course it is," Wesley answered instead. "Sylvan could do it."

Again, that young Warrior had that smug smile on his lips, like they could do everything we were doing, only better than us.

"The young ones," smiled Lars. "It seems to me that they're faster and smarter."

The compliment was well received by them. I pulled Sylvan aside and sat him on a chair beside Luke.

"Tell me how," I demanded, and the youngster blushed a bit under my scrutinizing look.

"We need closer access to them," answered Sylvan, rotating the images from left to right. "Like anything else, the ship is just a machine. It has codes and scripts, and it relies on satellites. I could cripple their system indefinitely if I could switch their satellite with ours."

"How can we accomplish that?" asked Octavian, and he came to stand behind the young warrior.

"We need a direct line of sight. If we could place our GPS on the ship, I could switch their system over to us and decrypt the signal."

"It *is* possible," agreed Luke, "but you can't use a helicopter—it'll fly too low and all that noise will activate their defense system."

"Octavian and I will fly our jet and sync with the satellite. Our aircraft won't be suspicious to them because many are likely to be in the area. Then we'll send down the device."

"I'll go with you," interrupted Artamian, who stood by the entrance, leaning against the wall.

"Still, the chances are that they'll shut us down," I said hesitantly, staring stubbornly at the monitors. I tried to look at him, but I couldn't.

"I know," he said calmly. "I'm willing to assume that risk."

"He could help," intervened Octavian, and for a second I remained quiet, trying to regain my composure. Why can't I fight a war without fighting my own feelings, too?

I found myself hating Artamian again. I hoped to retain that hate for a longer period of time. It was a good feeling.

"It seems that's the best plan so far," Octavian continued with a firm voice. "Luke and Sylvan will inform us when the switch has been made. The Europeans and the Americans will follow us in the speed boat and come on board at my signal. We need to have that ship dead in the water because the only way on it, from the speed boat, is to climb rope ladders. I need Julian's and Wesley's team to be our snipers. They'll be in the helicopter and attack the enemy from it. Those in the speed boat will keep your position until I clear you to come on board. We'll be in direct contact at all the times, of course, and we'll fight as the situation requires. We'll attack tomorrow night. Julian, is there anything else for us to know?"

"As I've said before, a destroyer isn't an open field," Julian responded, lifting his shoulders. "Be ready for a lot of close fighting."

"We may need to force them to come out in the open," I said, observing the exterior of the ship. "They'll come out for me, so I'm getting on board first."

"You can't be the first one to board the ship," said Andreas. "You're our Queen and Healer; we're bound to protect you. We need you in case we need healing. We can't risk losing you."

"It's true," interrupted Serban. "You're the one to heal our bodies and Octavian can bring us back from the Shadows. Raluca told us what you did for her—you two are priceless."

"Then, I'll go down first," Artamian suggested firmly.

"Agreed," responded Octavian, "but first of all, we are Warriors and our place is in battles with you. The traitor who killed our Master is on that ship. Rex *will not* prevail. Gallbor will be revenged. The mortals on that ship will be saved. Our children are growing into brave Warriors like these who're here with us now, and we have plenty of them. No, it's not too early to have them fight. They're ready. We'll build a new Order, stronger and better for us and for them. We'll win this war. Are you ready for it?"

Suddenly, the whole room lightened with glowing eyes. One by one, they all stood up and lifted their right hands, touching their foreheads and pledging themselves, saluting Octavian. Serban and Alex joined them, too.

"No," responded Octavian stepping back, "you can't salute me like that."

"We have a Master among us," said Serban. "Gallbor himself told me that I would recognize the new Master, and I do. It's you."

"We need a commander, someone with your skills, who's capable of leading us to victory," added Alex, and for the first time the brothers were in agreement. "There's one out there that wants to force himself to be our Master. You're the real one."

"Lady Safira is our Queen," Octavian insisted, and I was the only one who really understood his words. I was the one who could set everything right. I had the last word, so everyone turned to me in expectation.

"Octavian, you're the son of Gallbor. As the Queen of the Order of Warriors, I recognize you as our Master."

Saying this, I saluted him.

At that point, Octavian was undeniably the new Master.

28

OCTAVIAN CAME AND TOOK A seat beside me in the co-pilot's chair. It was a little after midnight and we had just passed over the destroyer's last known location.

"Safira, you're in love," he said without warning. He smiled, but he avoided looking at me.

"Are you asking me or are you making a statement?" I questioned him, surprised by his words. I turned my eyes towards the back of the plane at Artamian, who was strapping on the parachute. "What difference does it make?"

My brother continued to smile undisturbed. "It makes a huge difference. Love before the battle is amazing."

Did he know what had happened between Artamian and me? Of course he knew! Perhaps he was the one who had manipulated the whole thing. I wanted to rebuke him, but I realized that he wasn't referring just to me. Did Raluca give in to my brother's charm?

Probably! That wouldn't have been very hard.

"You're over the destroyer, but your altitude is too high," I heard Luke's frustrated voice. "I won't be able to connect with the satellite before Artamian makes it down. Can you make a turn and get lower?"

"If we go any lower we'll have to land or be shot down," responded my brother, who maneuvered the plane for a sharp bank to the right. Suddenly a voice blasted through the cockpit speakers. Octavian flipped on the communication switch of his radio.

"Is this jet flight 337? Do you hear me?"

"This is the pilot of flight 337," responded my brother, surprised. The voice on the speakers wasn't coming from the Miami tower control we had just passed. "Who is this?"

"I am the commander of the destroyer you are flying over," came the answer, and my brother turned to look at me. I shook my head in denial. The same people we wanted to deceive and take over had discovered us first. But Julian had warned us about this particular ship's capabilities.

"Miami cleared me on this flight plan," responded Octavian without hesitation. "I will be gone in a second."

"Do that," came the answer, "but before you fly on to Key West, you are going to circle around and release one of your passengers to us."

At first I wasn't sure I heard the command correctly, but then I saw the grimace of fury on Artamian's face.

"I am on board alone," responded Octavian, but now we knew who we were talking to. "You have no right to make such a request."

"You've been pinged," Luke whispered in our ear pieces. "I can see you on their satellite monitor. Get out of there immediately!"

"We should abort this mission," Serban's voice interrupted Luke.

"Just try ignoring me and you will suffer the consequences," said the voice again.

"OK," said Octavian, winking at me. "Who the hell are you and what do you want with me?"

We knew very well that this order was meant for me and not Octavian.

"I don't want you," came the answer. "Just send the girl down and you *may* live a little longer. Send Lady Safira down *now!*"

Four pair of eyes were on me. How did they know I was there? I gazed at both men in disbelief. It was the fulfilling of a prophecy. I couldn't run away and I couldn't escape my destiny.

"Ignore him," advised Alex, who was listening in from the Coast Guard boat, along with Serban and the rest. "Get away from there."

"I am flying alone," insisted my brother, trying to prolong the moment.

"You are not fooling me," the voice in the speaker said, louder and more impatient. "Let me tell you this, in case you still have second thoughts. I have two missiles aligned on course. They are about to fly out at my command."

"Then go ahead and shoot me down," Octavian responded angrily.

"Oh, but they are not for you. I have a certain target in mind. It's called *Rainforest Park*."

"The home of the Americans," whispered Alex in our ear pieces. "What do we do now? We're in range, only three miles from the warship."

"Stay put," said Octavian. "This isn't over yet."

"I'm going down," I loudly responded to the destroyer in my brother's microphone.

"Lady Safira," replied the man, and the tone of his voice turned softer. "I will be waiting for you on the upper deck. And please, come unarmed. Resistance is futile."

The fact that he used a quote from a movie made me even more furious. But who had I talked with? Was it Rex?

"I can't let you go," snapped my brother, and he pulled back on the yoke so that the plane climbed higher. "There has to be something else we can do to save you. I could go in your place."

"It has to be me—it's the only solution," I said, getting up from my seat and walking towards the back of the plane. "I'll parachute down there and I'm taking the device with me. He won't kill me, but the Americans in Key West are in danger if I don't wind up in his hands. It's going to work."

"I'm coming with you," Artamian demanded, and his eyes were fixed on me, deep and determined.

"No," I responded harshly. "I don't want him to act crazy. Once I start down, I need you two to turn around, get in the helicopter with the others, and wait for the right time to get on board. So far he's only mentioned that he'll destroy the island—he doesn't think that the Coast Guard ship is a problem. It's not too late. Our plan will still work if Luke and Sylvan do the switch."

There was a moment of silence. They both knew what was ahead for me. I took out the ear piece and handed it to Octavian. I couldn't risk the enemy hearing us talking or intercepting our plan. I was on my own.

"Suit up and wait for my signal," Octavian said, touching my forehead. His touch felt different—almost like the pressure of a healing touch.

Artamian helped me strap on the parachute. My eyes rested on his face the whole time he worked with me. I wished I could tell him the truth. Inside my own shell I felt differently. I wasn't courageous and I wasn't brave—I was afraid. A terrible man was on that destroyer, one who would overpower me because he was stronger.

My eyes lost contact with Artamian's. What I felt for him was something like love, from a little seed that had been planted deep in my heart, not long ago. And it was growing. The remedy was to not allow it to blossom. A love like that wouldn't make sense. A love like that was impossible.

I heard Octavian asking if I was ready, but I didn't answer. My hands were sweating, holding the handle of the hatch tightly. After all the planning and mental preparation we had done—it all came down to this.

Only Artamian understood me.

"I won't allow him to have you," he whispered, holding my face and forcing me to look back at him. "I'll come after you and kill him myself—I promise."

I nodded—I believed him. Before the hatch opened and I jumped, it was his face that I saw last. More than a century and a half ago, a similar face was looking down upon me when I died. But now this was different. It was him I wanted to see again, if I could live through this battle and this war.

*   *   *

I flew free for a few hundred feet until my parachute opened. The wind was against me, striking my face hard. I swung a bit to the left and turned on the satellite. Luke and Sylvan had only a few seconds to connect it before I reached the ground. The ship was there, underneath me. My eyes glowed with fury and their radiance lit the sky. I saw him there too—waiting for me along the forward deck with a scattering of his army. More than likely they were Amestec.

My feet landed on the hard steel on the forward deck of the bridge, and as I landed, I felt a heavier object than the satellite land at the same time. I knew what it was—the Vortex had followed me down—and I quickly covered them both with the parachute.

There were only seven on the deck. I was capable of taking down seven men, but I wouldn't accomplish much—the ship was full of them. Later I would attempt to kill as many as I could, but not right now. Now, I needed to know who killed my father.

The man in the middle didn't want me to recognize him. By the time I slowly walked toward them, he had donned a shining gray-ish mask that covered his face from his forehead to his nose and down his cheeks. The mask was strange and unsettling. It was similar to those that were worn in the old carnivals of Venice, Italy a couple of hundred years ago. It was in a very poor taste to me. And stupid.

I glowed my eyes and checked him out—he was unarmed. The Silver Sword wasn't on him. His choice of wardrobe was also bizarre: he wore a dark gray suit with an open neck pink shirt, while his men wore khaki pants and t-shirts.

He bowed and smiled at me, but I had no reaction to his show of civility. I was cold and unfeeling, but I had to stay calm. This man was dangerous and I couldn't allow him to take command of my feelings. He was the one who had murdered my father, and I would seek revenge or die.

"Welcome, Lady Safira," he said, and his voice was unusually pleasant. "You look the same way I remembered you, but even more beautiful and quite stunning with red hair."

He had an accent, too, and his eyes shone with lust in the dark night. I had seen those eyes before.

"Why did you force me to come here?" I asked, lifting my head and daring to look menacingly at him. My heart raced rapidly and painfully, but my spirit was aware and it was bold again. This would be over soon. Artamian would come for me—he had promised.

"Because, my dear, I have been looking for you for so long. A few times I almost got you, but I have stupid soldiers and they all failed to bring you to me. So, I decided to come and get you myself. Of course, I could continue to kill more Warriors in order to catch to you, but I thought I would be generous this time."

"Generous? You don't even have the courage to show yourself to me, covering your face like a stupid masquerade."

"My name is Rex."

He stepped toward me and all my nerves stretched and vibrated. I braced myself to fight him. My first instinct in my mind was to find the Vortex, but instead, he gently took my hand and forced me to follow him down inside the destroyer. It wasn't what I wanted, but in his mind, the fact that he had me on board was a moment of victory.

The interior of the ship was very well lit. He signaled to his men to leave us, and among them I recognized Nagoshi. Unwillingly I followed him down a long, narrow passage and through another long corridor to a set of stairs that took us deeper into the bowels of the ship. We passed a few Amestec and Hybrids who all did the same thing—they bowed to us.

I tried to remember Julian's floor plan of the battleship so I would know where I was, and I regretted not paying attention to all the details. However, the cabin we entered was of a considerable size, and it and looked like it had been transformed into nice living quarters. It was furnished plainly with two arm chairs and a small brown couch that had been pushed against the bulkhead. I guessed it also served as a bed, since that piece of furniture wasn't in evidence. It didn't have any portholes—only the massive steel door that he locked behind us.

He invited me to sit, but I remained standing to spite him—I wasn't planning to stay. He took a seat on a chair, never removing his mask.

"Why am I here?" I asked him again. I should just plainly hate him and ignore him, nothing else. He wasn't threatening—and that made him even more dangerous. I couldn't read anything into him at all. "What are you planning to do with me?"

He measured me intently for a moment. The glistening I saw in his eyes gave me chills—they blinked with pleasure and were undisturbed.

"I have wanted you since the first day I met you," he said, as he stood up to walk around the room. "So, I intend to keep you here with me as my wife. I remember you when you were just a scared little girl, lost in this world, not knowing who you were or what you could do. But *I* knew. And you proved it to me. The first time we fought, I felt your powers and I knew exactly who you were. And I fell in love with you. You were more than you were told, more than a Healer. And I wanted you."

His words struck me hard. He wasn't lying about events when had we met in the past. It had all happened, but I couldn't make any sense of what he was saying. Whoever he was, our paths had apparently intertwined very closely in the past. How could that be, when I had never known anyone named Rex?

My mind started to eliminate everyone I knew. Some were already gone, like Milos and Rares. The ones alive, Serban and Andreas, couldn't possibly be the traitor. I remained silent, allowing him to continue to talk as my mind was struggling to comprehend his story. There was nothing extraordinary about his physical appearance to make him special or easily recognizable.

"You are right about me," he continued, like he had read my mind. Of course he could do that, having Gallbor's gifts. "It is true, I am nothing special, or I should say, I *was* nothing special among the Warriors. Why was that? It was wrong! I should have been a leader; I was born with privileges, but I had to stay in someone else's shadow. I could not live like that. So I had a plan. I needed you and I needed some powers."

I knew what he was going to say. This time I lowered my eyes. He came closer to me, touching my chin. Then his hand slowly slid down my neck and onto chest. My skin trembled in revulsion, but I remained still. My mind concentrated on the moment when I would kill him and take his head off.

"So, fifteen years ago, I had the chance to bring my plan to life. I tracked down our Master, who was now nothing more than a mere Warrior, and I asked him for help. I had received a little help from a few devoted friends, who, I should say, I helped to become Immortals. Now, don't look me like that—I did it for you. It was a good plan and it worked.

When Gallbor refused to assist me with my plan, I killed him and left him headless on the side of the road. His spirit gave me great powers, greater than yours. Now, you see, I could finally be your Master and you could be my Queen. I could offer you what you do not have, now, and what you so richly deserve."

I gazed at him with hatred, but he didn't care. He came behind be and embraced me, putting his left arm around my waist and his other hand cupping my right breast, holding me tight. Then, one of his fingers moved to my shoulder and rubbed against something. I remembered the strange feeling I had at the mall when I bumped into somebody.

That's where the tracker was all the time—under my skin—on my body.

"For fourteen long years I pretended to be me, hiding my powers from the others. Nobody knew who I was—only the ones who were bound to me. I built an army greater than the Warriors, and last year I grew tired of waiting. I knew where you were and I needed to seek you out and fulfill the rest of my plan—to became the Master over all. So, I disappeared from my clan and I spread the rumor that an Amestec had killed me. The old me was dead. The new me, I called Rex."

I could barely breathe; I gasped for air.

Until then, I had no idea who he was, but now my whole body started to shake. It was impossible. The dead should remained dead!

"Aha," he said, releasing me and coming around to face me. "You think you know who I am? But you think it's impossible."

"You're my brother," I whispered, deliberately shedding some tears.

"I never believed that," he said, and he attempted to wipe the tears my face. "And it is *not* true, I am *not* your brother. I have never been you brother. I loved you from the day you raised your sword to fight me. Now, we *can* be together."

Saying that, he slowly removed the mask from his face.

It was Raluca's ghost from the mall.

Rares.

29

It was Rares!

Rares—who had died, and whose passing everyone had mourned – including me. Rares was Rex. Rares, who I had considered to be my brother for so long. I had loved him as my brother, but now he was nothing to me. He was the traitor, nothing more than a criminal, whose only fate was to be executed.

My mouth opened, but none of the angry words I had for him came out. I swallowed back their venom, along with my fury. Rex was a force to deal with and my powers couldn't measure up to his—I knew that very well.

I suppressed my thoughts about Octavian or Artamian and the other Warriors coming on board. He could read my mind, and I had no way of knowing if they could succeed in taking over the ship and cracking the code. It didn't matter for now. I had no powers while I was in his presence, except the will to break free from him. I couldn't show anger or my real feelings.

"Rares, I loved you once," I said, continuing to weep. I said it as a deception, not as weakness, hoping that Rares would fall for it. "Why did you let me believe you were dead?"

Rares didn't answer right away. His spirit searched for mine, coldly dissecting my thoughts and my feelings. But there was nothing I had said to him that was untrue. I had loved him as a brother, truly and sincerely, for so long.

"You loved me," he whispered, lowering his face and kissing my lips. My blood boiled with violence through my veins—I could have passed for a mortal that moment. I almost fainted. "Love me as I love you. I did all of this for you."

"You did all this for me?" I asked, pretending to be impressed. I needed to know more. "You took a lot of risks, coming for me. How did you succeed in taking over this ship?"

"Oh, don't worry about that. The mortals are locked up in the mess hall. This ship is safe; they cannot come to take you away. The Warriors are just a pitiful bunch of has-beens, now, just a hand full of them hiding in a retirement community. They will not dare to come against me, and they all will perish, soon."

"Where are we going now?"

"To prove my love for you and offer you a kingdom on the beach," he said, caressing my hair.

"I am having a problem breathing. I need air," I said slowly, so as not to break the moment's magic. "This cabin is so small. Could we go outside?"

My voice was imploring and he believed me. He took my hand again and we exited into the passageway. At that moment Nagoshi ran towards us.

"They're shooting at us from the air," he said, as he loaded his gun.

"Who is shooting?" asked Rares, as he stepped in front of me. I had already come out of the cabin, intending to run away.

"The Coast Guard," responded Nagoshi, and he looked furiously at me. "Some are in the air and some are on the water."

"How did they manage to come so close?" Rares furiously turned to me and grabbed my arm. It had happened. Luke had hacked into the ship's navigation and communication systems and he had taken control of the ship. Now Rares and his minions couldn't see or hear their enemy. And the Warriors were coming for them.

"Our radar is blank and the ship's power plant is shut down. We're completely dead in the water. The Coast Guard has climbed over the outer rails and they are attacking us."

"They are not the Coast Guard," Rares screamed, releasing my arm. "Go up on deck and take the Amestec with you. Let them fight for their immortality. And have those useless hybrids bring the ship back on line! I want those missiles up and in the air immediately."

Before I could take advantage of my freedom, Rares turned to me, lifted his fist and hit me hard on my right temple. The force of his blow shook me and I fell face down in the passageway.

There was no pain, but in the next moment I was blinded. I tried to force my eyes open, but I realized that they were already open, and I tried to glow. But nothing happened. I was in the deepest darkness I had ever known, blacker than when Milos had beheaded me.

"You must know without a doubt, and never forget, that I am your Master," Rares shouted to me, and I sensed him standing mercilessly over me. "Stay here! I will be back for you!"

I covered my face with my hands and I pressed them harder over my eyes. He had left in a hurry, leaving me collapsed in the passageway. I had won—I was outside the cabin! He hadn't imprisoned me.

I crawled forward until my head hit the bulkhead. I turned over and laid my back against it.

Shots were fired, erupting in different directions and locations on the deck. By now, Alex, Serban, and the Warriors should be on the ship. They were here and they were fighting. Leaving my phone behind had crippled my ability to stay in contact with my Warriors, and that was a huge disadvantage.

And I was blind!

It wasn't part of my plan to lie below decks, *blind*, instead of being out there, fighting alongside my Warriors. Rares was such a fool—I wouldn't stay still and wait for him. I had to know what was going on outside. I needed to take charge of my weapon, even if it was so far away from me.

Only my mind and my spirit were intact and still powerful. With my spiritual eyes, I traced back the way I had come here, following Rares. I saw the stairs clearly in my mind. I mentally flew over a few impostors who were sitting in the passageway, holding their swords. Next I was passing the Amestec who were in the passageway, waiting for their orders, before I saw the outside deck.

My mind paused for a moment, too tired to continue. It had never reached this far away from me. But I had to make it happen.

Outside, on the deck, my eyes saw the action through the power of my mind. Alex was fighting with two Amestec. He was holding a sword in one hand and a Cyclone disk in the other. I saw Ditmar flying in the air, followed by Lars. They had learned that from me. Far away, on the other side of the deck, I thought I saw Serban fighting with an impostor.

Serban...

My mind stood still again. I hoped Serban would never learn the true identity of Rex, that he would never know that it was his beloved brother, Rares. I closed my eyes tight to concentrate.

I couldn't fail now, I was so close to my weapon. And there, underneath the parachute, I found my Vortex. I tried to lift it, but it didn't move. Perhaps if I tried to get physically closer, my mind would be able to be control it.

I stood up and I blindly stepped forward slowly, following my memory, finding guidance with my hands as they touched the walls. Just then, something came my way, cutting me on my right shoulder. It was a Shuriken. I ignored it and continued to walk—I needed to get closer to the upper deck. Someone ran past me and shoved me roughly away. But by this time I had reached the steps and I hugged the metal railing. Instinctively, I touched my shoulder and the wound healed, as I knew it would. But why wasn't my blindness going away?

I concentrated and tried to lift my Vortex again, but it still wouldn't move. I saw in my mind's eye that Andreas and Cedric were fighting nearby. I saw their eyes glowing and I knew they were ready to go up to the bridge.

I concentrated again and this time the Vortex lifted up from the deck. The parachute blew off into the ocean as the weapon became uncovered. It came back to me. Two Amestec were in the way and they were killed. As it floated down the stairway, the Vortex caught up with an impostor—his head bounced down from step to step, stopping at my feet. I touched it with my foot.

Suddenly the total darkness began to turn a bit lighter, but my vision was still a dense fog and very unclear. I couldn't see three feet ahead of me, unable to distinguish anything but the vague shapes of objects. Then the Vortex landed in my hand.

Outside, the noise and commotion increased, a sign that the fighting was intense. I heard something similar to an explosion—I thought it might be a forced helicopter crash landing. By now, Octavian and Artamian should be here, too. My brother's presence was critical—he was the only one now who could fight Rares.

I needed to turn around and work my way back into every cabin on this lower deck, to find and kill the Hybrids in the weapons room. This ship must remain powerless—no missiles would fly over

Key West this night. Being blind wouldn't stop me for doing my part. Nothing would.

I raised the Vortex over my head. My hand released the weapon, but my hand remained in the air. My hands were my eyes now, and I still needed them to guide me around.

From my left, I heard rapid footsteps coming towards me. The Vortex started to rotate and flew in that direction. From the sound of the steps, I counted three people. When they turned the corner, the Vortex passed easily through their necks. They were killed instantly; they didn't know what had hit them.

I got down on my knees and searched the body of the one closest to me. I picked up some things that I felt sure were a rifle and a pistol.

I continued to keep the Vortex in the air and flying ahead of me. By the sound of it, the first room I encountered appeared to be some sort of command operations room. I heard the clicking of computers and the hum of monitors. The man who turned to me was just a shadow. My senses searched for his scent and I knew it was a Hybrid. I had found them and I must destroy them all.

Before he could react to my presence, I jumped and wrapped both of my legs high around his neck in a scissors movement. I twisted hard and his neck broke. The noise of his body hitting the floor created panic in the other Hybrids.

I bent under a rain of bullets as they made a swishing noise over my head, like a golf swing. They didn't hit me, but it was impossible for me to accurately judge their number or location. Julian had said that the weapons room was quite large, but it was filled with computers, monitors, and huge TV screens. They were located against the wall, as well being as randomly placed.

My right leg tripped over the body I had just killed, and I tumbled backwards in the air with my feet landing on a desk. From there, I floated onto something else and, continued to jump and rotate in the air over the objects that were in my way.

While my right hand kept me balanced, my left hand pulled the trigger as I swung my rifle around and shot continuously at everything. I heard glass smashing and bodies dropping, until I was the only one remaining who was shooting. I somersaulted and landed on my feet. Nothing moved or made a noise.

It was quiet. I had killed them all.

I had been hit by six bullets in my chest and four in my leg. I lay down on the deck and prepared my body, physically and mentally. As I brushed my fingers over the wounds, the bullets came out of them as my flesh grew back.

I heard movement in the next room and I peeked around the corner. My Vortex did the same thing, still rotating over my head like it was alive—but it was following the movement of my mind. I couldn't see anything, but my Vortex would. I sent it ahead me and I heard the sound of yet another body falling. I rose from the deck, shooting at an invisible enemy.

I heard quite a few Shurikens flying towards me, so I kept shooting until my pistol's magazine was empty. My hand felt the jamb of a hatch and I went through it, not knowing who was in the next cabin.

My mind began to grow tired, so I recalled the Vortex back to me. I held the weapon in my hand, ready to fight with it. The noises and the odors were my map and my defense system. I walked around touching things—it was just a storage room.

There must surely be more cabins down here on this level, I thought. I had no more time to rest. I got out from there and moved forward into the passageway.

I sent the Vortex towards every black shadow that I could detect, but it returned empty. I realized that I needed to find Octavian – he could heal me if I couldn't fight Rares' blindness blow on my own.

I needed to get out to the upper deck, but in the cabin to my left I thought I heard knocking on the bulkhead. I held my breath and listened. It was true—somebody was hitting the side of the cabin. I walked around touching the walls of the passageway I was in, but I couldn't seem to find a hatch release.

Just for moment I was overcome by helplessness. Rares knew exactly what he was doing when he made me blind. Seeing what was on the other side of the bulkhead wouldn't have been a problem if I had had my sight. All I needed to do would be to glow my eyes and see through the wall. Now, I could only rely on the knocking sound.

"Are you *normal?*" someone asked. It was the raspy, tired voice of a young man.

"Yes," I answered, smiling at his silly question. "Who're you?"

"Lieutenant Pollack. Captain Avery is sick," answered the man and I recognized his voice. "Well, you won't be able to help us if you are *normal.*"

"Be patient, Lieutenant Pollack. Give me five more minutes and I'll get you out of there."

"Safira!" exclaimed Pollack. "Thank you Jesus! We're saved! Safira, this hatch is sealed and programmed to open only from the bridge. Please hurry. We've been in here for a week now. How did you find us?"

"Just a lucky guess, my friend," I responded, and I took a deep breath.

I had found the mortals, and one of them was special to me—good old Lieutenant Pollack! He was vital to our victory in Greece. That meant that I was next to the mess hall. I remembered that Julian had said there should be another stairway that went out to the rear deck.

I stepped forward with one hand stretched forward, surprised to not encounter any more enemies. Perhaps they had all gone out on the deck to fight.

Julian was right; my hand grabbed the rail of the stairs and I climbed them, falling when I reached the top. The Vortex slipped out of my hand, and someone bumped into me. I lay motionless on the cold deck, but I recognized his scent.

It was Artamian. My whole body trembled, overwhelmed by mixed emotions – happiness that he had found me; sadness that I would not have him around for too long. That was the moment when I realized how much I wanted and needed him.

"Safira, what happened to you?" he asked, lifting me up into his arms. My eyes were wide open but I could hardly distinguish his features.

"I'm blind," I said, trying to smile while my hands softly touched his face. "Rex hit me. I'm afraid I can't be healed."

"There's no such a thing," I heard, as my brother joined us. "Come here!"

Octavian's touch on my forehead seemed as hot as a blacksmith's furnace. His fingers slid down over my eyebrows. I felt the heat burning inside my eyelids, and for the first time, I felt pain. Surprised and panicked, I opened my eyes. Now I could see! I saw him and I saw Artamian.

"I'm going to kill him," said Artamian, and his face flushed with anger.

He put his arms around me like a protective armor. I wished at that moment I could say something more meaningful to him, to tell him how much he meant to me, but I didn't. I had no doubt that he loved me deeply, but it was me who didn't open my heart for him.

"Where's everyone else?" I asked, without wanting to leave his embrace. He sensed that and he lovingly caressed my hair.

"Everyone's accounted for," responded my brother grabbing his Fire Sword from the deck. "They're on the other side of the ship, finishing the fight. Wesley and the youngsters killed all the Hybrids. We killed most of the Amestec and the impostors, but some managed to get away. Nagoshi was among them."

"The mortals are locked in the mess hall. Lieutenant Pollack is among them," I said. "Below decks is clear; I killed everything that moved."

"You fought blind?" asked Artamian, astonished.

I smiled at him in answer.

"Rex wanted to shoot missiles over to Key West," I continued. "Did anybody capture him?"

"We left Serban behind, fighting Rex," responded Octavian. "Rex demanded that Serban fight him."

I looked at him, frightened. My eyes instantly moved from my brother to the Fire Sword in his hand.

"Rex is actually Rares, Serban's brother. He's the one who killed Gallbor. Octavian, we need to help Serban! Rex is very powerful!"

"You're right," we heard from behind us. Rares came closer in the dark and his eyes were glowing with spite. "Too late for you to save my brave brother."

Saying that, he lifted the hand that was holding Serban's head. None of us moved or spoke.

Instantly I turned to Octavian. His hand gripped the Fire Sword, ready to attack Rares. My lips were closed but my spirit talked with his. I needed him to go after Serban in the shadows—he was the only one who could.

Rares was armed with the one sword I must take back, the one sword that could destroy me, the one sword that could certainly destroy Artamian. It was up to me to fight Rares.

"Who is next?" Rares asked, gazing at me in disbelief as he realized that I could see. Then he turned to Artamian who was still holding me. "Stay away from her! *I* am her Master."

"And I'm her guardian," Artamian responded, gently pushing me some distance away from them. What he said next was more addressed to me than to Rares. "You will not take her from me."

"I am her Master," repeated Rares, furious. "I do not have to ask your permission to possess her. You will have to fight me for her until one of us is dead!"

Before I could say anything, Artamian grabbed Octavian's Fire Sword from his hand and lifted it up. The Sword transformed into an immense flame.

Octavian grabbed Serban's head from Rares' grasp and ran towards the ship's forward deck.

I stood silent and frozen in time. There was nothing for me to do except to brace myself for the horror—Artamian doesn't fight with swords. Why did he do that? He chose a certain death.

Rares held the Silver Sword high and leaped very high in a forward motion, swinging rapidly and forcefully toward Artamian's head. The sword's blade came down with fury but it became invisible to the naked eye.

Suddenly I saw Artamian's body, still holding the Fire Sword high, falling over the rail and into the ocean.

30

MY HEART STOPPED BEATING!

My mind refused to believe what I saw. Everything inside me was paralyzed. Artamian's head was severed by the Silver Sword, and there was no recourse.

This time, the story wouldn't repeat—I couldn't save Artamian as I had saved Julian. I struggled to send my spirit to follow him into the deep water, but a stronger force took over my body. Rares wouldn't let me escape him. He demanded my defeat.

I was physically held hostage by my enemy's cruel display of power. Rares placed me in a void of time, and I felt like I was motionless while Rares' body flew around me over and over, like a carousel. He folded his arms, satisfied, but he measured me with such a dark intent. I had no doubt what my fate was about to become—he would force me to be his wife.

There was no love in his heart—just a violent desire to possess me.

Minutes seemed to pass like hours. Octavian hadn't returned, but the Fire Sword was gone and he had no weapon to fight with. What if it was hopeless for Serban? What if he had been decapitated with the Silver Sword?

I focused my thoughts on Serban, to find any reason to mourn—but not for Artamian—not for him. But I couldn't cry. In less than a second I was stripped of any hope I held for freedom and love.

Artamian was my hope and my love. The seed of love from my heart had grown with such an intensity that it had awakened my blood cells and it made my muscles vibrate. Rares couldn't hold his grip on me any longer. I wasn't about to bow down and obey him, not about to accept his terror.

The sound of voices and commotion coming from the front deck delayed my actions. I closed my eyes and my mind followed the direction Octavian ran with Serban's head. I found him, bent down over a headless body, while to his left, Ditmar lay injured on the deck. Raluca held Codrin who had fallen down with his feet hanging over the rail. He had been hit by shots fired at him, apparently out of nowhere.

My instinct was to rush to the injured Warriors and heal them, but I was distracted by what I saw out of the corner of my eye.

Wesley and Gianna started to shoot towards the port side of the ship. What was going on? I saw Octavian getting up and looking at somebody. I turned to see that it was Nagoshi coming towards me.

But no, he was coming towards my brother. It wasn't over! Nagoshi raised his sword and attacked my brother, but that was all I saw before my sight was obscured by Rares rushing over to challenge me again.

I composed my mind and ordered the Vortex to return to me. Rares' face became enraged.

"I see that you healed," he said, dangerously pointing the tip of his sword toward my eyes. "What is your intent, to fight me?

I am your Master, now. Everyone you ever cared for is dead, or is about to be—killed by me. My boat should be here in a minute, and we will leave together. You cannot win, so be a nice girl and accept it."

I shook the hair from my eyes, glowed them and I lifted the Vortex. My body was stiff from being restrained by him, but the fear I had felt disappeared. He would not spare me if I didn't gave in to his demands.

The only thing I had was control over was my own soul. My spirit wasn't my own—it was part of my father and part of my mother; and it was part of my ancestry as the Queen Healer of the Warrior Order of Immortals.

An arrow pierced my heart, however; it sank deep into that cavern of despair. I had lost it with the one man I had fought so much against loving; I had lost that battle. I had no heart remaining—just the energy derived from my intense hatred of Rares.

"I am Gallbor's daughter," I yelled, as loudly as I could. "*No one* tells me what to do!"

My hand released the Vortex, but my mind guided the weapon toward the arm that was holding the Silver Sword. I needed to separate that sword from him; however, he was fast and when the sword's blade turned invisible it also divided the Vortex in half.

My eyes followed my weapon to the ground, but my mind didn't disconnect from it. I used my mind to pick up the two pieces, and this time my target was his eyes—as a payback. And again, the Silver Sword caught up with the two halves and sliced them into many pieces.

"You cannot fight me," he responded, trying to stay composed. "Don't you see how much stronger I am by now? I have all your father's powers, Gallbor's daughter."

"You only have a sword that turns invisible," I provoked him, not too surprised that the Silver Sword had destroyed the Vortex. "Without it you cannot win over me."

My ruse worked. Rares laid the sword against the ship's outer hull, accepting my challenge at for a one-on-one fight.

We both knew that it was a lost cause for me, but he was eager to teach me a lesson, even though he would kill me by doing that. I didn't need my body when my heart and soul were absent.

No one needed me anymore. My Order was safe with a new Master who could also heal. I felt in my senses that he would kill Nagoshi. Octavian's spirit made me aware that he knew I was in danger, but I didn't need him.

I leaped. Both my legs left the ground at the same time, with one higher than the other, striking his head. I rolled down, but not before I grabbed his neck with my feet and flipped his body, crashing him to the ground. He got up in a hurry, surprised and enraged.

I waited for him to come closer as he prepared to jump and spin. I flipped backwards while my legs struck his chest, forcing him to step back a few feet. Running, he came towards me.

I leaped again, but this time he flew higher over my body and struck me hard as he sailed through the air. I fell down to the deck, almost unconscious under his powerful blow.

As he landed, he lifted me up and threw me forcefully into the air. I tried to keep my body floating against the force of gravity, but I crashed again to the deck. He picked me up again and slammed me against the inner hull. Physically, I was too weak to stand up.

I heard someone calling my name—it wasn't Rares—it was Ditmar. Then Codrin called my name. Then I heard Cedric and Alex. And one more voice I recognized—the young Wesley. Were they hurt? Why wasn't my brother healing them?

Suddenly, Rares ran to grab the Silver Sword and he picked me up, holding me against his body. His left hand was around my waist while his right hand held the sword against my neck.

When he turned me around, I understood why: Octavian and Serban were standing in front of us. Rares' body shook with hate when he recognized his brother he had killed—now alive and well. So, Serban hadn't been cut by the Silver Sword. Octavian found his spirit in the shadows and brought it back. I smiled happily, although the feared Sword's blade was just two inches away from my own neck.

The two Warriors stood still and silent. Rares growled, and I sensed that he was confused and scared. He couldn't understand why Serban was alive and who Octavian was. For the first time since he killed my father, he had met someone as powerful as himself.

"It's over," said my brother calmly. "Release my sister and you may leave."

"Lady Safira is your sister?" mumbled Rares, but his question was more rhetorical. "So *you* are the plane's pilot. Gallbor's son I would imagine, with some fancy powers. However, I am not impressed that you saved my brother. I am still more powerful, and Safira is now my wife."

"Why have you done this?" Serban asked Rares, and his voice diminished, overpowered with sadness. "You are the son of a prince."

"And you are a fool, my brother" he responded, spitting on my face with anger. Then he stepped back a few more feet, dragging me with him. "Don't you see? You are just a nobody and I am about to become the Master."

"We already have a Master," responded Serban, following us. "Release Lady Safira and bow allegiance to him. He can change you back to normal."

"I am not bowing to anybody," responded Rares. "Lady Safira is mine and we are going to leave this place together. I am her Master, I love her. If you try to oppose me, she will die. But I will not leave her behind for you to revive her. She will be lost forever, exactly like her Guardian."

His words hurt me, but in the next moment it was his heavy body that forced me down to the deck.

"That's not true," I heard someone saying, before Rares' head fell beside me.

Octavian and Serban rushed to drag him away from me. I turned to see who had dealt Rares his fatal blow.

My heart exploded inside my body, like a volcano. If I could bleed, I was sure all my veins would explode by the heavy overflow.

Artamian stood there over me, soaking wet, holding the Fire Sword. The flames from the sword reflected in his eyes. They were the flames of love. He helped me get to my feet. His body dripped water and I wiped his face with my palms.

He was real and he was back. Back for me and back to life. He did what he had promised.

"How did you…?"

"Unfortunately I didn't have the chance to face my enemy," he answered with a deep sadness. "I was forced to hit him from behind and I am not proud of it. I wish he could see his killer."

"You were dead, Artamian, I know what I saw. You were slashed by the Silver Sword!"

"There's a certain danger when you fight with an invisible blade," he said, but not very convincingly. "You can't be sure what you've cut, if anything."

I wanted to ask him more, because I didn't believe him, but Octavian grabbed my arm.

"We have a few wounded and we need you," he said, heading forward. "You two can talk later."

"Octavian why didn't you heal them? You could have done it! You did it for me."

"No," responded Octavian, "I can't heal as you do. I didn't heal you either—you did it."

"What are you saying?" I asked my brother, while I turned and looked back at Artamian who was gathering both swords and following us. All I wanted was to be with him, but I had to do my duty.

"Your spirit, Safira. It moved inside me and that's what healed you. I'm not a Healer. Your powers are like our father, and that's why your spirit can travel. As Gallbor said, I have to earn my own power one day, like yours. Now hurry up! They need you!"

"What about Serban? How did you bring him back?"

"He wasn't cut by the Silver Sword. Apparently Rares didn't know the real danger of his sword, other that it turns invisible. He was a coward after all, and he sent Nagoshi to eliminate his brother. Serban was lucky."

So were all of us!

* * *

Alex, Codrin, and Wesley were shot many times but Ditmar's left hand was severed. I ran to him first and reattached his limb. Cedric had been stabbed twice in his abdomen and I simply sealed the wound.

Removing the bullets was easy. As I did before, I had everyone stripped down and I checked their bodies. Andreas had many cuts, but none of them were severe. The armor over their hearts had protected the Transylvanians.

Raluca and Sabrina checked on the youngsters who were proudly standing on the deck, still holding their weapons, ready to fight.

My hands trembled a little while I healed my Warriors, but I smiled happily at them. I was thrilled. Everyone was here. Everyone.

Him, too. The man who had saved my life. He had killed Rares. The man I loved came to my rescue, as my guardian.

Gallbor knew!

*   *   *

When I was done and everyone was like new, they all hugged and congratulated each other, jubilant over the victory. However, our celebration was interrupted by an object in the air. As it drew closer, we saw a helicopter flying straight towards us. Octavian was the first one to glow his eyes on the craft, followed by everybody else. The helicopter was lit, glowing as if it were in broad daylight.

The helicopter landed on the warship, not far from us. Although the guests were a mystery to us, none of us grabbed our weapons. There was something in the air. A feeling of peace took over our senses. They weren't a danger for us—they were also Immortals. We all looked at the two men who emerged from the craft, and who were walking our way.

It was hard to comprehend what we saw. The men were tall, dressed in dark pants and dark untucked shirts. As they came closer, we could see that their hair was very light, almost white, and long to the waist. Their skin was clear and suntanned.

I started to remember. I knew who they were, and my mouth opened, astonished. I turned to Codrin, who smiled to me.

He knew too. I wanted to say something, but I couldn't. Raluca turned to me and looked at me suspiciously.

"Who are they?" she asked me, whispering.

"Your legends have come to life. They're the Enforcers."

The girl turned back to them, and she began to weep. The men smiled at us and bowed slightly. They were handsome and polite, but their aquamarine colored eyes didn't glow. We shut off our glowing eyes, too.

I supposed I would have many stories to tell my young Warriors, all that I had learned from Gallbor, but now wasn't the time.

"Congratulations, brothers. We were glad to learn that the magical swords are returning to our possession."

No one but Octavian and me knew what he was referring to, but we all politely bowed to them. My brother took the two swords from Artamian's hands and stepping forward, he handed them to the Enforcers.

One of them took the Fire Sword and the other took the Silver Sword.

"Rise and be strong, brothers."

Bowing once more, the Enforcers quietly returned to the helicopter. None of us moved as they rose into the air and disappeared in the night.

"What just happened?" Alex was the first to ask. "Who were they and why did they call us brothers?"

"They're the Enforcers, part of the Immortal Order, brothers to us," responded Octavian. "I'll tell you everything about them and the others. But now, we've got to release the mortal crew, take the hybrid and impostor bodies with us, and leave this ship.

Soon it will be morning. Tomorrow is a new beginning for us. It's time for the Warriors to rise again."

While everyone left to load the bodies onto the waiting speedboat, I called for Artamian. His lips were curved into that simple smile that drilled a big hole into my heart. This time I let him in.

"Lady Safira, I'm afraid you may have lost your Master," he said in a very serious tone.

"He wasn't my Master," I said, jumping into his arms while I let my tears flow. "You're my Master, Artamian. You always have been."

"You owe me an answer," he said, but my kiss interrupted him again. "You love me don't you?"

I nodded, and I laid my head on his chest. My father was right about him. He may deny it now, but I was certain that he had returned from the dead for me.

Our battles might not be over, but one of mine had been won.

My Master was here.

THE END

FUTURE BOOKS

The Warriors are featured in the following books:

- ➤ BREAKING MORTAL,
- ➤ REIGN OF FIRE
- ➤ THE HUNTED HUNTER.

The Enforcers are also featured in following books:

- ➤ BREAKING MORTAL,
- ➤ REIGN OF FIRE
- ➤ THE HUNTED HUNTER.

The Defenders are featured in the following books:

- ➤ BREAKING MORTAL,
- ➤ REIGN OF FIRE
- ➤ THE HUNTED HUNTER.

AUTHOR'S PAGE

Camilia John is author, publisher and founder of InTown Books. She grew up in a house full of story tellers, so it was natural for her to start making up her own. At the age of seventeen she earned the Gemini award for writing in her high school. Although she has had success in fashion design and business, she is a writer at heart. Her first paranormal series is *The Exiled Immortals* and will be followed by *The Invisible Kingdom*. She now lives in Atlanta, Georgia.